# FATAL DOMINION

POLITICS CAN BE DEADLY

Victoria M. Patton

Dark Force Press

Dark Force Press
www.darkforcepress.com

Publisher's Note: This is a work of fiction. Names, characters, places, and incidents are a product of the author's imagination. Locales and public names are sometimes used for atmospheric purposes. Any resemblance to actual people, living or dead, or to businesses, companies, events, institutions, or locales is completely coincidental.

Book Layout © 2016 BookDesignTemplates.com

Fatal Dominion/ Victoria M. Patton. -- 1st ed.
ISBN 13: 978-1-946934-07-9
ISBN 10: 1-946934-07-0


Library of Congress Control Number: 2017916081

Editor: Judith Bixby Boling
Cover photo "Madison 03" by Paul Frederickson is licensed under CC by- sa 2.0

## Dedication

To my beta readers: Amber, Janie, Judith, Tony, Susan, Jessica, Karen, and Gwen. You guys totally saved my ass. I can't thank you enough.

Amber Raley, thank you for providing all the names for my characters in this book. You and your clan helped a girl out. Love you girl.

Tony Michael Andrews, I could never thank you enough for the help you gave during the writing of this book. I will forever be grateful to you. You will forever be my best friend.

# CONTENTS

# CHAPTER ONE

Tuesday
3:30 a.m.

Lieutenant Damien Kaine maneuvered through the swamp-like parking area and pulled up next to the Crime Scene Tech van. He could just make out the giant monstrosity of a tarp through the sheets of pelting rain. Neither he nor his partner Detective Joe Hagan said a word as the roof of the SUV was battered by the angry storm. A warning of sorts, of the scene that lay under the tarp before them.

Almost simultaneously they exited the vehicle running to the protection of the covering. "Holy shit!" Damien said shaking the rain from his hair and clothing being careful not to contaminate the dead man before him.

"Damn, even mother nature says it's too early for this shit. You'd think the criminals could be a little more thoughtful and commit these murders at a decent fucking hour," Damien said shivering slightly, as he brushed the last of the moisture from his jacket. Januaries were bad enough in Chicago without a bone-chilling rain.

Dr. Bernard Forsythe smiled at his favorite lieutenant. "I'll be sure to post your request on the city's Facebook page and Twitter feed."

Joe let the last few raindrops fall from his chin. "What the hell do you think the killer used on him? There isn't much of his head left." Joe squatted pointing to the man's body. "Looks like the killer bashed in half his head and used a giant cheese grater on the other half." Joe stood stretching his back. He dragged his hand down his face. "Fuck, you think he was alive when all this happened to him?"

The man's semi-nude body showed signs of prolonged torture. Dr. Forsythe shook his head. "I'm not even going to hazard a guess until we get him back to the morgue. By the looks of the blood-soaked underwear, I have a feeling there is a surprise waiting for us when we get him undressed. We can't even ID him onsite." The doctor held up one of the hands with missing fingertips. "Our killer took a few souvenirs. It'll take us some time to figure out who our guy is." Dr. Forsythe glanced around. "With this rain coming down I want to bag him up as quickly as possible.

The CSTs are gathering everything in the general vicinity and will sort through it at the crime lab."

Damien ran his hand through his hair. He stared unfazed at the dead man. "Damn, I could've stayed in bed." He smiled at the raised eyebrow Dr. Forsythe shot his way. Over the years the Medical Examiner had become more than a colleague. "What? There's nothing for us here until you can give us a name." Damien looked around at the empty field.

"Oh, come on, Damien," head CST Roger Newberry said, "you wouldn't want to miss out on this case. Who knows who we have here, it could be Jimmy Hoffa."

"Yeah, that would be the find of the century," Joe said.

"Joe, how're things with Taylor? You know she is the bomb over at the crime lab. She has implemented some pretty impressive software to streamline the lab's efficiency, making our lives a lot easier," he grinned at the big Irish cop. "You know she has several admirers. I'd be careful if I were you. You piss her off, and she will have another man waiting to take your place."

Joe shot Roger a sideways glance. "Fuck you, Newberry."

Roger roared back in laughter. "You're so cranky."

"Joe, you ever come out here in high school?" Damien asked. The body had been dumped on a road located outside the city. The property jutted up against Lake Michigan. An area had eroded away, and crystal-clear water from the lake filled a large basin allowing swimming in the summertime. This area was notorious for high school students to hang out and party. "I remember a few late-night excursions back in the day, myself." Damien smiled at the men.

"I may have come out here once or twice." Joe snickered at the men around him. "Of course, nothing this exciting ever happened to me." He wiggled his eyebrows. "Our lovebirds over there had one hell of a damper put on their night." He nodded towards the young couple who sat in the back of a patrol car.

"Hmm, I bet. Let's go interview our happy couple. I seriously doubt they can tell us anything. It looks like our guy has been here a while." Damien turned towards the car. "Doc, as soon as you know the identity, will you call me?"

Dr. Forsythe looked up from bagging the body. "Yes, Lieutenant, I will. I plan on working on this right when we get back to the morgue.

Give me a few hours. Hopefully, I will have something for you."

Damien nodded to Joe, "You ready?"

Joe sighed. "Yeah, let's get this done and then get something to eat before we head into Division Central. No way I'm facing the day this early on an empty stomach."

# CHAPTER TWO

Damien and Joe walked into VCU at seven fifteen. Joe sat at his desk to finish up paperwork from a previous case. Damien was on his way to his office when his cell rang. He looked at his screen. "Hey Dr. Forsythe, got results already?"

"Yes, son, I do. I'm giving you the first call. My next one will be to Captain Mackey and Chief Rosenthal."

Damien sat in his chair. His pulse pounded in his ears. "I'm not going to like who our victim is, am I?"

"No, you're not, and the shit will hit the fan. I wanted to let you prepare yourself. This case is not going to be easy."

"Okay, Doc, now I'm scared. Who is our dead guy?"

"Your victim is Glenn Rossdale."

Damien forced himself to breathe. He rubbed his hand on his jeans. "Oh, fuck no. You've got to be kidding me." Damien's head rested against the back of his chair.

"No, I wish I was. I'm calling Mackey now. I'm sure everything you do from here on out will be scrutinized. Damien, if I can give you any advice, use your family ties and stick to your guns. Don't let anyone force you to clear this case before you're ready. I will be working this end. Whatever you need, you call me."

"I will, Dr. Forsythe. Thanks for the heads up." Damien hung the phone up. He glanced at his watch. He figured he had roughly fifteen minutes before being summoned to the captain's office. "Joe," Damien yelled from his office.

Joe sauntered in and grabbed a handful of jelly beans. "Yeah, oh, wise one, what can I do for you?" He picked out several of the same color beans popping them into his mouth.

"Got the identity on our dead guy. Glenn Rossdale."

Joe coughed. He inhaled and coughed again. "Oh, holy shit." Joe fell into the chair across from Damien's desk. "We are screwed until we solve this case. You realize this, right?"

"Yeah, I do. Have you ever listened to Rossdale's radio show or watched any of his televised interviews?" Damien asked.

"Oh yeah. I loved it. Rossdale always hammered the liberal pundits.

He never let them get away with anything. But in all fairness, he hammered the conservatives too. He made sure politicians did what they said they were going to do. If they didn't, they got grilled." Joe leaned forward on his elbows. "Do you understand how many fucking suspects we have?"

Damien leaned back. "Hell yeah. And getting them to answer questions for us will take an act of Congress." Damien's desk phone rang. "The circus is about to start. Hey, Captain. Yes, Sir. Joe and I will be right up." Damien hung up, smiling at Joe. "C'mon, sweetheart. Let's go."

Joe rose and followed Damien out. "You know, we could both turn in our resignation papers and build that bar we always talk about. This would be the perfect time."

"They'll never let us leave, my friend. We have checked into the *Hotel California.*"

# CHAPTER THREE

Damien and Joe stepped into Captain Mackey's office and waited for instruction. The captain stood in front of his window. Even with his back facing them, the captain was formidable looking. His shoulders were broad and made of one piece of solid muscle. Even in his fifties, he had the body of a younger man. And, as a former Marine, he had the skill set to back up his mass.

Captain Mackey continued to stare out the window as he spoke. "This is going to be a clusterfuck. We are going to have the news crews following our every move." He turned to face his two best detectives. "Under no circumstances, are you to give any kind of statement. Our communications department will have a high-ranking official provide scheduled briefings. If you find yourself in a situation where press corps personnel are asking you if you took a dump today, you will answer 'you can contact the Division Central Communications Office for statements.' Then walk away. Do not engage. Am I clear?"

Damien nodded. "Yes. I hear you loud and clear."

Captain Mackey dragged a hand across his face. "If you need to pull in uniformed officers to help with this investigation, do it. Use Fuentes and Grimer from Traffic Core. They are the biggest guys in the group, put them in plain clothes for the duration. We're going to have tons to interview, and having them in plain clothes may keep the press from following their every fucking move." He stared at his lieutenant. "Do you have any idea why someone would want Rossdale dead? I mean I know his reputation, but he gave it to both sides even though he was a conservative."

Damien looked at Joe.

Joe shrugged. "Don't look at me. I don't pay any attention to politics. Aside from catching his show here and there, I didn't keep up on his affairs."

Damien's lips twitched. "No, Sir. I haven't heard of anything going on that involved him. I'll call my dad. I know he may have dealt with him on occasion. I think he requested some security not too long ago, but I'm not sure what it was for. Personal or for appearances."

"I would appreciate any help your father can give. At the rate we use your family; eventually, we will have to put them on the damn payroll." Captain Mackey leaned back in his chair. "There was a party I went to about three weeks ago, for State Senator James Lockhart. I know Rossdale was at that party. He and the senator's personal secretary, Tyler Bryce, got into it."

Damien leaned forward. "Do you have any idea what they argued about?"

"Well, the word at the bar was Bryce didn't like the way Rossdale interviewed another senator on his show a few weeks ago. He came down hard on some of his policies. Are you aware Senator Lockhart is being touted as the next governor? According to those in charge, he is so favored to win, that the Republicans aren't even putting forth the good fight. Some have said the election is nothing more than a formality. Ever since James became a state senator, his father, Robert, has groomed him for this position. At thirty-five, look for him to run for president in the next seven years, or less."

"Do you know if there is anything else? Anything you know, Captain, will go a long way to giving us someplace as a starting point," Damien said.

Captain Mackey stood and walked to his window. "I'm a conservative. Have been all my life. Senator Lockhart has some damn good ideas that could bridge the gap between conservatives and liberals. He still slants his major policies towards the far left, but when it comes to public safety, he is an ally to this division. The chief and I had decided to support him in his upcoming bid for governor." He turned back to his men. "You need to be aware there will be people who want to make sure nothing comes back on the senator."

Captain Mackey walked back to his desk. "You have my full support. But I want you to understand the shit-storm you two are walking into. You are going to come up against a brick wall. I will help facilitate whenever I can."

Captain Mackey came around in front of Damien and Joe and leaned against his desk. "I don't need to tell you how to run an investigation. Be prepared for the FBI to get involved if this gets anywhere near the senator. I want daily written updates. I'm going to have to keep the communications department in the loop so they can craft their news release updates."

Damien nodded. "I understand. Joe and I are heading to Rossdale's office. See if his assistant or secretary can give us an idea of his movements yesterday."

Captain Mackey nodded. "Be careful. Tread lightly when you can."

"Yes, Sir," Damien said. He and Joe left the office.

***

Neither spoke until they were in the security of Damien's office.

"This is going to be a bitch of an investigation. Get your shit together. I'm getting Detective Travis from Electronics and Cyber Division on this. Call Fuentes and Grimer's lieutenant. Explain to him what Captain Mackey wants. Let him know to send the two over later today. I want him to have enough time to cover whatever they may be doing. I'm going to have them help Detective Travis execute search warrants for his computers and mobile devices. He's going to need some muscle."

"You got it. I'll be at my desk. Holler when you're ready." Joe walked out of the office grabbing a hand full of jelly beans as he left.

Damien called Detective Travis and asked him to come to his office. He texted Dillon. She was in California on a case for the City of San Francisco. She was due back in a few days. *Hey babe, I got some news for you.*

*Yeah, what is it?*

*Glenn Rossdale was murdered last night.* Damien stared at his screen. There was a long pause before she responded.

*Looks like I'll be back sooner than I thought.*

Although he didn't like the reason she was coming home, he smiled knowing she would be sleeping with him that night.

Detective Travis walked in and snagged a handful of jelly beans. "What's up, Lieutenant?"

"Glenn Rossdale was killed sometime last night."

"No fucking way. I loved that guy. He never let anyone get away with mamby pamby answers. He hounded his guests 'til he got them to respond to his questions. Shit." Travis grabbed another handful of jelly beans.

Damien frowned. "I had no idea you were a political pundit."

"I'm not. I did enjoy watching Rossdale's televised interviews when he grilled these politicians. He pissed a lot of people off over this governor's race."

Damien smiled. "Well, I guess you got your dream job. I need you to contact ADA Flowers. Get her to give you warrants covering everything but especially ones including his computers, home, and work. All his devices, phone, anything electronic. Tell her I need search warrants for his office and home. Those should be easiest to get. His communications may take longer. As soon as you get those, shoot them to my phone. His death allows us access, but the warrants would make our lives easier." Damien eyeballed the detective. "I want my warrants yesterday."

Detective Travis nodded. "I can get you the home and office warrants by the time you hit Rossdale's office." Travis typed out something on his small handheld device. "Warrants like that are almost rubber stamped. The comms will take longer for sure."

"I've got two traffic cops coming in later. Fuentes and Grimer. They can assist you. They should be here by the time you get those warrants. Take them with you."

"No problem. Fuentes is a poker buddy of mine. Grimer has come to a few of our tournaments. I will send him a message, letting him know to come to ECD."

"Listen, if you have any trouble and you need action fast, call Mackey. Tell him what I have you doing and what you need. He will facilitate it."

Detective Travis stood. "Okay, Boss." He grabbed more jelly beans.

Damien turned to his computer and downloaded one of the photos from the crime scene. He placed the gruesome picture of Glenn Rossdale on his murder board. He studied the photo as he plotted out the next steps in his investigation.

The first stop would be Rossdale's place of work. Damien thought the answers were more than likely there. He knew the guy wasn't married and had no kids. He lived alone in a high-rise apartment smack in the middle of downtown. His office was four blocks from the James R. Thompson Center.

Most of the legislative body worked out of there, making it a source of contention amongst the voters. Almost all state representatives and senators lived in Chicago. They traveled to Springfield when they had sessions to attend. The James R. Thompson Center had long been referred to as the State of Illinois Building. Damien now referred to it as the State Building.

Damien thought it was ironic, knowing Rossdale's profession, that his office would be so close to that building. After searching his work-space, they would have a short hop over to see Senator Lockhart. Not something Damien was looking forward to.

# CHAPTER FOUR

Damien pulled up outside the office of Glenn Rossdale. Four news crews were already set up. "Oh, fucking kill me now," he said looking over to Joe. He placed his on-duty police sign in the window. There was no way he would spend endless hours searching for a spot, even if it meant he blocked traffic. He turned on his blinking blue and white lights. He texted Detective Travis and asked him to send a uniformed officer to stand outside Rossdale's residence. He didn't want anyone entering or exiting until the home had been secured and searched. Damien's phone pinged with a text. "We have warrants for both his home and here."

"Well, hot diggity dog. Let's go in and bust some balls," Joe said laughing as he exited the vehicle.

Immediately, Damien and Joe were rushed by the news reporters.

"Lieutenant Kaine, can you give us any information on the death of Glenn Rossdale?"

Damien merely strolled through the crowd not answering anything. Questions continued to ring out as they entered the building.

A doorman ran up to them. "I'm sorry, unless you have business in this building you are going to have to leave the premises. The offices of Mr. Rossdale are closed today. As are most of the other offices in this building."

The man stood like a sentry. Allowing no one to pass. Damien tapped the shield located on his belt. "I'm Lieutenant Kaine."

"Oh, yes, Lieutenant. Sorry, I didn't notice your badge. Rossdale's secretary and personnel are all in his office. Just through those doors." The security guard pointed to an ornate set of double doors. "Due to the coverage on the news, several other businesses in this building have closed for the day."

"Who else is in this building?" Damien asked.

"There are two architectural firms. One specializes in residential and one in commercial. There is a personal injury attorney and a graphic designer. To the best of my knowledge, they are all working from their homes for the next few days."

"Could you get me all their information, along with all their contact details? We are going to need to speak with anyone who might have seen Mr. Rossdale in the last twenty-four hours. How about you, what can you tell me about yesterday and Mr. Rossdale?"

The doorman had moved to his computer. He spoke as he typed out a series of commands. "I'm here daily from eight a.m. to five p.m. The front doors are locked around that time. There is a panel located between the two sets of entry doors. Each office has a buzzer so anyone coming in after the five o'clock hour can buzz wherever they need to get in."

The doorman turned to a printer as a piece of paper came out. "Here's all the tenants' information." He handed the paper to Damien. "As for last night, I stayed until roughly five-thirty. One of the architectural firms expected a delivery, and they asked if I would stay until it showed up. After the delivery, I left."

Damien glanced at the sheet. This was a job he could give Fuentes and Grimer. Having two big men show up at these people's homes would no doubt help get the information they needed. "Thank you for this." Damien held the paper up. "Was there anyone here with Mr. Rossdale when you left?"

The doorman's eyebrows wrinkled. "I'm sure his assistant can help you more. She has his schedule. But, as for last night, I don't think anyone was in there. I didn't stop in before I left. I had to head out, but I can tell you he had plans for last night. He'd mentioned he had dinner plans. He didn't elaborate, though, so I'm afraid that is all I know."

"Do you have any idea with whom he had plans? Do you know if he was seeing someone regularly?" Damien asked.

"No, but I think it was a woman. He seemed excited about it. He had changed into a nicer shirt and pair of pants. Usually, he wears jeans and casual shirts, unless he has something major."

"Thank you for your time. Can you get me a copy of the security disks before I leave? Do you think you can you go back, say, four or five days?"

"No problem, Lieutenant. I can have the information for you before you leave. I will also print out any key lock entries occurring after hours."

Damien tilted his head. "What do you mean?"

"Oh, after hours if you want to come in, you have to use a special key card and a unique passcode. Every time the code is accessed, an electronic record is made. The information will have who and when they entered and left. To exit the building, you must repeat the process. Unless you leave via the emergency exit, but an alarm will sound, and the police and fire are automatically called."

"Thank you. Go back a week for me on those disks. I appreciate it." Damien turned to Joe and nodded towards Rossdale's office doors.

Joe leaned in. "Do you know how expensive an office building like this has to be? It's very exclusive."

"Yeah, and there are going to be limited people coming in and out. Hopefully, that will make our jobs easier." Damien held open the door for Joe. "Age before beauty."

"We are practically the same age, dufus," Joe chuckled.

"Okay, fat ugly Irishmen before sexy Italians."

"Oh brother, now you're delusional."

As they entered, a teary-eyed brunette looked up from her desk. "Oh, I'm sorry. Mr. Rossdale is unavailable."

"Yes, ma'am, we know. I'm Lieutenant Kaine, and this is Detective Joe Hagan. We are going to need to go through Mr. Rossdale's office, and we need to speak with everyone who was here yesterday."

The young receptionist's eyes widened. She rolled her chair back from her desk. "Oh my, I don't think I can let you into his office." The young lady shifted her gaze from the door to the two men before her.

Damien leaned over the counter. He pulled his phone out. "I have a copy of the warrant which allows me access to his workplace and his home. I can email it to you so you can print it. But we have the authority to go through everything. How about if you call someone?" Damien smiled at the young lady, hoping to calm her.

Her eyes were glossy with moisture. "Oh—okay." Her hand shook as she dialed a number. "Yes, Sandra, two detectives are up here. Okay." She looked up at Damien. "She will be right up."

Damien and Joe stepped away from the desk. They had the authority to walk in and do what they wanted and needed to do, but Damien wanted to make friends, not make his job any harder than it had to be.

A smartly dressed woman, Damien estimated her age around twenty-six, walked towards them. Her dark hair had been cut in a style that enhanced her heart-shaped face and her bright blue eyes sparkled like pieces of glass in the sunlight.

"Hi, I'm Sandra Kirkland, Mr. Rossdale's assistant. Why don't you two tell me what I can do for you."

Damien smiled. "I'm sure you know why we are here. We have a warrant to search these premises as well as Mr. Rossdale's home, in hopes of garnering any information which will help us find out who killed him."

Sandra sighed. "Would you follow me, please?" She turned and led them down a skinny hallway past one office and one conference room.

"Is this where he does his radio show from?" Joe peeked inside what looked like a state-of-the-art media room. The room was filled with high-end recording equipment. The walls had been covered in a thick material helping absorb background noises.

"Yes. Mr. Rossdale had this room built specifically for recording purposes. He didn't want to have to go to a studio." Sandra led them to a large office.

Two oversized leather chairs faced a rich mahogany desk. The inlay of wood gave the desk a rich and robust color. Sandra looked around. When her gaze landed on Damien, he could see her eyes glistened.

"Forgive me. I didn't want to discuss anything within earshot of Anna. She is very young and not always trustworthy. I don't need any search warrant. You are welcome to go through everything. You can have officers come in and search everything in his office and mine. As well as every other room in here." The tears spilled over. "I have worked with him for over six years. Right out of college. I loved him." Sandra used a handkerchief to dab the corners of her eyes in hopes of stopping the deluge of tears.

Damien glanced at Joe. When he returned his stare to her, she had a slight smile on her face.

"Not that kind of love. He treated me like his daughter. He didn't have kids. Said he never wanted them." Her lips pressed together in a tight smile. "Truth be told, he did want kids. He was just a tough man to live with, and keeping a serious relationship intact would have probably killed him. I lost my father and mother when I was younger, so he filled that void in my life. I never took his sarcastic humor to heart. I knew when he needed to vent and learned early on not to take anything personally."

Sandra moved to sit behind the desk. "I need to sit." She gestured to the two chairs in front of her. "What do you want to know from me?"

"First, who did he have plans with last night?" Damien shot a quick glance at Joe. Damien turned back to the attractive woman. He listened intently, waiting to catch her in a lie or slip up. Her quickness to help had him both leery and grateful. At the moment, he wasn't sure which would win.

She reached into the center drawer of the desk. "According to Glenn's ledger, he had a dinner date. He wouldn't tell me who it was with."

Damien watched Joe walk over to look at photos on the wall. He turned back to Sandra. "Was he seeing someone special? Dating anyone?"

Sandra laughed in a sexy husky tone. She looked at Damien, the corners of her mouth twitched. "Do you know anything about Glenn, his personal life at all?"

Damien frowned. "No. I don't. Should I?"

"For as much as that man was in the news, his personal life never was. I don't know how he managed to be so secretive and get away with it. It must have something to do with all the secrets he knew. I always figured, those in fear of being outed for various activities made sure Glenn's personal stuff was never spoken about."

Sandra reached into her pocket and pulled out the key. She stood and moved to a wall sconce. She twisted it to one side revealing a hidden door behind a wooden panel. Sandra used a combination, and a key to unlock a door roughly the size of one square foot. She retrieved a notebook-sized leather journal.

When she turned around to see the wide-eyed expressions on both Damien and Joe's faces a giggle escaped. "He put this in a long time ago. Only he and I knew of it. I need to clarify a few things. When you check his will, you will see I'm a benefactor. He told me years ago he would make sure I was taken care of. I'm going to try to keep his work going. I learned a lot from him. And I hope I can continue to hold these politicians accountable."

She sat at the desk. Sandra placed the journal in front of her and stared at it. A few tears dripped on the leather. She gently wiped them off the rich brown material. She glanced back up at the handsome detectives. She smiled at Joe as he took the seat next to Damien. "I understand that statement puts me at the top of the list. Whatever you need from me to clear me, just tell me. The sooner you move your suspicions from me, the sooner you can widen your search." Sandra pulled a card from a desk drawer. "This is our attorney. He already has permission to answer any of your estate questions."

Damien raised an eyebrow. "Could you tell me where you were last night?"

She wrote another note, handing it to Damien. "I was with one of my girlfriends at the hospital. She and her husband are having their first child, and Joseph, her husband, didn't get in until after three a.m. I stayed there all night even after he showed up. Here is their information. I was there from four p.m. until six a.m. this morning when I went home and changed for work."

Damien glanced at the piece of paper. He looked over at Joe who gave him a cheeky grin. He turned back to Sandra. "I don't think my partner and I have ever had such cooperation before in a murder investigation. Especially one like this."

When Sandra smiled, her eyes lit up. "I imagine that makes you even more leery of me."

Damien sat back in his chair. "I am curious as to why you are so forthcoming."

Sandra sighed as she gripped the edges of the journal on the desk. "My father was a detective in California before he died. He instilled in me that if more people would lay everything out from the beginning instead of trying to make the police work for the information, cases could be solved easier and quicker, at least he hoped they would be."

"That explains it. So, tell us what you know." Damien waited for her response.

Her expression softened as she gazed at the detectives. "Glenn dated a lot of women. Occasionally even the odd man. He preferred women, but he enjoyed a sexual encounter with a man occasionally. If a man caught his fancy, he would spend the night with him. He was happiest in the company of someone. He didn't like to be alone. Yesterday before I left, he had mentioned he would be dining with a friend. I asked him where, but all he did was smile at me and said that was his secret. He often did that. I think his ability to keep secrets to himself helped keep his own out of the news."

"Do you have an educated guess who it might've been?" Damien asked.

"My guess, it was a male. If Glenn dated a woman, he kept it very casual, nice jeans maybe slacks. But for some reason, if he went out with a guy, he dressed up. Don't ask me to explain the psychology behind it."

Joe noticed Sandra's hands rested on the journal as if to keep it safe. He glanced back to the wall then back at her. "I guess that cubby hole was built for the book."

Sandra looked over at Joe. His eyes were emerald green with gold flecks. A darker green circle encompassed the pupil making the lighter green color glow. She tilted her head towards the wall. "That's correct. I know this sounds cloak and daggerish, but that was Glenn. He always figured one day something would happen and I would need this."

She leaned back. "Tonya Fairchild and Josh Temple were the two people he spent most of his time with. I think they even spent time together, although Tonya and Josh didn't mingle without Glenn present. I figured his date was with one of them. I will give you their contact information."

Damien watched her. Sandra Kirkland was damn efficient and prepared. Well prepared. Her excuse about her father made sense, but he still didn't trust her. No one ever *wanted* to give information voluntarily to the police. He wasn't sure of her motivation, but he was willing to see where it went. "Why is that book so important, Miss Kirkland? And do you think that's what got him killed?"

She shook her head. "I'm not sure. He said if anything ever happened to him, I was to give it to you, Lieutenant Kaine."

Damien looked over at Joe turning back to Sandra. "I don't understand. Me specifically or me the authorities?"

"You specifically. Glenn was aware of Belgosa's womanizing. He also knew about his book, Bishop Cantor, and the sex scandal. He was mindful when that book never came out in the news, he decided then he could trust you." She turned her attention to Joe. "And your partner."

Damien bristled at the comment of his last case. He knew there was one other copy of Belgosa's book on his sexual escapades. The original was stashed in the Chief's safe at DC, and the other was at Damien's father's security company. Locked away in a safe. A young woman distraught at the suicide of her mother had held priests responsible for her mother's death and murdered them in some wicked ways. Each one punished for a perceived sin they had committed. Although the killings had been hard to deal with, the realization the Catholic Church had purposely withheld information and stonewalled the investigation never did sit well with Damien. He and his staunchly Catholic Italian family had several discussions over the issue, not always resulting in a warm and fuzzy feeling.

Sandra's gaze shifted between the two detectives. "We are the only three who know about this book. I don't plan on telling anyone else. There is a letter inside, addressed to you. When you showed up this morning, I knew what I was supposed to do. Before you turn this in as evidence, you need to read the letter and the book."

Damien's jaw tensed. "I'm baffled. Why would he want me to have this book? He had to know, as an officer of the law, I am required to turn over all evidence collected during an investigation."

She roared with laughter. "Glenn knew a lot about you. He made you his business after the Jason Freestone case in Springfield. I think he secretly wanted to be your lover, but he knew that would never happen. He always said you were the sexiest most masculine man he had ever seen."

Joe snorted. All eyes turned towards him. "What?"

She smiled at Joe. "You don't get off that easy, Detective Joe Hagan. He had his eye on you too. He often thought a threesome between both of you would send him to heaven."

Damien held in his laugh. "Yeah, Joe. What about that?" Damien looked back at Sandra.

She handed him the book. "Read the letter and the book, you'll know what to do. I don't think the book got him killed, though. No one knows of this book. But they do know he knows things. I believe the person responsible for his death isn't in this book. But I think Glenn found out something that led to his murder. I don't have any insight for you, but I'm aware he was working on something having to do with Senator Lockhart. Maybe not the state senator himself, but someone close to him. He had me gather a lot of research on the man, his family, and his staff."

Sandra reached into a drawer and handed Damien a folder. "This has all his research. I have read it several times, but I can't figure out what he was looking for. You may be able to piece it together."

"Why the senator?" Joe took the folder from Damien.

"Glenn told me about it several weeks ago, he had come into some information. By mistake really. But he wasn't sure what to do with it. He was looking for something, something specific."

Damien's eyebrows drew together. "Was that after the party held for Senator Lockhart?"

"Yes. Something happened at or before the party. He didn't elaborate. But shortly after the party, he asked me to start researching the senator. Glenn was great at taking a morsel of information and turning it into a meal."

Sandra nodded towards the book. "That book is the holy grail. It has information on senators to representatives, both state and congressional, as well as presidents to governors. Glenn was privy to a lot of information. Why do you think his questions always struck a nerve with his interviewees? He had enough to get them to talk. He may not have known everything, but he knew enough to make them nervous. The questions he asked let them know: answer me, or you'll have a problem. But he never would use any of the information. That wasn't his style. And I think most knew that."

Damien focused on the book in his hand. He didn't like having it. He didn't know what he was going to do with it. "Do you have anything else for us?"

She smiled at him. "Yes, I do. I know you are working on a warrant for all his communications. I set up all his mobile accounts. So, I'm the primary account holder." She held out another folder to Damien. "That has all his communications for the last sixty days. I can go back further if you need me to. There is no reason for the warrant. Whatever you need access to, you can have.

"I asked the phone company if there has been any activity on his phone since yesterday, they said no. One last thing," Sandra reached into the side drawer and pulled out an electronic bag. "Inside you will find jump drives. I have downloaded every file from his computer. You can take his laptop." She pointed towards the corner of the desk. "He may have a hidden file on there. If you guys find one, I may have the code, and I don't realize it. Let me know, and we can go from there."

She laughed at their expressions. "Glenn often did things like that. He would tell me to write something down, then if he ever mentioned something like cupcakes, I was to remember that was the code for whatever he had given me. He was a little paranoid."

Damien nodded to Joe who took the laptop from the desk. He watched as her eyebrows drew together. "What is it, Sandra?"

She shook her head. "You are welcome to search here anytime. If what I have given you leads you to something and you need my assistance, please call me." She handed him her card. "Oh," Sandra reached into her pocket. "Here are the keys to his home. I own that. He transferred the title to me some time back for tax purposes. He said I could do with it as I needed when he died. I will keep it the way it is until I let him go." She wiped her cheek. "When you are finished there if you would let me know I will have the locks changed. Attached to the key is a code. You need to enter it before you put in the key. Otherwise, it won't work."

Damien smiled. "My family has a similar system set up at their house."

She laughed at him. "Of course, it's the same. It's from your father."

Damien nodded. "I remember. Rossdale had my Dad hook up his home security a few years back."

"Glenn liked your family very much. Another reason he wanted you to have the book. He said you would do right by him." Sandra sighed. "Is there anything else I can do for you two?"

Damien glanced at Joe, shrugging his shoulders.

Joe laughed. "Damn, I wish all our interviews went like this. You've been a fantastic help."

Damien stood. "I can't thank you enough." He held out a card to her. "If you need me for anything, you call me."

Her lips formed a thin smile. "Thank you. I will." Sandra held up her forefinger. She bent over and brought up an empty box she had sitting at her feet. "Here, put everything in this. It will keep the vultures outside from knowing what you are taking out."

When Damien reached for the box, she grabbed his wrist.

"Promise me you will find his killer. I loved him." Her voice choked on her tears. "He treated me like his daughter, and I loved him. I was lucky to have had two fathers in my lifetime. I miss him." Now the tears streamed down Sandra's cheeks.

"Joe and I will find who killed him. I promise you. Thank you for everything today. I think we have enough to start with. We will be going to his residence in the next few hours. I will phone you as soon as we are finished."

They left her sitting in her boss's chair. As Damien pulled the door shut behind them to give her some privacy, they heard the soft sobs. Exiting Glenn's office, the doorman met them in the foyer.

"Here is everything you asked for. I pulled the security for the last two weeks. Anything after that time is stored off-site for thirty days. If you need any more, please call me, and I can have the videos for you." He held out a bag with several items in it.

"Thank you very much. If we have any questions, we will contact you." Damien took the bag from him. He and Joe headed out to the truck.

The press corps seemed to have multiplied. Questions came at them lightning fast. An overzealous reporter shoved a microphone into Damien's face and barked out several questions. Damien gave the reporter a cold hard stare. The man took a step back and stumbled trying to retreat to a safe distance. Damien pulled away from the curb before he and Joe spoke.

Joe raised an eyebrow at him. "Sandra saved us a lot of work."

"Yeah, she did. Text Travis, tell him to meet us at Rossdale's residence and let him know he doesn't need a warrant. Tell him to be there in an hour or so. Tell him to bring Fuentes and Grimer if they are there. In a separate vehicle."

"You got it." Joe typed away on his phone. When he was finished, he thumbed through the file that held the research on Lockhart. "There doesn't seem to be anything but dates and accomplishments regarding James Lockhart in this file." Joe closed the folder. "If it is as Sandra says, then Rossdale had to be researching the Lockharts for a reason."

"Well, I'm hoping when we have a chance to go through that book that we will find some correlation to the research."

Joe glanced around realizing they were headed in the opposite direction of the State Building. "Let me guess, we're going to your house?"

"Yeah, I want to drop the book off. I will go through it and you can too. We will decide what is best." Damien ran a hand through his hair. "I don't like being put in this situation, but I have a feeling he did it for a reason. No one will know of this book. I'm not telling Dillon. The fewer who know of it, the better."

"What book?" Joe asked offering a bemused expression.

# CHAPTER FIVE

Damien pulled up outside Glenn Rossdale's high-rise apartment.

Joe whistled as he looked at the doorman. "I have a feeling Sandra is going to be set for life. I guarantee this property alone is worth several million."

"I'm sure she won't be hurting. She also seems like she has a good head on her shoulders," Damien grabbed the box from the back seat. The officer he asked Detective Travis to send over had done an excellent job at keeping the press corps away from the entrance. As soon as they walked in, a man in a black suit greeted them. "I guess you are Lieutenant Kaine?"

Damien tilted his head towards the man. "Yes, I am. This is my partner, Detective Joe Hagan. We need to go up to Mr. Rossdale's residence."

"Yes, Miss Kirkland phoned me. She said to send you on up. His residence is on the top floor. Take the elevator marked private." The doorman pointed to the last elevator in the bank. "I've already opened it for you."

"Thank you. Some other officers should be showing up. Would you send them on up when they get here?"

"Yes, Sir."

Damien nodded and followed Joe to the elevator. "Have we stepped into another universe?"

"Ha, wait until we get to the State Building. All the cooperation we are getting now will be gone. And we will be back to reality as we know it. And assholes. We will be back to working with assholes."

They exited the elevator to an opulent entry, and they weren't even in the residence yet. Damien used the code and the key, and when the doors opened, the smell hit them like a tidal wave.

"Oh, fuck me. I think we found our crime scene," Joe said.

Damien pulled out his phone. "Hey, Roger, it's Kaine. You need to get over to Rossdale's residence. We found our crime scene. Okay. No, we will be here." Damien went to the phone on the wall that linked to the security desk at the front door.

"Yes, Lieutenant Kaine, what can I do for you?" The doorman asked.

"Listen, I need you to pull all the security logins and video for this property. There will be Crime Scene Techs coming here. You need to keep any traffic away from this area until we release the scene."

"Are you telling me this is where he was murdered?"

"Yes, Sir. Thank you for your assistance." Damien hung up. He pulled his phone back out and called Sandra Kirkland. He wanted to let her know it would be several days before she could get into the residence. Damien also gave her a number for a cleanup crew who could have it cleaned and sanitized before she ever came in. The last thing he wanted was for her memory of this place and Glenn tarnished by the blood, tissue, and brain matter that covered most of the living room area.

Joe stood at the edge of the room. "Well, I think we know what the killer used on his head." Joe pointed to a chair in the center of the room. Laying on the floor next to it was a spiked metal bat. One side had a metal sheeting attached to it that literally looked like a giant cheese grater. "I don't think you can buy that kind of bat at Uncle Dan's Sports store."

Damien raised his eyebrows. "Really? I figured this was a stock item. Maybe if we're lucky, we can get a lead from it."

Since they didn't have any booties on their shoes, they stepped gingerly around the scene. It looked like the man had been tied to a chair and beaten to death over an extended amount of time. There was a noticeable void in the middle of the floor.

Damien looked around. "I'm betting the killer had something he wrapped him up in so he could get him out of the building. Look at this area. I'm not sure what it was, probably a tarp of some sort. I don't see any drops, so it covered the body completely."

Joe moved from the living room to the master bedroom. "Hey, come in here," he yelled out to Damien.

"What's up... oh." Damien glanced around the room. "I think before he was killed he had a damn good time." Several condom wrappers were on the floor of the space. The sheets on the bed were rumpled, but the room didn't look like a struggle had taken place. It read as if consensual sex had occurred. A lot of it. "Maybe we'll get lucky, and some of that stuff is the killer's." Damien pointed towards the condoms.

Joe frowned. "We need DNA to tell us who wore the condoms. But I can't see the killer leaving his *spunk* in a condom on the floor."

Damien snorted. "Where the hell do you come up with these words?"

"Oh, should I say semen?"

"Well, that is the correct terminology." Damien walked around the room. "You think it was a woman, and the beating came later?"

Joe ran his hand through his hair. "How the hell should I know? Do I look psychic to you?"

Damien laughed. "What's the matter?"

"I was thinking how much this is going to make our lives even more complicated, and it's pissing me off." Joe walked out of the room when he heard a noise in the foyer.

Damien and Joe walked out to find Travis, Fuentes, Grimer, and Roger. "Well, the clan is all here." Damien pointed to Roger. "Did you bring help?"

"Yes. Jacoby is bringing up another kit from the van." Roger looked around. "Wow. You think they sell that bat at Uncle Dan's?"

Joe high-fived him. "I said the same thing. Hopefully, we will get some evidence off it. It seems like a pretty specific weapon of choice."

Damien nodded over his shoulder towards the master. "It looks like he had a lot of sex in there before he died. There are several condoms strewn about the floor."

Roger smiled. "Dang, I don't have that much sex."

"Roger, you don't even have sex," Joe said mockingly.

"Fuck you, Hagan. I have a few side pieces I have sex with. Can't tie myself to one girl, where would the fun be in that?" Roger was about to say something else when a sound off to his right caught his attention.

Fuentes and Grimer weren't prepared for the blood and tissue surrounding them. Fuentes had fallen against a table inside the foyer. Damien noticed they both paled as they stood there. The smell of decomposing flesh and brain matter wasn't something traffic cops were used to. "Fuentes, you gonna be alright?"

Fuentes waved a hand in front of his face. "Yeah, wasn't prepared for this. Shit, you see some pretty bad shit in traffic accidents, but that's a different environment."

Damien nodded. "Listen, Grimer, I have a list of people who work in the same building as Rossdale. I'd like for you guys to go to each one of their homes, and interview them. Find out if they saw anything in the last few days. Ask them if they have seen anyone coming and going in and out of Rossdale's office." Damien reached into his back pocket and pulled out the folded piece of paper with everyone's contact information from the office building. "If they aren't at home, call them and find out where they are. Go to them. Don't call before you go to their residences. I want the element of surprise on your side."

Grimer reached out and took the paper. "You got it, Lieutenant. We'll contact you when we've questioned everyone." He held a hand out to Fuentes. "C'mon big boy. Let's get the hell out of here."

Fuentes smacked his hand away. "Suck it, asshole." He chuckled. "I saw the color drain from your face. Don't act like this smell isn't getting to you."

Grimer laughed as they exited the residence.

Damien glanced around the apartment. "Detective Travis, I have a box over by the door. It has Rossdale's laptop from his office. Several jump drives, and all his cell phone activity. As well as all the security footage for the building. If you need anything else," he handed Sandra's card to him. "Call her. She will get you whatever you need."

Travis took the card and placed it in his pocket. "You got it. I'm going to take everything back with me."

"The doorman will have the security film from this building too. Make sure to pick it up when you leave. I need you to get on that security footage ASAP. We need to see if there is anyone on it." Damien pointed to the bat. "Our killer had to get that bat into the building somehow." He moved towards Joe. "We can come back here later after Roger does his job. I don't want to get in his way of collecting evidence."

Joe nodded. "I like that idea. This place stinks."

"See you guys later. Seal the door with an electronic lock. Text me the code," Damien said to them. He and Joe headed back out to the vehicle. "Let's go hit the senator's office and see if we can find out what the argument at the party was about. I have a feeling we will get one shot at asking Senator James Lockhart any questions before the FBI shuts us down."

Joe lifted his chin and inhaled the fresh January air. "How much you want to bet we will be in and out of there in under an hour with no answers?"

"Are you saying members of our legislative branch of government, won't be willing to help us?"

"That's exactly what I'm saying. How much?"

Damien looked at his watch. "Lunch from Carlitto's or Kaufman's."

# CHAPTER SIX

Damien pulled in front of the Thompson Building. He placed his on-duty placard in the window and turned on his flashing lights when a security guard approached him.

"You're going to have to move your vehicle." The man pointed at Damien as he spoke.

"Not in this lifetime. I'm on official business." Both Damien and Joe held their badges up.

The security guard stepped closer to them and studied each badge. He pulled out his handheld. "Hey Alvin, grab Carlos and tell him to get his scrawny ass out here. I need him to do a standby." The guard held out his hand to Damien. "I'm Mark. Head of security here."

"Nice to meet you, Mark. What's a standby?" Damien asked as he clipped his badge back on his belt.

"Carlos will stand out here at your vehicle, even with the flashing lights and placard, Robin from the parking squad will try to have your vehicle towed. She's a bitch and likes to take her miserable life out on others. Carlos will make sure she doesn't do anything."

"Thank you. I appreciate your assistance. Can you tell me anything about Senator Lockhart's assistant?" Damien asked.

Mark lifted an eyebrow at the lieutenant. "I can tell you a lot." He glanced over his shoulder. "You better have a warrant to get any information out of his tightwad ass. He thinks he knows everything about everything. Takes his job as attaché to Lockhart like he is a superior ass." Mark glanced around again. He handed Damien a card. "You call me later, away from here, and I will answer all your questions. I'd rather not look like I'm cooperating with you. I like my life the way it is."

Damien took the card he held out. "I understand. You ever hear of Mulligan's?"

Mark's nodded. "You can't consider yourself a damn Chicagoan and not know Mulligan's."

"Good. We will set up a meet there, yeah?" Damien pocketed the card.

"Sounds good. Let me know when," Mark said.

A short, muscled Mexican man walked up. "Hey, Carlos. Make sure you know who doesn't try to have the Lieutenant's car towed. She seemed extra pissy at the briefing this morning."

"*No hay problema.*" Carlos smiled at Joe and Damien. "She hates her life. So, she makes ours even worse. Don't worry about your vehicle, Lieutenant."

Damien nodded. "Thank you, Carlos." He and Joe headed into the foyer of the State Building. They raised their badges at the security officer.

"Yes, Lieutenant, Mark just tagged me." He motioned for them to take their weapons off. "After you go through the scanner, I will hand your weapons back to you." Security Officer Johnson placed their weapons in a special container passing them to another officer on the other side of the body scanner.

Both Damien and Joe proceeded through the scanner and retrieved their weapons. As Damien holstered his gun, Johnson held out visitor's badges.

"You'll need to wear these while you are in this building. If you take the third elevator over there," he pointed to a bank of elevators, "push the fifth floor. Lockhart's assistant, Tyler Bryce, should be there to greet you."

Damien scrutinized the security officer. "How does he know we are here?"

The guard shrugged. "He phoned me this morning to let us know we should be expecting you. As soon as Mark buzzed me to let me know you were here, I phoned up to his office. As per his instructions."

Damien shifted his feet leaning into the man. "Can you tell me what time this morning he called you?"

The officer held up his finger and looked in a log book. "Yeah, I logged the call at eight forty this morning."

Damien nodded. "Okay. Thank you for your assistance." Damien's skin tingled. If he hadn't found out the identity of Rossdale until seven thirty that morning, how the hell did Tyler Bryce know they would be coming today? He was running the timeline in his head when he and Joe entered the elevator. Damien noticed the small camera in the corner and nudged Joe. "*L'ascensore ha le orecchie e gli occhi. Attento a quello che dici.*"

Joe smiled at him. "Oh hey, I got the camera guy lined up for the party, I know he will take video and stills. This party should be a helluva good time."

Damien smiled knowing his partner got the hint. He started to say something else as the doors opened. There stood a tall, lithe man holding a clipboard in his hand. He spoke rapidly into a Bluetooth earpiece as he held up a finger. His stylish, dark blond hair was cut a little longer on top and was parted and swept to one side. The man's beady brown eyes bore through them.

"Listen, Charlie. Do whatever you need to do, but the senator wanted those files yesterday. Well, that's not my problem, is it? Do your damn job, or I can have you replaced." He tapped a button by his ear and glanced at his watch. "I'm Tyler Bryce, the assistant to Senator Lockhart, who is a very busy man. He can give you approximately fifteen to twenty minutes. Please follow me."

Damien didn't say anything. The words of his captain echoed in his head. He and Joe fell into step behind the assistant. They were led down the long wide corridor. As they passed opened doors to various offices, Damien could see men and women dressed in suits and skirts huddled over computers or large open files splattered on top of desks. The offices bustled with activity. As they neared the end of the hallway, Tyler led them through a large oak door. They entered an immaculate outer office. Not a file out on the desk or a cabinet drawer left open.

Tyler brushed a piece of lint off his jacket as he spoke to the detectives. "Give me a few moments?" He turned and went into another office, closing the door behind him.

Damien leaned into Joe, "It took everything I had not to shoot this fucker. All I kept hearing was the captain telling me to play nice."

Joe smiled at him. "I saw the smoke pouring from your ears. Good job on keeping your weapon holstered."

The door opened, and Mr. Bryce motioned for them to come into the inner sanctum. Behind the desk sat Senator Lockhart. Damien had seen his picture several times but was still taken aback by his youthful appearance. He knew the senator was in his thirties, but he sure as hell didn't look like it. If Damien weren't familiar with the man, he would have thought he had recently graduated from college.

The state senator stood and extended his hand. "Lieutenant, please have a seat. What can I do for you two today?" He motioned to two chairs in front of his desk. The senator ran a perfectly manicured and delicate hand through his sandy brown hair, adjusting his tie as he took his seat.

The man was fit and toned. He was average height, but he had an air of superiority. But something nagged at Damien. Even with his position of power, the senator didn't seem all that comfortable with power.

Tyler Bryce stood off to the left of the senator's desk. Like a guard ready to stop any unwanted intrusion. Damien removed a small notebook from his pocket. "Senator Lockhart, I'm sure you are aware of the circumstances that bring us to your doorstep."

Senator Lockhart glanced over his shoulder and was met with an almost unnoticeable nod from his assistant. He smiled faintly. "Yes, I am aware of the untimely death of Glenn Rossdale. I'm still confused as to why you are here to see me. I don't know what I can help you with. I didn't have any reason to hold regular meetings with the man. He often ran in my circle of acquaintances, that's it."

Damien noticed as the senator shifted slightly in his seat, leaning back with a slight grimace on his face. Damien glanced between Lockhart and his assistant Tyler Bryce. Unspoken instructions were passing between the two. "Senator, did you have any meeting scheduled with Rossdale or any appearances planned on his talk show by chance?" Damien waited for the senator's response.

He quickly glanced at an open agenda on his desk. "I don't have anything on my schedule, anyway. Tyler, was I supposed to appear on Rossdale's show anytime soon?"

Tyler frowned, shaking his head. "No."

"Do you know if Rossdale had contacted anyone in your office," Damien nodded towards Tyler, "other than your assistant, trying to gather any information on you or someone associated with you?"

Senator Lockhart's eyebrow's smashed together. He shook his head slightly. "Why would Glenn Rossdale want to talk to anyone in my keep? He wasn't planning on an interview nor was I scheduled to do one. I'm not sure why you think I have something to hide, but I have no idea why the man would want to question those around me."

Damien raised an eyebrow. "Why would we think you had something to hide, Senator?"

The senator leaned forward placing his elbows on his desk. "I'm sorry, I misspoke. What is it that I can help you with?"

Damien didn't want to give too much of his investigation away, but he needed to get a handle on the situation with Tyler Bryce and the senator. "Are you aware of an argument Rossdale had with your assistant Mr. Bryce?"

Senator Lockhart turned in his chair and stared at his assistant. He eyes narrowed, but he didn't say anything. Senator Lockhart turned his attention back to the detectives. "I'm not sure what you are referring to."

Damien had the impression the senator had no idea anything had occurred between the two men. Damien focused on the senator. "At the party held in your honor, several weeks back. It seems Mr. Bryce got into an argument with Mr. Rossdale." He turned towards the assistant. "Can you tell me, Mr. Bryce, what the argument was about?"

Tyler took a half step forward. His face had a pinched expression. He sighed heavily. He folded his arms across his chest. "I think you have been misinformed. There was no argument between Mr. Rossdale and myself. We were simply discussing the senator and his appearance, or lack thereof on Rossdale's show."

Damien looked over at Joe and gave him a slight grin.

Joe smiled at the assistant. He spoke with his melodic Irish lilt. "Ah, Mr. Bryce, we were under the impression the senator wasn't scheduled in any way for an interview with Rossdale. Are you telling us Rossdale had approached you about the senator doing an interview on his show?"

Tyler Bryce's face became rigid, and all pleasantness left his expression. "I think I need to explain. Mr. Rossdale had approached me the night of the party and asked if the senator would be interested in doing his show. He wanted to set something up to coincide with the announcement of the senator's official entry into the governor's race." Tyler shifted his stance. "I informed Rossdale that Senator Lockhart had no intention of doing his show. That must be the argument you are referring to. Glenn didn't take the refusal gracefully. I walked away after that."

The senator had a lost look on his face. It seemed evident that whatever occurred between Bryce and Rossdale, the senator was unaware of the incident. That added to Damien's suspicion that had nothing to do with the argument between the two men.

Joe leaned in slightly towards the senator. "I find it slightly odd that your assistant would have a conversation about you doing a syndicated, highly watched show, and you wouldn't be privy to the contents of that conversation. Especially if it is as Mr. Bryce stated, and that Rossdale wanted to interview you before your announcement into the governor's race." Joe smiled deliciously and looked at his partner. "Lieutenant Kaine, don't you find that slightly odd?"

Damien nodded in agreement. "I do." He focused on the senator. "Are you telling us, Senator Lockhart, that you would turn down that kind of opportunity?"

The senator shifted in his seat. As he was getting ready to answer the question, his assistant stepped forward and whispered into his ear. The senator frowned and looked at his watch. "Gentlemen," he said, rising, "I am sorry that I need to cut this short, but I'm expected in a cabinet meeting. I would be more than happy to schedule an interview later, to answer any more of your questions." He gestured towards the door with his hand. "I would like a little notice before the next interview, however. I think in a case as high profile as this, it would be prudent to have my counsel in the next meeting."

Damien and Joe took their cue and followed the silent instructions of the senator asking them to leave his office. Damien moved towards the door and stopped. He turned towards the assistant. "One last question, Mr. Bryce. How did you know we would be coming to see you this morning?"

Mr. Bryce shook his head. "I'm not sure what you mean."

"You phoned the security guard downstairs and told him to be expecting us. How did you know that?" Damien asked.

Tyler Bryce's eyes squinted together. "Senator Lockhart called me on his way in and told me." Bryce glanced at his boss.

Senator Lockhart smiled. "Yes, I did. I have a friend in the press corps that keeps me informed about a few things. I can't tell you who, but he let me know."

Damien focused back on the assistant. "Mr. Bryce, I need to schedule a time to get your official statement regarding your interaction with Mr. Rossdale. Could you please have your secretary call me with a date and time at your earliest convenience?"

Tyler Bryce's gaze narrowed in on the lieutenant. "I have already told you what I know, why do I need to give an 'official' statement?"

Damien handed one of his cards to the man. "Since you were involved in a heated discussion with a man who was recently murdered, you can understand that we need to clarify a few things about that conversation." Damien started through the open doorway. "Oh, by the way, Mr. Bryce, where were you last night, say, from nine p.m. until roughly three a.m.?"

"How dare you! I had nothing to do with this man's murder. I don't have to answer your questions." Tyler Bryce's eyes flamed red from the heat that burned there.

Damien's posture stiffened making his muscles rigid. He sighed heavily with exaggeration.

Joe took a small step towards the man. He rose a good five inches above him. "Actually, you do. You can answer the question now or at our station in one of our interrogation rooms. We are giving you the benefit of your association with Senator Lockhart. Please don't make us revoke that benefit."

Tyler took a deep breath and shifted slightly from one foot to the other. His mouth downturned and he bowed his head. "I apologize. The senator is a big supporter of our men in blue, and I'm aware of what you are up against. I had a late evening meeting with the senator and his wife, Amber. I left their residence around twelve thirty a.m. and arrived home at roughly one a.m. You can check with the security of my building. They can verify that."

Damien nodded and smiled. "Thank you. That is one more person we can remove from our suspect list. I do apologize if our questions offended you. That was not our intent. We can find our way out. Thank you again."

Damien and Joe stepped out into the hallway. As they made their way back to the main bank of elevators, they were intently aware all eyes were on them as they passed several offices.

As they reached the elevators to take them back to their vehicle, a young lady walked towards them. She stumbled forward grabbing Joe's arm as she lost her balance. As she reached out to grab the extended hand of the Irish cop, she leaned into him and quickly slipped a piece of paper into his hand.

"Oh, I'm so sorry. I'm such a klutz." She smiled up at the handsome man. "Please forgive me. I just purchased these shoes, and I seem to be a walking disaster." She straightened her skirt and adjusted her shirt.

Joe angled his head towards her. "That's okay. It isn't every day I get to keep a beautiful woman from face planting on the ground."

She smiled again and hurried away. Joe pocketed the note and stepped into the elevator. They rode in silence to the lobby.

They were greeted by the cold Chicago wind, as they walked out to Damien's truck. Carlos stood guard, arguing with who Damien assumed was Robin.

"I'm going to have you fired, and this truck towed. Get out of my way, Carlos." The woman huffed at him like a bull in a china shop ready and itching to break a whole lot of glass.

"Listen, Robin, you can't fire me. Mark told me to watch the lieutenant's vehicle. So, bug off, man." Carlos turned towards the footsteps behind him.

Damien noticed the immediate wash of relief over the man's face. "Hey, thanks very much, Carlos. The city of Chicago appreciates your assistance." Damien smiled and nodded in the man's direction.

"No worries, Lieutenant." Carlos almost ran into the entrance of the building.

Damien heard Joe snicker behind him as they both stepped up to the vehicle. He caught the surprised look from the young woman.

She quickly regained her composure. "You have no right to park here and block traffic."

Damien took a small step in her direction. "Miss, I have every right to park wherever the hell I want." He pointed to his badge and the placard in his window. "These two things give me that authority. I suggest if you have a problem with that you can call my superior. He will tell you the same thing." He smiled as he opened his car door. "You know, I have the right to arrest your bitchy ass, too. You seem to be hell-bent on blocking my duties as an officer of this state, and, last I looked, that was an arrestable offense. I suggest you pull your panties out of the uncomfortable wad they seem to be in." He left the young woman stunned and climbed into his truck to the laughter of his partner.

"Damn, I don't think our Robin here has ever been spoken to like that." Joe continued to chuckle as he buckled in.

"Yeah, I don't think so either." Damien pulled away from the front of the building. "What did that girl give you?" Damien chuckled. "You know, Taylor won't take kindly to you getting some random chick's number."

Joe wiggled his eyebrows at him. "She doesn't have to know..."

Damien smacked him in the chest. "If she doesn't kill you, you know Dillon will. And if either of them don't, I will."

Joe rubbed his chest. "You're a fucker, you know I wouldn't do that to her. Not to mention, she would torture my ass before she killed me." He reached into his pocket. "Well, let's see." He pulled out the paper and unfolded it. Scrawled messily across the paper was a written note. Joe read it out loud. "I have information that may help you. Call me tonight at this number. Laura." He looked up at his partner, "What the fuck kind of top-secret shit are we involved in? What do you think of that?"

Damien's lips pressed together into a white slash as he pulled to a stop at the red light. "Beats the fuck out of me. Evidently, no one wants to talk at the building. But they sure as hell have a lot to say. What about what the senator said about his press corps friend?"

Joe shrugged. "I can see that. He probably has a shit ton of informants that tell him all kinds of shit so he can stay out of any messes." Joe pocketed the note he had just read. "You owe me—Kaufman's. Let's go eat."

"Why do I owe you Kaufman's?"

Joe tapped the face of his watch. "Under an hour. You owe me lunch."

"Fuck. Damn Irish luck."

# CHAPTER SEVEN

Damien led the way from the garage to the house. Coach greeted them gleefully the minute they stepped through the door. "Hey, buddy." Damien reached down and scratched the top of his head. The cat darted ahead of them and ran into the kitchen circling his food bowl.

Joe laughed as he walked past the kitchen. "Does that cat think of nothing but food?" He placed the sandwiches on Dillon's desk and opened his diet soda.

"I know someone else who thinks of nothing but food," Damien muttered.

"I heard that," Joe said.

Damien chuckled as he watched the cat storm through the office door and jump onto Dillon's desk. Sitting with a glare, Coach glanced between the sandwiches, Joe, and Damien. "This cat would eat himself to death if we left a big bowl of food out." Damien caught the sandwich Joe threw his way, "C'mon, Coach. I'll share my food."

The cat jumped down and trotted happily to Damien's side of the room. He jumped up on the desk and pranced the length of the hard-top waiting for the food to be unwrapped. Damien tore off some bread and a few pieces of the meat and cheese placing it in a pile for the cat to nibble on before he walked over to the wall and accessed a hidden safe. He pulled out the book Rossdale's assistant had given him.

Joe wiped the corners of his mouth as he chewed on a large bite of his meatball sandwich. "What do you think is in that thing?" He nodded towards the book.

"Well, we are about to find out." After taking a bite, Damien opened the book and placed the sealed envelope off to the side. As he began to scan through the pages, he kept one eye on the cat. "Holy shit. Rossdale had all kinds of crap on people."

Coach tried to sneak a piece of meat dangling off the side of the sandwich only to be thumped lightly on the head. He looked up at Damien and huffed at him. Damien shook his finger at the cat. "Listen, fatso," he tore off more bread and meat, placing it in front of Coach. "I'm sharing my food with you. Quit trying to steal it."

The cat growled as he ate the morsels.

"Is there anything in there that would get Rossdale killed?" Joe guzzled his soda.

"I mean there is some stuff in here about affairs and some back-room deals. As I read this, though, these secrets don't strike me as something to get someone killed. Particularly in the manner that Rossdale was murdered. If what Sandra said is true, and we are the only ones who are aware of this book, I'm not seeing anything that sticks out as a glaring motive." Damien chuckled. "There is some good shit in here, though."

"Yeah? Like what?"

"Well, did you know that the former governor had a mistress?"

Joe's eyes widened as a big smile filled his face. "Get out. Not old man Tarleton? That guy was like a hundred when he left the office."

Damien laughed. "According to this, he had a long-time mistress. Like twenty-five years. And the wife knew about it. Rumor has it that," Damien held up his finger as he scanned the page. "It says here that the wife knew about it, but she let it go as long as the governor didn't divorce her."

Joe wiggled his eyebrows. "Damn. How come I can't find a woman like that?"

"You wouldn't want a woman like that, and you know it." Damien wadded up his trash. He heard the garage door alarm engage. "Shit, that must be Dillon." He quickly gathered the book and the letter, stuffing it inside and placed it back in the safe. He shut the safe door and sat back at his desk right before Dillon walked through the office doorway.

"Hey, babe," Damien said. He rose and walked around the desk to meet her. He took her in his arms and kissed her passionately, forgetting Joe was in the room.

"You have never once kissed me like that when I walk into a room." Joe wiggled his eyebrows when Damien and Dillon's head turned towards him.

"Which one of us are you referring to?" Dillon asked as she bent and picked up the cat as he weaved his way through her legs.

"I'd be happy with either one of you greeting me like that." A wide grin filled Joe's face.

"Never happening from either one of us," Damien said, leaning against the desk. "They rushed you back because of Rossdale, huh?"

Dillon sat on the corner of her desk situating herself between Joe and

Damien. "Yeah. I was supposed to go straight to the office for a series of briefings and meetings. But I had to come home and change my shirt." She pointed to the front. A big stain of ketchup and mustard adorned the front of the pink blouse. "I have my bag of clothes, but I really wanted to just take a few minutes to myself before I went into the office."

"Do you think you will be late tonight?" Damien asked her.

"Oh, for sure. Don't expect me at a decent hour." Dillon glanced between the two handsome men. "That's another reason I wanted to stop by here. Do you have any information yet? I was hoping you two would have the case solved by now."

Joe snorted. "Ha, fat chance on that. We have established he was killed in his residence." Joe raised an eyebrow at Damien behind Dillon's back.

"We're still going through the footage of the office and residence to see if we can see anyone. Detective Travis has that as we speak." Damien didn't say anything about the interview with Senator Lockhart and his assistant. He hoped for one more sit down before the FBI got fully involved and shut him and Joe out of the investigation altogether.

Dillon rose, still holding the cat in her arms. "I'm going to go up and change. Then head to the office." She gave Damien a quick peck on the lips and headed towards the hallway.

"See ya later, Agent," Joe called out to her.

She waved as she disappeared around the corner.

"Fuck. I guess we need to head back to the office." Joe threw his trash away and stood, stretching his back.

"Yeah. Let's go see if Travis has anything for us. Maybe he has the killer on the surveillance tape, and we can have an arrest by the end of the day."

Joe laughed heartily. "Keep dreaming, buddy. Keep dreaming."

# CHAPTER EIGHT

As Damien and Joe walked back into the VCU a little man with wire-rimmed glasses stepped out of Damien's office.

Joe leaned in. "Looks like someone was snooping in your office." Joe scampered off to his desk before Damien could respond.

Turning his attention to the man, Damien cursed under his breath. He didn't want to talk to him. Not now. "Hey, Mr. Wendell, what can I do for you?" Damien walked past him and sat at his desk. A quick glance around told him his visitor had shuffled some of his paperwork around on his desk.

Mr. Wendell huffed as he stood rigid in front of the desk. "Lieutenant Kaine, have you interviewed Senator Lockhart regarding the Rossdale case?" He remained standing.

Damien leaned back in his chair. "Yes. I asked him some questions about the current case."

"Well, I am sure you are aware, some steps need to be followed before one can be careless and question the next governor of Illinois with questions regarding a heinous murder." Mr. Wendell sat on the edge of the chair.

Damien leaned forward on his elbows. "Are you suggesting that because of someone's standing in the political fabric of this state that we should give them special treatment?"

Mr. Wendell flapped his hands, "No. I didn't say that at all. However, I don't like receiving calls from lawyers associated with the legislative body telling me his client was harassed by the local police." He scooted back in the chair. "I'm sure you can appreciate the politics involved in this case."

"Are you telling me that Senator Lockhart said we harassed him?" Damien raised an eyebrow at the little man before him. He may be the head counsel for DC, but this man had no idea how an investigation needed to be carried out.

"Tyler Bryce, Senator Lockhart's assistant, complained to the senator's legal representative and wanted him to call us, me. He wanted to make sure that you weren't going to overstep the boundaries again."

"Mr. Wendell, my partner and I interviewed the senator about an ongoing investigation regarding the heinous murder of Glenn Rossdale. Now, as a detective, I don't randomly pick people out of a hat to question. I let the facts of the case dictate who I question. I'm sure you can appreciate how murder investigations are conducted." Damien leered at the annoying man.

Mr. Wendell stood. "Lieutenant, I don't want to have to tell Captain Mackey to take you off this case. I..."

"Go ahead and try," Damien said, rising.

Mr. Wendell moved towards the door. "I'm not the bad guy here. You need to tread carefully. You are dealing with some significant people."

"The dead are my concern."

"That may be a noble thought, Lieutenant Kaine, but you are employed by Division Central and the State of Illinois. You need to remember where your priorities lie." Mr. Wendell turned on his heels and left.

Damien closed his eyes and inhaled through his nose, exhaling through his mouth. He sat there in the quiet of his office. He cracked an eye open at the sound of a knock.

"Hey, Boss. What did the little guy want?" Joe took a handful of jelly beans.

"That fucking prick of an assistant called the Senate counsel and complained. Said we harassed the senator." Damien threw a pen across the room. "I don't like that fuckwad." He dragged his hand through his hair.

"Well now, why don't you tell me how you really feel?" Joe giggled. "How long do you think it will be before the captain calls you?"

The phone rang. Both men turned towards it, then looked back at each other. "Fuck," Damien said. "Now?" He picked up the phone. "Kaine." He watched as Joe took another handful of jelly beans, picking out the ones he liked best first. "Yes, Captain. I will be there."

"Ahh, the perks of being a lieutenant." Joe quipped. His wicked smile pushed his cheeks up high.

"I don't know what you're laughing at me for. Your ass is going with me."

Joe's hand stopped midway to his mouth. "What the heck for?"

"Hey, you're my partner. And I'm your boss. Need I say more?"

"Fuck me," Joe said. He glared at his best friend. "I really hate you right now."

Damien laughed, smacking him on the shoulder. "C'mon, big boy. We got about thirty minutes before the captain wants to see us. I'll buy you a soda from the canteen. Let's go."

Joe grabbed one more handful of jelly beans. He looked at his watch. "Damn, this day is dragging on. It's three-thirty, and I'm tired as hell."

"Yeah, well, a few more hours and we will hit Mulligan's. Since Dillon is working late, we might as well grab a bite to eat." Damien hit the button at the elevator.

"You buying?"

"You're not only tired, but you're also delusional."

# CHAPTER NINE

Dillon sat at the long oak table in the conference room. Her immediate supervisor AD Reynolds and SA Marks were sitting across from her. Two other agents from the office joined them as well as Director Sherman via telecom. This kind of case normally wouldn't be of great concern to the FBI. At least not until a second or third body showed up. But, being that it was Glenn Rossdale, the whole damn Bureau had been put on high alert.

She didn't keep up with political affairs. Lord knows she had to deal with the politics of the Bureau. Dillon didn't give a rat's ass about politicians.

"Agent McGrath?" AD Reynolds squinted at the young agent across from him. Evidently, she was in her own world, "Agent McGrath, are you going to join in?"

Dillon's head snapped up to her AD's glare. "Oh, I'm sorry. I was thinking about this case." She smiled at him. Hoping her lie disarmed him and the other agents at the table.

AD Reynolds tilted his head to the side. "Uh huh. The Director is about to join us. I was bringing everyone up to speed."

Dillon nodded. When the Director came on the big screen TV, she smiled inwardly at the man before her. That past holiday season they had come into town to meet her grandparents. Sherman and his wife had gotten along with what was left of her family. She tried to rein in the happy memories. Not everyone was privy to her relationship with the Director, and she liked it that way.

"Good afternoon, everyone." The Director said as he scanned the room. "I see you made it back safely, Agent McGrath. You will need to follow up with the San Fran bureau on the case you were pulled from. I'm sorry for that. I know they need you there. Do what you can while you are working this damn case."

Dillon nodded. "Yes, Sir. I told Agent Furrows to keep me updated. I did give them a partial profile. Hopefully, that will give them some direction to narrow in on."

"Good. Now, AD Reynolds, what do we know so far?" The Director rested his forearms on his desk and stared at the group around the table.

"Well, not a lot. I spoke with Captain Mackey. He assured me he would keep us in the loop. I did make it very clear that we want this case to be on media lockdown. He assured me that all the officers and detectives involved have been briefed on maintaining communication silence when it came to the media.

"All press releases will come from the Press Secretary for DC. Nothing will go out without his knowledge and approval." The AD glanced around the table before settling his stare on Dillon. "Have you had a chance to speak with Damien about their investigation?"

She twisted her head to the side looking at the AD and glimpsing the Director out of the corner of her eye. "Have they been instructed to share all information with me on an open basis? If not, Damien won't share the information unless he is told to."

Murmured snickers filtered around the table.

She smirked at their response. "Listen, just because we live together doesn't mean we talk about cases. Trust me. The last thing I want to do is discuss work with him on my off time."

The Director rubbed the back of his neck. "We need all the information we can get. AD Reynolds, make sure the captain knows I want him to tell us everything. I understand that Damien—Lieutenant Kaine has already questioned Senator Lockhart and his assistant. I don't want that to happen again." He paused to take a drink of his water. "I got a phone call from Lockhart's counsel, he has expressed that all questioning will now be directed to his office."

Dillon bristled. "I don't understand. If the senator or anyone associated with him needs to be questioned because of their ties to Rossdale, why are they getting special consideration? They aren't suspects, why can't they give us or the VCU information?"

AD Reynolds eyebrows pinched together as he frowned at his profiler. "You can't be seriously asking that question. You aren't a naive woman."

All eyes turned towards Dillon. She shook her head. "Oh, I see. Because he is a Senator, he gets special treatment. Too bad the average citizen isn't afforded the same considerations." She leaned forward.

Director Sherman's voice boomed around the room. "Seriously, Agent? You know this is an election year for the governorship, and you know that Lockhart has already been slated to win. That's how the politics of this state works. Unless he murdered Rossdale, this needs to stay as far away from him as possible. If someone on his staff needs to be questioned, that is fine. But they will not be made to look guilty unless they are. This has come from the top. This stays away from the senator."

Dillon clenched her lips together. She bit down on her tongue to give her brain enough time to catch up with her mouth. "I'm not stupid. I know you want me to use my relationship with Damien." She shook her head. "I will do my job as an FBI agent, but I won't use my personal relationship to get the information you want to feed it to those pulling strings."

AD Reynolds leaned across the table making direct eye contact with Dillon. "No one has ever asked you to use your personal relationship with Damien to do anything. Give us some credit. But this case is sensitive in nature. Surely you can see that?"

She sighed as she leaned back in her chair. "Yeah, I see that. Damien and Joe wouldn't put someone in the guilty column unless that's where they belong. They will figure out if there is any connection to the senator. They are also smart enough to keep the shit from splattering."

The Director excused everyone from the room except Dillon and AD Reynolds. Once the room had emptied, the Director spoke. "Listen, this case is a fucking nightmare. Of all the people to get his ass murdered it had to be Glenn Rossdale. Dillon, I don't think you are aware of the importance this man had. He knew shit going back decades."

AD Reynolds chimed in. "With respect for the dead, Rossdale never divulged anything unless it was for a noble purpose. He was damn good at getting information from people without them even realizing they told him anything."

"The problem is, he was murdered, and that means he had to be onto something. And if it has anything to do with Senator Lockhart, talk about shit hitting the fan. Several people's futures are riding on this man getting into the governor's house. Rumor has it, he is going to run for the presidency in three years," Director Sherman said.

Dillon glanced between the two men. Both had become more than her boss and supervisor, and sometimes those fond feelings collided head-on with her increasing distrust of the people running the Bureau. "I get it. I do. There is a lot at stake. I'm not disagreeing."

"Dillon," Director Sherman addressed her in a tone, not of a boss. "I would never put you in a compromising position with Damien. At least not intentionally. But I am going to ask that you put the Bureau first. Your job before his, not your relationship."

She nodded but didn't say anything. She glanced up to see the AD staring at her. "I get it." She turned towards the larger than life man on the screen. "The Bureau first."

# CHAPTER TEN

Damien and Joe walked into Catherine's office. Her position was more than the captain's secretary. She had been with him in the Marines, and she was more formidable than any woman Damien had ever met. Neither of them said anything. They had learned over the years to wait. Catherine moved at her pace. She would send them in when the captain was ready for them.

Catherine glanced up raising one eyebrow at the men. "Captain Mackey is on a call. As soon as he is finished, I will tell him you are here." She went back to typing something on her computer.

Damien looked over at Joe who had a sheepish look on his face. Damien jumped at a noise, causing Catherine to look quizzically at him as she picked up the receiver.

"Yes, Captain. Lieutenant Kaine is here. I will." She peered over her glasses, "You two can go on in." She watched them enter the office, wondering how much of their ass they would have left at the end of this meeting.

Damien led the way. The captain sat this time. He was engrossed in something on his desk but managed to wave them in and motioned to the chairs in front of him. Damien didn't dare look at Joe.

Captain Mackey looked up as he leaned back against his chair. "I just got a call from Director Sherman. He wants us to coordinate with Agent McGrath and AD Reynolds. They want to know everything we know." He scooted his chair closer to his desk. "You will send your report to me, then I will forward everything to them. You are my lieutenant, and you work for DC. Not the FBI."

He rocked in his chair before he spoke again. "Damien, this case is a hornet's nest. Mr. Wendell called me after he left your office." He glanced at his favorite detective. "Don't worry, I made sure he understood you were well within your right to ask the senator and his assistant questions. Especially after what I shared with you earlier."

Damien glanced over at Joe before responding to the captain. "When we asked the senator questions about Rossdale and the party, we both had the distinct impression he was unaware of any conflict between his assistant and Rossdale. To be honest, it seems like Senator Lockhart was pretty clueless about anything having to do with Glenn Rossdale."

The captain frowned at his lieutenant. "If that is the case, maybe this doesn't have anything to do with the senator at all. Which would make our lives a helluva lot easier. 'Cause as of this minute, you aren't supposed to interrogate anyone from the James R. Thompson Center. Unless you have something that directly ties Senator Lockhart or his assistant to anything, you need to tread very lightly. And that came from the chief."

Damien dragged his hand through his hair pulling on the ends. "I don't get it. Anyone else on our radar concerning a murder of a major player in the political world and we would have them in here in the hot seat. But I guess the senator and his asshole assistant warrant special treatment."

Joe reached over and tapped Damien's leg. Shaking his head when he caught the glance from him.

Captain Mackey roared back in laughter. "I never cease to be amazed by you. I wish I had the luxury of being so dogmatic in my thinking. I hope you are never corrupted by this job Damien. This is politics. Lockhart is on the shortlist for the presidency in seven years, possibly even three. His father has put in place the wheels that will spin his son's race for the White House. And trust me when I say that man has more power and money than God. You can't beat this."

Damien drew back. He blinked rapidly and gawked at the captain. "Are we even supposed to investigate, or let this case fall through the cracks?"

The captain's demeanor shifted. "I don't think I ever said anything about not investigating this case. Follow all the evidence. If it brings us back to the senator's door, we will knock loudly. Do you have anything yet?"

Damien's fingers tapped on the arm of the chair. "No. Not yet. We are waiting on Fuentes and Grimer to get done interviewing the people from the office building. I was giving them until tomorrow to track everyone down. I will have a report on that to you by then."

"What about the security? Anything there?" The captain rocked in his chair. The intensity on his young lieutenant's face caused him to pause. He wondered if—after the last case and the shooting—Damien was mentally or physically ready to deal with this new case.

"Detective Travis is going through everything now. I will check in on him before the end of the day. See if he has anything." Damien peeked over at Joe. He remained stoic and silent.

Captain Mackey leaned forward, placing his elbows on the desk. "Damien, how is the wound healing?"

"The staples came out shortly after the Christmas party. Other than a nasty scar that is still a little raw, it's healing up fine. No residual problems at all." Damien's heart raced faster.

"How about your head, son? How's that? Are you ready to deal with a case of this magnitude after dealing with being shot and having to kill a young woman?"

Damien's leg bounced. His heart rate sped up, causing his pulse to pound between his ears. "I have gone through the psych evaluation and passed."

"That's not what I asked, son." The captain peered at the man before him. Waiting to hear the correct response.

"Captain, the last case was difficult. My body is healing, and I'm at peace regarding having to shoot Caroline. I have no problem with the way the case ended. There is nothing from that previous case that will interfere with this current case. I don't hold on to things like that." Damien's stare didn't waiver. He maintained eye contact with his captain.

Mackey smiled. "I have no concerns about you, Damien. I know you are capable and ready to move on." He sighed. "This case is going to be hard. There are a lot of things in play and a lot that we have no control over. If you are having any problems let me know. I trust your judgment, Damien, and I will support and back you one hundred percent." He motioned for the two men to leave.

With the office empty and quiet, Mackey leaned his head against his chair. The chief had made it clear he wanted this case closed. But Mackey knew Damien wouldn't close the door on this case until the man or men responsible paid for the death of Glenn Rossdale. He hoped his lieutenant was prepared for the fight.

# CHAPTER ELEVEN

Damien entered the pen, followed by Joe. He motioned for him to go into his office. Damien spotted Officer Ivanski across the room. He scanned the room, looking for his other two uniformed officers but didn't see them. "Ivanski?" he yelled.

Ivanski looked up "Hey, Lieutenant, what do you need?" He made his way across the VCU.

"Do me a favor. Check on Detective Travis, see where he is on reviewing the surveillance, computers, and communication records from the Rossdale case. Also, ask him to tell you where Fuentes and Grimer are on the interviews."

"Will do," Ivanski said as he left.

Damien walked into his office to see Joe's feet on his desk and his friend almost asleep. He smacked him on the back of the head. "Wake up, sleepy head. If I can't sleep, you can't sleep."

Joe abruptly put his feet on the floor. "I wasn't sleeping. I was resting my eyes." He grabbed a handful of jelly beans hoping the sugar would give him a much-needed boost of energy.

Damien flopped into his chair. Like Joe, the day was catching up with him. About to close his eyes and rest for a minute, his cell phone rang. "Kaine here." Kaine motioned for Joe to shut the door. "Okay, Mark, hang on. I'm going to put you on speaker. My partner is here, and I would like him to hear this."

Damien hit the speaker button and placed his phone on his desk. "Okay, Mark, go ahead. Start from the beginning."

They heard a shuffling sound and what sounded like a door closing. "Hey, sorry about that. Okay. I wanted to phone you instead of meeting in person. I'm not comfortable putting myself out there where someone may see me speaking with you. I know that may be a punk move, but I promise you everyone at the State Building knows everything."

"Do you have any information that may help our investigation?" Damien asked.

"Well, I don't know if it will help the actual murder investigation, but it may help to shed some light on a few key people. I don't usually partake of gossip, but this is something I have first-hand knowledge of.

Senator Lockhart's assistant is having an affair with his wife, Amber."

Damien's mouth fell open while Joe's eyes widened. Damien regained his composure, "Are you sure? Have you seen them together?"

"Yes. They regularly show up here in the same vehicle often after an extended lunch date. I know that several times the senator has been in Springfield and his assistant remains here. And I have known him to spend the night at the senator's mansion when he is away." Mark coughed into the phone. "Sorry about that, I think I'm coming down with a cold."

"Mark, are you sure about this? Do you think you could be misreading those cues?" Damien scribbled on a notepad.

"I was up in the corridor one evening after hours. Lockhart was in Springfield. I was doing a late-night round of the offices and heard laughter from inside the senator's office. I didn't go in, I can't explain why I did this, but I ducked into one of the doorway wells. I heard the door open, and a woman giggle. That hallway carries conversations. You don't have to be right next to someone to hear them. I heard her say, 'I always wanted to have sex on that desk.' I heard Tyler Bryce say, 'Well I'm glad I could fulfill that wish for you.' When the two stepped out of the office, it was Bryce and Mrs. Amber Lockhart."

Damien rubbed his temples. "Mark, I appreciate you giving me this information. It sheds some light on this case. I know it took a lot for you to tell us this."

"No worries. I wanted to make sure you knew what you were up against. If I hear anything else, I will let you know."

The phone went dead. Damien sat back, interlocked his fingers, and rested his hands on the top of his head. "Well, fuck me running. This may explain some of the reaction we got from the assistant today. He made sure nothing was said in front of Lockhart."

Joe made a tsk sound. "I think Lockhart has his head in the sand. Either that or he is so wrapped up in this election process he can't see anything going on around him."

Damien looked at his watch. It was getting close to five o'clock. "Tomorrow how about if I pick you up and we go to the senator's residence. We will make sure Lockhart is gone before we go."

Joe whistled. "Are you sure you want to do that? The captain said not to interview anyone associated with the senator."

Damien stared at Joe without flinching. "No, he didn't. He said not to question anyone at the State Building. Big difference."

Ivanski walked through the door. "Fuentes and Grimer are still out on the interviews. And Travis is still going through everything."

Damien raised his chin. "Thanks, buddy."

Joe reached into his pocket and pulled out the paper with the girl's number on it. "Let's see what my new girlfriend has to say." Joe dialed the number on the piece of paper. "Hey, this is the guy from the elevator, Detective Joe Hagan." Joe nodded. "Yeah, sure, how about in an hour or two? Mulligan's, meet us there. Okay. Thanks." Joe laid his phone on the desk. "She said she would be there. How about we get the hell out of here and go now?"

"Yeah, sounds good." He texted Dillon, asking if she would be able to get away for dinner. She responded with no chance in hell, but be ready to give her a back rub when she gets home. Now that was something to look forward to.

# CHAPTER TWELVE

*David pulled out behind the SUV. He drove an ordinary Ford truck. However, he had the windows tinted as dark as the state law would allow. He followed them to Mulligan's and parked on the road just down from the entrance. The man he worked for told him to stay away from the detectives five years ago, and he did. But damn if those two weren't like two little nits.*

*He watched the two men walk through the front doors of the famous Chicago landmark. David thought back to the murder several years ago. It wasn't his first murder, but it was the first one his current client paid him for. If the man hadn't had the pull he did, the picture Kaine got from the two teenagers, might have made its way onto the news. But his customer had Officer Thadd Lynn remove the file from the evidence locker. David tried to convince him to let him take care of the officer, but his employer had said no.*

*David had tried to tell this guy not to involve so many people, but the man insisted he knew what he was doing. Now loose ends were popping up everywhere.*

*He glanced at his watch. He was about to pull away when a familiar car pulled up and parked. He keyed into it immediately. She was here to meet them. Why else would she be at Mulligan's? From what he knew of the blonde, she didn't hang out at this kind of place.*

*Pulling his phone from his pocket, David hit the redial button. He had one number stored on this burner phone. "We have a problem."*

*"What's the problem?"*

*"The blonde from your office is at Mulligan's. She's meeting Kaine and his partner."*

*"Are you referring to the little girl who saw you at the party?"*

*"Yeah. I should have taken care of her that night."*

*"Well, I told you not to talk to anyone that night, but you just had to. So, this is kind of your fault."*

*"You asked me to be there to garner information for you. Don't blame me for this shit." David said.*

*The man on the other end sighed. "Fine. Take care of her but make it look like an accident. We don't need any more heat on us."*

*The man in the truck glanced around. "I thought you were going to get*

Kaine and his partner shut down. Removed from this case."

"I tried to shut them down. They are the fucking golden boys of DC. I did manage to get them where they can't interview anyone here at the State Building without going through the legal counsel. I wouldn't have to even do this if you had just killed Rossdale and made it look like an accident. Instead, you had to make it appear like a fucking psycho killed him. You had to know that would bring Kaine and his partner into the investigation."

David sighed as his fingers tapped on the edge of the steering wheel. "I wouldn't have to worry about Kaine or all these other people that keep popping up if you had let me do my job five years ago. And let's remember, you hired me. So, I will take care of the targets any way I see fit."

"Well, all I'm saying is you could've killed Rossdale in a less conspicuous way. Why did you kill him like you did?"

"I was going to make it look like he drank too much and had an accident, but the fucker came on to me at the bar. And that pissed me off." David stared out the window. "I should go ahead and take care of Kaine and his partner. Get them out of the way as well."

"Do not do anything to those two detectives. Killing them now will bring more scrutiny. I don't need that. Do you understand? Plus, I have someone I think can put the pressure on Kaine to close this investigation. I think Kaine will listen to him more than anyone else, anyway."

"Yeah yeah. I understand. I think you're making a mistake, but I understand. What about the one other person who knows about the case from five years ago? He poses the biggest threat of all." There was an awkward pause on the phone. "Hello? You still there?"

"I'm here. I trust him. Plus, I promised him the vice presidency. He will keep his mouth shut for that opportunity." Silence filled the line once more. "Just make sure whatever you do to her looks like an accident."

David opened the driver door. "Whatever you want. Just make sure the money for this chick is deposited by tomorrow morning."

"I'll do it as soon as we hang up. Anything else?"

"Nope. That'll do it."

The line went dead. He tossed the phone on the passenger seat. The question about why he killed Rossdale the way he did bothered him. David shouldn't have gotten so fancy with wiping that first victim's identity five years ago, but he was young and thought he was being clever. David had been completely surprised Rossdale had figured it out.

David exited the truck and moved towards Laura's vehicle. He released air from the two rear tires. Not enough for them to be flat, but enough to serve his purpose. David got back in his truck. He thought back to Rossdale and that night he killed him. He had worked Rossdale over pretty good and the man never revealed if he told anyone else what that name meant. David was sure, no one could withstand that amount of pain and not tell their secrets.

David sat and waited for the blonde to leave Mulligan's. He knew the route she would take home. He'd followed her before. He should've taken care of her a few weeks back. This time, she wouldn't make it past the first curve.

# CHAPTER THIRTEEN

Joe looked up as Laura, the pretty blonde from the State Building entered the bar. She was a looker. But nothing compared to Taylor. Even though this woman was attractive, there was no way he would mess up his relationship. Not to mention, Damien would whip his ass. Joe stood and waved her over.

Damien stood and pulled out her chair. "Hey, Laura, thanks for meeting with us. Are you hungry? Can we get you anything?" he asked.

She glanced around the bar. Her eyes darted back and forth as they scanned the room. She sat but didn't remove her coat. "Nah, I'm not hungry." Her slight southern accent was barely audible over the gathering crowd in the bar. "I feel foolish. This may not have anything to do with anything, but I thought you should know when I heard the news that Rossdale was murdered." She shuddered at her last statement.

Laura reached out a trembling hand as she grabbed the water glass on the table. She took a sip as her eyes darted around the room one more time. When her focus landed back on the table, both men stared at her. "I went to a party recently. It was the one held for Senator Lockhart."

Damien nodded. "We are familiar with that party. What did you witness Laura?

She tucked a strand of hair back behind her ears. "I saw the senator speaking with this man at the bar. I hadn't seen him before, and I hope I never see him again."

"What made him stand out to you? Make you scared of him?" Damien stuffed a fry into his mouth.

"The man had these piercing slate blue eyes, surrounded by a dark rim. Making them look black and empty like the devil's soul. I saw him speaking with the senator, for a long time. I couldn't hear what they were saying, but the man kept pointing. I tried to see what or who he was pointing at, but I couldn't figure it out. Finally, the man left, and the senator went back to mingling. Glenn Rossdale approached Mr. Bryce. Bryce kept shaking his head, and he kept mouthing the word no. Their argument seemed to be heated as well. Both men were very animated. No one but me seemed to notice."

"Do you know what they were arguing about? Bryce and Rossdale?"

Joe asked before taking a big bite of his sandwich.

"No, not really. I heard bits and pieces, but I think part of it had to do with Senator Lockhart's wife."

Damien and Joe glanced at each other. "Can you tell me anything about the senator's wife? Why Rossdale and Bryce would be arguing over her?"

Laura shook her head. "No, I really can't. I've met her at a few galas or parties." Her head hung, and she sighed. She looked up at the handsome detective. His dark hair made his sapphire blue eyes burst with color. She hadn't seen such an attractive man since she moved here from Texas. "There is one thing. But I have no proof."

Joe leaned over and patted her hand. "Listen, Laura, whatever you tell us stays between us. If you have any information that can help us in our investigation, we can keep your name out of it. No one needs to know you told us anything."

She smiled at him. The scar above his left eye made him even more ruggedly handsome, and a little scary. "Well, every time Mrs. Lockhart is around Mr. Bryce, they are always exchanging glances. They stand off to the side and giggle and laugh. I know that he escorts her to a lot of things. I have never seen them hold hands or be physical at all. But I would swear they have something going on."

Damien craned his neck to one side. "Laura, would you like us to follow you home?"

She shook her head, glancing down at her hands. "No, that's okay. I'm not that far from here. I'm not worried about anything happening to me. I just didn't want anyone from my work to see me. I like my job. I was afraid if anyone saw me speaking with you, they might think I was giving office secrets away."

"Don't worry. No one will find out you have spoken with us. You won't lose your job," Damien said. "Before you go, can you tell me anything about Senator Lockhart and the scary man he was speaking to?"

"No. I hadn't ever seen him before. The senator has a lot of functions. But he always tries to attend these types of parties. I hadn't seen this man ever before, let alone seen him speaking with the senator."

Damien's brow wrinkled. "I think I must be confused who the scary man was speaking with? I thought you said he was talking to Senator Lockhart?"

Laura's eyes narrowed. "Well, now I think I'm confused. He was speaking with the senator."

Damien and Joe turned towards each other.

Joe rubbed his chin.

Damien pulled at the ends of his hair. He shook his head as if he were trying to clear the cobwebs away. When he looked back up, Laura had a funny grin on her face. "Why are you smiling, Laura?" Damien asked.

"I think I figured out why we are all so confused. You think I am talking about the current Senator Lockhart."

Joe looked quizzically at her. "Uh yeah, who else could you be talking about?"

"The father. Former State Senator Lockhart."

"Wait, you're telling us that it was the old Senator Lockhart that was talking to the scary man? Not James Lockhart?"

"Yes." Now she giggled. "I'm sorry. All this time you thought I was talking about the current senator. I shouldn't be laughing, but there is no way in heck that the sitting senator would have the guts to speak with that guy. The junior senator is not near as tough as his father."

Laura stood, tightening the belt on her coat. "I hope I've helped you. I'm not sure I did. But I do feel better for telling you." She smiled sweetly at them.

"We can't thank you enough. You have helped us more than you know." Damien extended his hand. "Thank you again."

Laura shook their hands. "Thanks. See you guys later."

Damien watched the young woman exit the bar. He turned towards Joe. "What did you think of that?"

"I think the former senator is the one pulling all the strings." Joe took the last bite of his sandwich. "I also believe he is the one telling all the powers that be to shut down this case."

"What I don't understand is, why does the son let him do that? James must know what his father is doing. If anything the former senator is doing comes out, James Lockhart will pay the price." Damien motioned for the check. The waitress raised a finger in his direction as she finished with customers on another table.

"We need to talk to the wife," Damien ate the last fry from his plate.

Joe lifted an eyebrow. "We already went over this. The captain told us not to interview anyone associated with the senator."

"Again, with the rule enforcement. He said don't question anyone associated with the senator *at the Thompson Center*. Very different."

"You're splitting hairs."

"I understand if you don't want to be involved. After this conversation with Laura, we need to get some answers. I think we can only get those from Amber Lockhart. In the morning, I'm going to go to the senator's house and question his wife. You go on into the VCU. Do some paperwork or something, don't tell anyone where I am." Damien took a long draw of the last of his beer.

Joe reached over and smacked him on the side of the head.

"What the fuck was that for?" Damien rubbed his temple.

"You fucking asswad. I never said I wasn't going with you. I'm your partner. If your ass in on the line, mine is too. All I said was you were splitting hairs."

"You could've just said that instead of hitting me." Damien took the check and paid the bill. He stood, stretching as he put on his jacket. "I'll drive you home and come get you in the morning. Are you seeing Taylor tonight?"

Joe pouted. "No. She had to go to a conference in Springfield. She might be back tomorrow or the next day."

They waved to the bar personnel as they walked out the door to Damien's SUV.

"Well, I don't know about you, but today was the longest day I've had in a long time. I for one will be glad to stretch out in my bed," Damien said.

Once in the vehicle, Joe laid his head against the seat. "Onward home, slave."

Damien sneered at him. "I'd kick your ass, but I'm too tired."

# CHAPTER FOURTEEN

Laura belted out the words to one of her favorite songs. Chicago had one decent country music radio station—US99. The music blared through her two working front speakers. The little Honda Civic wasn't the newest car, and it lacked some of the high-tech gadgets and audio, but it was hers. She didn't have to share it with a bank.

Her eyes filled with moisture as she thought of her dog Charlie riding with her on the plains behind her family's ranch. After her last visit home a few months ago, she considered moving back to Texas, leaving the cold winters of Chicago behind. But she worked hard for this position, and she couldn't give up now.

Laura's mind drifted back to the handsome lieutenant, the moisture in her eyes quickly drying up. Her cheeks flushed as a warmth flooded through her. "Damn, he was a cutie." She giggled. "What I wouldn't give for one kiss." She'd kissed men before, but that was it. She wanted to wait and save herself for that one special guy.

Laura swayed to the music. She glanced in the rearview and saw an approaching car. She figured it would go around her. Although she had driven this route several times before, she wasn't used to the tight turns, and she tended to drive slower than most like to go.

Lost in the song, she didn't notice the speed of the approaching car. She caught a glimpse of headlights as they came up alongside the rear of her vehicle. It looked like it was going to pass her.

She pulled over as much as she could. But the road was about to curve, and she would be right next to a huge boulder jutting out. That thing always scared her. The turn required just the right amount of speed, or the car would lose traction on the loose gravel lining the bank of the road.

The vehicle sped up, crashing into her rear bumper. It maintained its pace and pushed her car off the road. Laura screamed as she lost control. She hit the gas, thinking she was hitting the brake, and her wheels spun out on the loose gravel. By the time she realized what she had done, the boulder was right in front of her.

Laura screamed as her car collided with the massive rock. Glass exploded as if a car bomb had gone off. The sound of crunching metal reverberated in Laura's ears as her car came to an abrupt stop. Her head smacked the steering wheel. Dazed and halfway unconscious she heard someone at her shattered window.

# CHAPTER FIFTEEN

*"Miss, are you alright?"*

*Laura squinted at the figure standing there. "I—I don't know."*

*The figure yanked on the door. It made a screeching noise.*

*Laura attempted to turn her head. "Please help me." She tried to reach up and grab her neck, but her right arm was dislocated. She cried out, "Please help me. I'm hurt."*

*The figure leaned into the car. "Don't worry. I'm here to help you."*

*Laura turned her head as best she could. The man was visible in the glare of his vehicle's headlights. Laura's chest stopped mid-rise. She tried to swallow, but her dry throat almost swelled shut. "No." She squeaked out the word. "Please. I don't know anything." Staring her in the face was the blue-eyed man from the party. "Please, I don't know anything." Her voice choked, she tried to move, but the man had grabbed her hair.*

*"Don't worry. This won't hurt for very long." The crunch of bone and cartilage echoed as he repeatedly smashed Laura's face into the steering wheel. The man stayed crouched, listening as the young woman struggled to breathe. Blood dripped from her facial wounds as her head rested against the steering wheel. The gurgling noises lasted a few moments, then silence.*

*David stood, admiring his work. When the authorities found the wreck, it would look like an unfortunate accident. Lucky for him, this older model car didn't have airbags. He walked back to his truck and drove off.*

*Loose ends were beginning to unravel. If his client didn't take care of it, the need to protect himself would far outweigh his client's wishes. He checked his rearview as he rounded the corner. He should've taken care of those two detectives five years ago. He didn't care how much heat it brought on his client. If those two got too close, they were going to have to be dealt with.*

# CHAPTER SIXTEEN

Damien pulled into his garage. The clock on the dash read eight forty-five p.m. His body told him it was way later than that. He entered the living room to Coach who sat like a gargoyle with a nasty scowl on his face. "Hey, buddy." Damien reached down and scratched his head and chin. Coach turned and stuck his butt in Damien's direction. Damien laughed. "Okay. I know you're pissed at me. I do have to work, you know?"

He followed the cat into the kitchen. Coach sat and stared at his empty bowl. Damien filled it with his wet stinky food. "Damn, how can you eat this shit?" He washed his hands after he threw the empty can away. He headed into the office and grabbed a glass, filling it with whiskey. He sat in his chair and placed his feet on his desk. Damien took two long swallows of the amber liquid and rested his head against the seat.

He bolted up at the sound of the garage door alarm. He glanced at his watch—9:25. Shaking the sleep from his head, he dragged a hand across his face. Damien left the office to find Dillon placing her keys and credentials on the table by the front door. She looked tired and stunning at the same time. Her honey blonde hair had fallen loose from the bun she wore. Strands fell across her shoulders.

She turned around and stared at him. Her eyes looked heavy-lidded. He moved across the room to her. Taking her by the waist, he pulled her into him. "Hey there, gorgeous."

Dillon glanced up staring into those fuck me blue eyes. "Hey there yourself." She bit his bottom lip before devouring his kiss. The taste of whiskey swept across her tongue. She broke away from the kiss and laid her head against his chest. Lost in his woodsy scent, the stress of the day melted away.

"I'm guessing your day was as long as mine?" Damien lifted her chin.

She smiled at him then turn to lead him towards the stairway. "Very long. Are you done working?"

"No more work for me tonight. I was thinking of taking a hot bath. You want to join me?"

"Hmm. That sounds perfect." She stopped in the office and grabbed two glasses and the bottle of whiskey. She waved them in front of him.

"It's been one of those days. I don't think the wine will be enough."

"I knew I fell in love with the right woman."

She laughed as they entered the luxurious bathroom Damien had built. She placed the bottle and the glasses on the shelf that lined the back of the tub. The word tub didn't do it justice. It was a mini pool. Probably big enough for four or five people easy. She nodded to the built-in audio system. "Put on some classic rock."

Damien did as she asked while she started the water. He grimaced knowing she would make the temperature hot enough to boil small fish. "Please remember my skin is not as tough as yours. Maybe you could put in a tad bit of cool water?"

"You are such a wuss. It's a wonder you're even a guy. I keep waiting to see you wearing panties one day."

Dillon had stripped and stood there in a pair of pink panties and nothing else. She had pulled her hair from the elastic, and it hung loosely around her shoulders, grazing the top of her full round breasts. Damien's mouth watered at the sight of her.

She reached over and turned the flow of water to a little more than a trickle then moved towards him. "Do you need help getting undressed?"

"Are you offering?"

She lifted his shirt over his head. "Yes." Her husky voice made his skin tingle. He let her undo his pants and slide them down his legs. She lifted each foot helping him step out of his jeans. Now on her knees in front of him, she slid off his boxers. He was hard, and she had to ease the waistband over his erection.

She raised an eyebrow as she looked up from her perch. "My my, you are pleased to see me, aren't you?" Her fingers gently traced the gunshot wound on the side of his abdomen. She kissed the tips of her fingers then placed them on the scar. The skin had smoothed out, and the redness had dissipated. The scar was a daily reminder of those few days before Christmas. That day still made her shudder when she thought of how close she came to losing the one man she had ever loved. She dragged her fingertips across his torso and inched her way down his body. She took him in her hand and slid him into her mouth.

The warmth and wetness made his legs quiver. Dillon teased the tip of him with her tongue. Slowly sliding it along the side of his dick. She gripped him tighter as she sucked on the length of him. She slid her hand up and down in unison with her mouth.

Damien held onto the sides of her head. One of her hands grabbed his ass. Damien's lips parted, as he looked downward. His climax growing closer. "Oh, Dillon. That feels incredible." His legs trembled as his hips thrust forward. "Dillon, I'm going to cum, don't stop. Baby..." his words trailed off. A gasp escaped his lips as his orgasm exploded from him.

Dillon looked up as she swallowed the last of him. She teased the tip of his dick one last time before rising. His eyes had glossed over, and all the muscles in his face had relaxed. She found more pleasure in doing that for him than she thought most women did. "Hmm, you liked that huh?"

"No. It was awful. I had to force myself to enjoy it."

She smacked him on the ass. "Sure. And if I said I won't do it again, what would you say?"

He pouted. "I'd cry."

"Yeah, that's what I thought." She pulled off her panties and turned off the water. A light mist of steam rose from the water in the tub. Dillon stepped up onto the platform and lifted her leg over the side. She sighed as she lowered herself into the bliss.

Damien stuck his toe in and sucked in a deep breath through his clenched teeth. "Jesus woman. Are you trying to boil me alive?" He eased himself into the tub. Once submerged up to his chest he poured two whiskeys and handed her one. Damien pulled her towards him nestling her between his legs. After a long sip of his whiskey, he set his glass on the edge of the tub. He massaged her upper arms moving slowly upwards to her shoulders.

"Mmm, that feels so good." Her head hung low rounding her shoulders. "I think I'll keep you around."

"Is that so?"

"Yeah. At least until someone more handsome shows up."

"I feel so used."

"Ha, and you love it." Dillon moaned as he moved to her arms. She took a drink of her whiskey and laid her head back against Damien's chest. "I had to have a conference about your case today."

"A conference with the AD and the Director?"

"Yeah. They are pushing to have this case shut. Have you been advised to do the same?"

"Yes. And we have been instructed to share all our information with the FBI."

She laughed. "Well, you can share tomorrow. I have had enough of the senator and his family. Not to mention I have learned more about the politics of this state than I ever cared to know."

Damien's hands made their way to her breasts. "I bet I could find a better topic." One hand stayed on a breast, and the other slid between her legs. She spread her legs further apart and reached her hands up around his neck. Opening herself to him.

"I don't think I want to talk anymore."

"You don't have to say anything baby. Just let me pleasure you." Damien could feel her hips as they ground against him. He slid two fingers into her as his thumb rubbed her clit.

Dillon sank against Damien. His fingers teased her, coaxing her climax closer. The man knew where and how to touch her. When he squeezed her nipple a shock of electricity shot right through her. "Oh my God Damien, I'm so close. Please don't stop." She wiggled against him. His pace sped up. He pinched her nipple again, and that was all she needed. "Yes, yes. Oh, Damien." She held on as her orgasm overtook her.

Damien eased his fingers from her and slowly rubbed his way back up to her shoulders. She was limp and sated. "You ready for bed baby?" He kissed her shoulder.

"Hmm, yes. I hope I can walk to the bed."

Damien stepped out of the tub and grabbed two towels from the heated towel rack. He wrapped one around his waist and took the other to Dillon. "C'mon stand up, and I will get you dry."

She obeyed. Her eyes half closed. "I'm all rubbery."

Damien raised an eyebrow. He wrapped the towel around her and lifted her. She swayed as he dried her off. Picking her up, she held onto his neck and laid her head on his shoulder.

"I could get spoiled having you carry me around like this," Dillon said.

Damien laid her under the covers, moved to his side of the bed, and crawled in next to her. She snuggled her ass up against him and pulled his arm around her waist. "Are you done?" Damien asked.

Dillon giggled. "Yes. I was getting comfortable. I'm comfortable, now I can go to sleep."

Damien started to say something but heard Dillon's soft snore. He closed his eyes enjoying the citrus and vanilla aroma of Dillon's hair. Coach jumped on the bed and walked across Damien to get to his favorite spot. He opened one eye and peered at the cat. Coach spun in circles before settling next to Dillon's stomach. Damien heard the cat sigh as he curled up and drifted off to sleep.

# CHAPTER SEVENTEEN

Wednesday

Damien noticed Joe stared out the window as he drove to Senator Lockhart's house. "Hey, you're awfully quiet. Something wrong?" Damien took a long sip of his ritual morning diet soda.

Joe turned towards his friend and partner. "No. I miss Taylor. She called last night and said she wouldn't be home until tomorrow, maybe the day after. I was thinking about her cat."

Damien grinned. "Is that code for something else?"

Joe laughed. "No, you *neddy*. I was thinking about her cat, Muffin. I had to go over and check on her last night. I swear to God," Joe made the sign of the cross, "I prayed the cat was still alive."

Damien couldn't help but laugh, even being called a fool. "Why would the cat be dead?"

"That thing is like one hundred and fifty fucking years old. Her hair is so thin in spots, she looks like she has mange or something. She's almost blind and can't hear a damn thing." Joe chuckled. "Every time I walk in, I slam the door in hopes the vibration will wake her up. It doesn't. I always tap her to make sure she's breathing. I swear I hold my breath each time."

Damien laughed so hard he couldn't see to drive. "Stop—stop. I can't take it," he said laughing.

Joe laughed at his friend's reaction. "You are such a goof."

"Oh hell. You know that damn cat is going to die when you're watching her, right?"

"Yeah. I have already resolved myself to that fact. I just don't know when." Joe sighed as he leaned back. "How do you know the senator won't be there?"

"I don't. That's why we are getting there so early. I'm betting he doesn't go in much before nine. We are going to sit out front and watch his house. See when he leaves."

"You're going to sit and watch the house. I'm going to rest my eyes."

Damien pulled over a few houses down from the senator's large Tudor style home. The houses in the neighborhood were spread apart, but they were located on a wide neighborhood street allowing for parking.

He parked far enough away as to not be noticed by the senator's staff. Damien pulled out a pair of binoculars. The autofocus zoomed in on the driveway. A car was pulled in front, but no one sat in the driver's seat.

Joe grabbed the high-tech equipment from Damien's hand. "Sweet. Are these from your dad?" Joe focused on the house across the street.

"Yeah, they are a new model. They have a range of 1500 yards." Damien frowned as Joe aimed the binoculars towards the house across the street. "Why are you looking at the wrong house?"

"Uhh, hoping to see a gorgeous naked lady in the window. What else?"

"You're such a pig."

"Yes, yes I am." Joe smacked Damien on the chest. "Hey, someone is getting into a car. Not sure who it is."

"It's got to be the driver. I don't think the Senator drives himself anywhere."

Joe continued to look at the senator's house. "Wait, the senator is coming out."

Joe and Damien both crouched as the vehicle left the driveway.

Damien waited until the car turned the corner. He pulled his SUV into the senator's driveway. "Well, we get one shot. If that wasn't the senator, we're screwed."

They exited the vehicle and walked up to the door. Glancing around the property, Damien noticed the many surveillance cameras which surrounded the property. Ringing the doorbell, they stood and waited.

A woman opened the door. Her hair had been pulled back into a ponytail, showing off her high cheekbones. Her hazel colored eyes coruscated against the dark brown eyeshadow that filled her eyelid. "Yes, may I help you?"

They both held up their ID's. "I'm Lieutenant Kaine, and this is my partner Detective Joe Hagan. Is Amber Lockhart available?"

"Yes. Why don't you come in and have a seat in the parlor? I'll go and let Mrs. Lockhart know you are here."

Damien and Joe sat on a large half-circle shaped sofa. Damien watched as Joe sat, stood up, then sat again. "What the hell are you doing?" he asked out of the corner of his mouth.

Joe looked over with a frown on his face. "Seriously, why the hell would someone buy a fucking couch like this? You can't lay down. My fat ass can barely sit on it without my balls hanging off the edge."

Damien snorted as he tried to hold in his laugh. "You're a fucking idiot."

The doors to the parlor opened. The woman seemed to glide into the room. She wore a pair of tight yoga pants and a colorful workout bra. Her ample breasts spilled over the front making Damien question whether the bra was for show or actual support.

"I'm afraid you have wasted your time, Lieutenant Kaine. My husband expressly told me that I should not speak with you without our lawyer present," Amber Lockhart said.

"Mrs. Lockhart, we have come into some information that I think may change your mind." Damien smiled at her.

She moved towards a phone located on a small side table. "I think I should call our lawyer and let him know you are here." She picked up the receiver.

"Mrs. Lockhart, I think you should hear me out first. Then if you think you should call your lawyer, that's fine. But your husband will be privy to what we know. I don't think you are going to want him to know this information." Damien again smiled at her.

She looked up and huffed at him. "What could you possibly know that I wouldn't want my husband to know?"

Damien looked at Joe, who had a sly grin on his face. Damien turned his attention back to the senator's wife. "We know you are having an affair with Tyler Bryce."

Amber Lockhart stepped away from the phone. "I'm afraid you have made a horrible mistake."

Damien pressed his lips together. "No Mrs. Lockhart. We have not made a mistake."

"Yes, you have. And I am extremely offended that you've made such a comment. I need you and your partner to leave. I will be calling your superiors."

"Did you enjoy having sex on your husband's desk?" Damien asked Amber Lockhart.

Mrs. Lockhart's eyes widened. She opened her mouth then closed it. She moved towards a winged back chair and fell into it.

"You were seen coming out of the office, and your conversation with Mr. Bryce was overheard." Damien moved to the empty chair next to her. "Listen. We don't care about your affair. We haven't even told anyone we came here. We need some information from you."

Amber let out a long slow breath. "I'm not going to give you information to help you railroad my husband on a trumped-up murder charge."

"Mrs. Lockhart, we don't think your husband had anything to do with the murder of Glenn Rossdale. But we do believe that you can help us figure some things out."

"If you don't want information about my husband, what can I possibly know?"

Joe sat on a footstool across from Mrs. Lockhart. "We want you to tell us all you know about your father-in-law."

She guffawed at them. "You must be mad. I'm not going to tell you anything about James' father."

Damien tilted his head back and to the side. "I find it interesting that you didn't say he wouldn't have anything to do with this murder. Why is that?"

Amber wrung her hands in her lap. "The former senator is a powerful man. He almost always gets what he wants."

"What do you mean by that?" Joe asked.

She looked between the two men. "He has always meddled in James' life. James wanted to be a lawyer, but his father talked him into going after a political science degree. He practically forced his son to run for senator five years ago."

Damien leaned into her. "The senator, the father, how did he force James to run for the Senate?"

Amber sighed. "You need to understand something. Robert Lockhart has a lot of power and a lot of money to throw that power around. Brock Avery, the senator who held the seat prior to James, was a shoo-in to win. Then out of the blue, poof, he resigned his position. Since it was so close to the election, and no one else had run in the primaries, it pretty much opened the door for James to take the win."

"What exactly happened to Avery?" Joe asked.

"Not sure. All I know is that after someone close to him died, Avery resigned his seat and moved to Baltimore, where he lived when he was younger, and opened a restaurant." Amber leaned back in her chair. "Look, you don't want to mess with Robert Lockhart. He doesn't like messy to get anywhere near his family. When James was in college, he was dating this girl. She came to him and told him she was pregnant. When James told his father, Robert had the girl shipped off to somewhere. She opened a beauty shop or something like that, out on the East Coast. She doesn't have a baby. No kid."

"What happened to the kid?" Damien scribbled in his little spiral notebook.

"I have no idea; James doesn't even know. He tried to find out, and his dad warned him off. I made sure after James told me about that, shortly after we started dating, that I didn't cross Mr. Lockhart." Amber exhaled and wrapped her arms around her waist. "I'm telling you, don't mess with Robert Lockhart. You guys don't want to mess with him. He can cause a lot of problems for you and your families."

"Mrs. Lockhart, is there anything else you can tell us?" Damien rose from his seat.

"No. I've told you everything I know. I hope that you will use your discretion on what you know." She walked them to the front door.

"You don't have to worry, we have no need or desire to tell your husband about your affair. Thank you for answering my questions." Damien nodded towards her as they exited the house.

Once in the vehicle, Damien looked at Joe. "What do you think?"

"I think Daddy gets whatever the hell Daddy wants."

"Yeah. I think even if his son had anything to do with Rossdale's murder, Robert Lockhart is going to make sure nothing sticks to his family."

Damien left the Highland Park area via US-41. "Damn this traffic always sucks."

"Before we head back to the VCU, let's get something to eat." Joe glanced at his watch. "It's close enough to lunch, and I'm hungry."

"Your gonna need a scooter to carry your fat ass around you keep eating the way you do."

Joe smiled. "You know something? I've noticed you mention my ass a lot. You want a piece of it?"

Damien grinned. "Yeah Joe, don't tell Dillon. She'll shoot us both."

# CHAPTER EIGHTEEN

Damien walked into the VCU, Detectives Hall and Alverez sat at their desks typing up reports. Officer Baker stood talking to another uniformed officer. Damien still didn't like how she looked at him. Googly eyes, Joe had called it. But Baker was one of his best-uniformed officers, and she would one day make a great detective. "Officer Baker?"

Officer Baker turned and smiled, "Oh hey, Lieutenant, what's up?"

"Can you find out if Detective Travis has anything on the video evidence, and if he does can you tell him to come brief me on it?"

"Sure, thing, Lieutenant Kaine." Baker excused herself from her conversation and headed into the Electronics and Cyber Division.

Damien nodded to his detectives, but didn't see the need to interrupt them. He thought about Detective Kyle Travis. He was the best electronics officer Damien had ever worked with, and ECD was lucky to have snagged him from the academy several years back.

Damien sighed as he entered his office. "Shit, I leave my desk clean and overnight shit just magically appears." He sat and began the long process of sorting his mail, filing and answering what he needed to, and throwing away what he could.

Twenty-five minutes later, Detective Travis walked into his office. "Hey, Lieutenant Kaine, I got some video for you to look at."

"Joe," Damien yelled through his open door, "get your Irish ass in here."

Joe moseyed in from the pen with a cheeky grin on his face. "Again, with my ass." Joe laughed. "You are so in love with my ass, aren't you?"

"I'd like to kick your ass from here to Sunday."

Detective Travis laughed. "You two kill me," he said as he took one of the seats in front of Damien. He placed a tablet on the desk. He glanced between the two detectives, "Okay, so I'm still tracking Rossdale's phone records. However, I have pulled all the video from the residence. I figured I would start there since it was the crime scene." He pushed play on the tablet, and a silent video started up.

"Now, this is at approximately nine p.m. You can see Rossdale goes into his apartment with a male and a female."

Damien nodded to Joe. "That must be Tonya Fairchild and Josh Temple."

"Yeah, I bet it is." Joe scooted a little closer to the desk.

"These three go in and are in there for several hours. Which explains the sex party scene we found in the bedroom. Now you see them leave at approximately twelve a.m. They seem, hmm, very happy." Travis laughed.

"Jeeze I wonder why," Joe said.

"There is no activity until shortly after one a.m." Detective Travis fast forwarded to the time stamp on the video. "Here, you see Rossdale come off the elevator with a man. The man keeps himself hidden from all cameras. He's wearing gloves and what looks like blue work pants and boots. He resembles a maintenance worker. That may be what the guy intended. Because..." Travis again fast-forwarded the video, "at one thirty the man exits the residence. He disappears down the hall, comes back and you see he has the bat. At two thirty a.m. the man exits the residence again, this time carrying the body." Travis stopped the video.

Damien looked at Joe. "This guy has some balls. He leaves the residence and gets the bat, then comes back to finish the job. He carried Rossdale out in that damn tarp. Which would account for the large void on the carpet at the crime scene."

Joe frowned at both Detective Travis and Damien. "If he didn't use the elevator, how the hell did he get the bat into the building and the body out of the building?"

"Well," Travis said, "after I saw this video, I wondered the same thing. So, I called the building management. On every floor, there is a maintenance elevator. On this floor, the elevator is at the end of the hallway. Which you can't see from this vantage point."

Damien nodded his head. "Okay, that explains why we didn't see it when we were there, but aren't those elevators locked, where you need a key to get the elevator to work?"

"No. These elevators aren't secured. They may be after this incident. Especially when the residents get wind of it. They go all the way down to the underground garage area." Detective Travis laid the tablet on the desk. "I haven't spoken to the CSI team, the lab, or the Morgue. I mean I can't do your entire job for you."

Joe chuckled. "Why the hell not? This is a damn good job, man."

Damien put his hands on his head and leaned back. "It's totally feasible he brought the tarp with him. It would have to be a new tarp. Unopened and new, those things are packaged pretty small."

Joe smacked his leg. "No shit, right? I have never once been able to get those damn things folded up like they are when you buy them. That and tents. Everything comes in this one bag, and the first time you put the tent together, BAM, you can't get that fucker back in the bag. Next thing you know you're throwing the whole fucking thing away because it fills your entire garage."

Damien lifted an eyebrow at his partner. "When the fuck have you ever been a camper?"

An evil smile filled Joe's face. "Girls love to go camping. Especially college girls."

Both Damien and Travis roared back in laughter. Detective Travis stood taking his tablet with him. "You are a fucking nut, Hagan." He headed towards the door and turned back to the men. "If I find anything else, I will let you know ASAP. Grimer and Fuentes should be coming in shortly with their interview notes. I'll send them your way."

Damien laughed again as he looked at Joe. "You amaze me."

"What?" Joe giggled. "Alright, so now we know how he got in and how he got the body out. The timeline fits with when the kids at the park discovered the body. If you could identify the man in the photo, we could have this case solved by dinner time."

"Yeah, not gonna happen. I'm gonna call the lab and the morgue, see what I can find out. Call Tonya Fairchild and Josh Temple, ask them about the few hours they spent with Rossdale. Let them know up front they aren't suspects; we need them to tell us what they know. See if they can tell you where Rossdale went afterward. It would be nice if we could get a bead on this guy. If we are lucky, we might catch a break there."

"You got it." Joe gave him another cheeky grin. "I know you want to stare at my ass, it's okay. Go ahead."

"Go the hell away." Damien laughed as he picked up the phone to call Roger Newberry, lead CSI Tech. Damien rubbed the side of his face. Concentrating on his temple area. His stomach was in knots, and he wasn't sure why. Something about this case wasn't making sense, and he didn't like it at all. No evidence, no leads, and someone wanted the investigation stopped.

"Yo, Newberry here."

"Hey, Roger, it's Kaine. Can you tell me what you guys got so far on the Rossdale case?"

"Hey, buddy. Yeah, hang on let me get the file." Roger shuffled items around on his desk until he found what he needed. "Alright man, let's see. The sex scene looked like a damn good time happened. There were two males and a woman donor to the samples. One obviously was Rossdale."

"We got a lead on the unknown man and woman, we can have them confirm they were there, and get samples from them. Do you have any other unknown samples from the scene?" Damien wasn't expecting any evidence from the guy to be present since in the video their suspect wore gloves.

"Well, funny you should ask that. During the autopsy, they found one lone gray hair on Rossdale's body. I think Rossdale got ahold of one small piece of evidence during the struggle. They will run it for DNA, but without a match, it won't do us any good. But you never know, we might get lucky."

Damien sighed. "Alright buddy, thanks for the information. I'm gonna call the morgue. Later."

The line went dead before Damien set his phone on his desk. He leaned back and closed his eyes. The case and all its crappy clues sloshed around his head. He knew in his gut this all tied to the senator. Either the former senator or his son. But Damien had no doubt this would end at their doorstep. He also recognized if he couldn't catch a break, this case would never get solved.

# CHAPTER NINETEEN

An hour later, as he was about to call the lab, Fuentes and Grimer walked through his door. Damien smiled at the two men. "Hey, guys. Tell me you have the identity of my killer, and you two have single handily solved this case?"

Fuentes looked at Grimer, "Let's see, we could lie to you if you'd like us to."

"Fuck," Damien let out a heavy sigh as he leaned back in his chair. "No, just tell me the bad news."

Grimer pulled his notepad from his pocket. "We interviewed everyone from the businesses. Not one person saw anyone suspicious hanging around. No one mentioned anything out of the ordinary or anything that would have led them to think Glenn Rossdale was in any kind of trouble."

Fuentes cut in. "Everyone liked Rossdale, even those who didn't agree with his politics. They all said he was a super likable guy and always willing to help."

Damien rested his head in his hands for a moment. "Okay, I want you two to go over to his residence and interview his neighbors. Also, talk to Detective Travis before you go. See if he found anything on the tape of the business that matches the guy he saw entering Rossdale's residence." He saw the furrowed eyebrows on both men.

"He'll know what I want when you mention that. Interview the security guard at the residence, get him to tell you what he knows about Rossdale's habits. Like where he likes to hang out, or if he uses a car service. If he does use a car service, get the company and follow up on that lead."

Both rose. Fuentes looked at Grimer who nodded in his direction. "Hey, you might get a call from one of the idiots in Traffic. We know our supervisor knows we are working with you guys, but there's this asshole that thinks we were trying to get out of an early morning wreck out on US-41."

Damien raised an eyebrow and tilted his head to the side. "Seriously?"

Fuentes nodded. "Yeah. The wreck happened sometime last night but the young girl, some college kid, wasn't found until early hours of this morning. Anyway, we wanted to give you a heads up."

"No worries, fellas. I'll make sure they know you aren't slackers."

Fuentes and Grimer left, and Damien picked up his phone to call Dr. Forsythe. The phone rang several times, and he almost hung up when he heard panting on the phone.

"Uh, Dr. Forsythe's office."

"Yeah, this is Lieutenant Kaine, is Dr. Forsythe there?"

"He is. He is washing his hands. Here he comes now."

Damien heard a muffled discussion before he heard his old friend's voice on the other end.

"Ahh, Lieutenant Kaine. How are you doing today?"

"Well, that depends on you. Please tell me you know who killed Glenn Rossdale."

A hearty laugh filled the phone. "Oh son, I wish I could. Unfortunately, I don't have that info. But I do have a lot of other stuff."

"What do you have?" Damien pulled a notepad from his desk.

"Give me a moment, let me open this file. I already sent it to the FBI and your captain, as per their instructions, and I was about to call you. Okay here, Mr. Rossdale picked up a very nasty man. We found a hair..."

"Roger told me that."

"I'm assuming that the probability this is a male's hair is more than fifty percent. It was a coarse hair and long. Lends to possibly more than likely a man's. Also, very few women let their gray hair grow out that long."

Damien laughed. "Damn, that isn't much of a scientific profile, Doc."

"Hey, I'm not a magician. We are still waiting on DNA. As for Rossdale, he was tortured, and most of it took place prior to death. If you remember, he wore bloody underwear, that lovely instrument that was found at the crime scene, well your killer used the spike part on his genitals."

"Oh, hell," Damien said. He shuddered at the vision of Rossdale being beaten. He grabbed himself and adjusted his jeans.

"The damage was extensive. This guy was pissed at Rossdale. Now I'm not a profiler, but this had to be a rage or sexual kill. That should placate the FBI. Those damn guys are breathing down our necks. I assume they are doing the same to you."

Damien ran a hand through his hair. "Someone somewhere is making it very hard for us to do our job, that's for sure. Is there anything else?"

"Nothing much you can't read in the report. The killer worked him over damn good. No other evidence leading to the murderer's identity was collected. The scene at the park was nothing more than a body dump. Everything happened at the residence."

"Okay, Doc. Thanks."

"You're welcome, Damien."

Damien placed his phone on his desk. His murder board had nothing but a picture of Rossdale's body. "*Cazzo!*" Damien threw a pen across the room. "I got *niente.*" Glancing at his watch, he saw it was almost five thirty. He grabbed his jacket and called out his office door. "Joe, you ready for me to take you home?" He was about to walk out when his cell phone rang. Damien's eyes lit up at the name of the caller.

"Hey Papa, cosa c'è?" Damien put his father on speaker phone and laid it on his desk while he finished putting on his jacket.

"Damiano, what is this about you hounding Senator James Lockhart?"

"Dad, what are you talking about? I'm not hounding Senator Lockhart." Damien shrugged his shoulders at Joe's raised eyebrow as his partner walked through his office door.

"I understand you are questioning him in this horrible murder of Glenn Rossdale. Although I am deeply saddened by the loss of Glenn, I don't see any reason for you to hound the senator. He could not possibly be responsible for such a disgusting act."

Damien pinched the bridge of his nose. "Dad, why the hell are you calling me about an ongoing investigation? And how the hell do you know who I am questioning?"

"Damien, don't take that tone with me. If you questioned Senator Lockhart like this, it is no wonder Robert Lockhart is upset with you."

"I'm sorry, I must have missed something," Damien said. "Why are you bringing up Robert Lockhart?"

Joe looked up from his phone, wondering why Damien's father was bringing up Robert Lockhart.

"Damien, I'm good friends with the Lockharts. Robert called me to ask for my help. He isn't thrilled that my son is trying to pin a murder on James."

Damien closed his eyes. His head pounded to the same rate his heart beat. "Dad, I love you, but I don't care about Robert Lockhart's feelings. I'm in the middle of a murder investigation, and I will question anyone I need to. If you don't understand that, you don't understand my situation."

"Damien, I wanted you to realize that you are way off base here and you need to stop harassing Senator Lockhart. Your mama sends her love."

Damien looked fixedly at the dark phone screen.

"What was that all about?" Joe asked.

"What the hell is going on with my fucking dad? I can't believe he said I was harassing Robert Lockhart's son. Or that he told me to stop."

A smirk crept into place on Joe's face. "I'm so glad I'm not the son of Giovanni Kainetorri."

Damien tugged at the ends of his hair. "I know my dad has a lot of pull, but did Robert Lockhart really think he could call my dad and get him to make me stop an investigation? The man is an arrogant fuck."

Joe started to exit the office but stopped. "I have a feeling Mr. Lockhart is more than that." Joe languished at the office door.

"You don't seem to be in much of a hurry to leave," Damien said.

"Yeah, I'm really not."

"I thought you'd be happy to leave."

"I am. Unfortunately, it means I need to go over and check on that damn ancient cat."

Damien laughed. "I'm sure the cat is fine. Doesn't Taylor come home tomorrow?"

Joe nodded. "Hopefully that thing will still be alive. Answer your phone if I call you."

They headed for the parking garage.

Damien looked over at his partner. "Okay, why?"

"Because, if that fucking cat is dead, you're helping me box the damn thing up."

# CHAPTER TWENTY

Damien sat in his SUV in the garage for a few minutes before entering the house. The phone call with his dad lingered in the back of his mind. He wanted to push all the crap about the case to the side. He didn't want to bring it into the house with him. He rolled his shoulders and twisted his head from side to side causing a crack-like sound to fill the silent vehicle.

He walked into the living room from the garage. Coach wasn't there. "Now that's odd." Damien took off his jacket. He knew Dillon was home because her car was there. He had a sneaking suspicion he knew where he would find Coach.

Walking into the kitchen, his assumption was right. Dillon stood over a pot on the stove and Coach sat right next to her on the counter. Every few moments she would share a morsel of food. "That can't be sanitary. I'm sure the Health Department would fine you for that."

Dillon turned, and her breath caught her throat at the sexy man before her. She moved towards him and kissed him. "I'm making chili and cornbread. It's almost done. You can help set the table."

Damien gave the cat an evil eye as he grabbed glasses from the cabinet, two for water, and two for wine. "You feel like wine or beer?" he asked as he held the two wine glasses in the air.

"Beer. Beer and chili."

Damien put the two wine glasses up. "Whatever the lady wants, the lady gets," he said as he scratched the cat.

"Hey now, you asked. And a cold beer and chili go together." Dillon opened the oven and pulled out the golden-brown cornbread. "Grab a stick of butter and slather it on while it's hot." She loaded two big bowls with chili. After placing them on the table, Dillon grabbed a jar of jalapenos, sour cream, and a bowl of shredded cheese. She rubbed her hands together. "Let's eat. I'm starving."

They sat in silence as they ate. Coach took his usual seat at the table and waited for his morsels of food.

Damien looked across the table at the love of his life. "Dillon, this is fabulous. Where did you get the recipe?"

"From Taylor. She told me how to get the most flavor without having to let it simmer for hours."

"Well, it's fantastic. Thanks for cooking it."

They continued to eat in silence. Not an awkward silence, a nice calm, comfortable quiet.

***

Once the kitchen was cleaned and the food put away, they both headed towards the office. Damien opened his computer and pulled up the ME's report. He wanted to read it and see if he missed anything that would help direct him.

"Did you see the ME's report on Rossdale?" he asked Dillon.

"Yeah, I did. Looks like Rossdale picked up the wrong guy. I also got the CSI tech's report. The man must have had the stamina of a bull to go from the crazy sex party he had to pick up another man, not a few hours later."

Damien chuckled. "No shit. How much sex can one man have in a day?" He wiggled his eyebrows at her.

"According to you, never enough."

"With you as a girlfriend, can you blame me?"

"You just need a girl, it doesn't matter who." She winked at him. "Back to the case, it looks like he picked up a crazy sexually depraved person. That's how the profile seems to be evolving. At least based on what I've been given."

Damien struggled. He never worried for a moment that he couldn't trust Dillon. "Okay, let me ask you this. Detective Travis found Rossdale on his security video. It shows him entering with his two companions, leaving with them later, and then returning with the killer."

Dillon frowned. "I haven't seen the video yet."

"I had Travis send it to me. Let me pull it up. I'll put it on the screen there." He nodded to the oversized monitor that hung on the wall. One of three. Within a few minutes the screen filled with the security video.

Dillon came around her desk and leaned against it as she watched the video. "Pause it."

Damien did as she instructed.

She turned towards him. "It's obvious this guy was familiar with the building. He doesn't look in the direction of any of the cameras. Start it up again."

Damien started the video. When the killer left the apartment with the tarp, he paused it. "We didn't know this until later, but there is a service elevator around the bend in the hall. We were focused on getting over to the State Building, so we didn't see it."

"When you say the State Building, you mean the James R. Thompson Center, right?"

Damien chuckled. "Yes. Chicagoans affectionately call it the State of Illinois Building. Because most of the State government operates out of there. A lot of traditionalists are pissed. They say Chicago is becoming the shadow capital of Illinois. They don't like it."

Dillon nodded. "Okay. I wanted to make sure I knew what you were talking about."

Damien pointed to the video. "Why would a random stranger be prepared with a tarp and know where the service elevators were? I don't think it was random."

Dillon stood shaking her head. "Just because Rossdale was murdered, doesn't make it a fact Senator Lockhart had anything to do with his death."

Damien's head hung. He wanted to tell her everything. He tugged at the collar of his shirt. The pressure to shut this case had become a noose around his neck. He wasn't sure how far Dillon would be willing to go if it meant going against the FBI or Director Sherman.

"Listen, Damien. I know how you work. You seem to think there is always a conspiracy going on. You thought that in the last case you had."

"Duh, and I was right. There was a massive conspiracy within the Catholic Church."

"This isn't the same thing, Damien. The death of Glenn Rossdale has nothing to do with Senator Lockhart."

"How can you be so sure?"

"Hello, I'm a fucking profiler." Dillon hissed out a breath. "This is what I do. I profile. Rossdale's killer doesn't fit a pattern of a cover-up or conspiracy. That's what the evidence shows anyway."

There was a heavy silence between them. Dillon walked back and forth. She stopped and gaped at Damien. "Unless I don't have all the evidence. Is that what this is about? You know something that you haven't shared with the FBI. That's it, isn't it?"

Damien's shoulders sagged. "It's not that I didn't want to share it."

"Damien, what the hell do you know?"

Damien eyed the ceiling. "Merda." He dragged a hand through his hair. "Okay. We had an informant, I can't tell you who, come forward and tell us about a conversation between Mrs. Lockhart and Tyler Bryce, the senator's assistant." He considered Dillon's whiskey-colored eyes and swore he saw a flame ignite.

"What was the conversation about?"

"Amber Lockhart and Bryce are having an affair. Now you can't tell anyone. I'm telling Dillon, not Special Agent McGrath."

She shook her head. "What the hell is that supposed to mean?"

"It's not intended to mean anything. I'm telling you this in confidence. It isn't in a report for a reason. No one knows but Joe and me. I want to keep it that way."

"First, you ass, I've never betrayed your confidence. I wouldn't now. Second, what does a sexual affair have to do with the senator and Rossdale?"

Damien breathed deep. "We went to the senator's house to question the wife. We let her know we knew about the affair..."

"Back the truck up. Weren't you instructed not to interview anyone associated with the senator without their counsel present?"

"Since when do you care about that shit?"

"Since I got the entire FBI wanting me to keep you on a fucking leash."

"Excuse the fuck out of me. Keep me on a leash?"

"Oh hell, Damien you know what I mean. You always go off half-cocked. Look at this situation. You think the senator is involved in a murder simply because his wife is banging someone."

Damien's nostrils flared. His neck throbbed where his vein had become engorged. His pulse pounded at the base of his skull. "Dillon, Amber told us Robert Lockhart has always kept messy from his family. She explained over the entire course of James Lockhart's life, his father has controlled everything. Making things, people, and even fucking babies disappear. It isn't a stretch that Rossdale knew something and Robert Lockhart didn't want it getting out."

Dillon's head pounded. Each beat intensifying. She grabbed at her temples. "You can't be fucking serious. You are now trying to tie in the former senator, to this murder. That now he has something to hide? You are so fucking crazy I think you need medication."

"Really? You're the fucking profiler, and you can't even see the connection."

"What fucking connection? You don't have a connection. You have your crazy Italian mind working overtime that Rossdale had a huge secret and now the senator is hiring hit men to shut people up. Do you hear yourself?"

"Well, at least I'm not worried about my ass. I'm more concerned about solving this case than you are. It seems like you don't give a rat's ass about the dead."

Dillon's fists clenched as she pulled her elbows in close. She inhaled through her teeth. She took a step back. "You have some fucking nerve. Telling me, I don't care about the dead. I care more about the dead than most of the living assholes I must deal with. Especially the one I fucking live with."

"Well, you can move out anytime you want. I'm not forcing you to stay here."

"Fuck you. I'm going to bed. You can put your theories together. I have a long day tomorrow, and I want to sleep." She bent over and picked up the cat who cowered under the desk. "I'm taking Coach upstairs. You can sleep on the couch or in your car. Hell, you can leave if you want. But you are not welcome in my bed." Dillon walked out, stomping up the stairs.

Damien heard the bedroom door slam shut. He picked up the stapler from her desk and chucked it across the floor. He didn't want to deal with this anymore tonight. This case was a fucking nightmare. His stomach rolled. He had no way of proving what his gut told him, that Robert Lockhart was connected to this case. And if he kept going, searching for the connection, he might not have a girlfriend or career by the end of it.

# CHAPTER TWENTY-ONE

Thursday

Damien and Dillon shuffled around the next morning. Neither of them spoke, and even Coach gave Damien the cold shoulder. Damien stood in the doorway of the kitchen. He watched her put up her breakfast dishes. The heaviness in his chest made it hard for him to breathe. He looked down before he spoke. "Do you have any idea when you will be home tonight?"

She didn't look at him as she brushed past him. "Hmm, I wasn't sure this was still my home." She kept her back to him. "I don't want to fight this morning. I'm not sure when I will be home. I'll let you know if I think about it." Dillon walked out of the house without another word.

Damien raised an eyebrow at Coach, who sat with a slant-eyed glower on his face. "Listen, you fat ass. I'm the one who saved you, fed you for years before she came along. If she ever leaves, you're still gonna be stuck with me. Just remember that."

Coach swung his ass to Damien and pranced away. Ignoring his warnings.

"Can't believe my fucking cat isn't even loyal to me." Damien left the now cold empty condo and headed into the VCU.

***

As he entered the pen, Damien noticed all his detectives at their desks. "What the hell, you guys take a break from catching scum bags?"

Everyone looked up.

"Well, look what the cat dragged in. You keeping banker's hours now?" Detective Hall asked.

Damien pointed to the clock on the wall. "Dude, what are you talking about, it's not even eight a.m. I'm early."

Detective Davidson smiled. "Yeah, but we beat you, so you're late."

Damien frowned at his only married detective. "Whatever. How're everyone's cases going?"

They all nodded or shrugged. Each team gave a quick oral report. "If you guys need me for anything let me know. I appreciate the good work you guys do." Damien's feet seemed to drag across the floor as he headed to his office. The fight with Dillon cloaking him like a five-hundred-pound weight.

He sat at his desk and held his head in his hands. A knock rattled the door. "Yeah?" he said without looking up.

"What the hell is wrong with you?" Joe took a handful of jelly beans and plopped into the chair. "What happened?"

Damien sat back and sighed. "Dillon and I had a horrific fight. She wouldn't even let me sleep with her. Hell, Coach was even mad at me."

"What did you do?"

"Why does it have to be my fault?"

"You're a guy. So, what did you do?"

Damien shoved the desk. "I didn't do a damn thing. Except try to tell her there was more to this case than a random sex killing. She said I was pretty much delusional. I told her she cared more about keeping her ass covered than solving this case."

Joe's raised one eyebrow. "Yeah, that was really stupid. What were you thinking?" he shrugged. "You weren't thinking. That's the problem."

Damien rubbed his face. "I know something is going on with Senator Lockhart. Both of them." He pulled a pad of paper from his desk when his phone rang. "Don't leave," he said to Joe. "Kaine here."

"Lieutenant Kaine, it's Mark from Thompson Center."

"Hey, Mark. What can I do for you?"

"Look, I wanted to give you heads-up. I'm taking my family out of town. We will be gone for about two weeks. Maybe longer."

Damien's forehead wrinkled. "Umm, Okay. Why are you telling me? Am I missing something?"

"Did you not hear about the girl from Senator Lockhart's staff?"

Damien sat up straight. "What girl from Lockhart's staff?"

"One of his girls died a day or so ago. I think two days. I think I shouldn't have spoken to you. Call me paranoid, but it seems like there is something not right going on here."

"What was the girl's name. Do you know?" Damien locked eyes with Joe and nodded. Joe stepped out and made a phone call.

"No, I'm not sure. I know one of the girls in his division died. I think she died in a car wreck. Look, I know you won't tell anyone about the information I gave you unless you can't help it. I want you to keep my name out of it. I don't want anyone knowing I spoke to you. I like my job, but more than that I like my life."

"Don't worry Mark. I won't tell anyone about our conversation. Please send me a text weekly letting me know where you are. Don't worry, Mark. Okay?"

"Yeah. I'm not. Thanks, later."

Damien looked up to find Joe standing stone cold still.

"It was Laura. She's the one in the car wreck." Joe said.

"*Figlio di cagna*," Damien said. "That son of a bitch. I don't know who is killing these people, but I swear if it's the last thing I do I will hunt that bastard down." Damien grabbed his coat. "Let's go over to the morgue. I want to see her."

# CHAPTER TWENTY-TWO

Damien stormed through the front door of the morgue. He walked right past the receptionist, through the double doors and straight to Dr. Forsythe's office. "Hey, Doc."

Dr. Forsythe looked up from his desk. "Well, Lieutenant Kaine and Detective Hagan, how are my favorite detectives?"

"Did you do the autopsy of the girl in the car wreck? The one from US-41?"

Dr. Forsythe studied each of the men's faces. They were long and rigid. "What's up boys?"

Damien marched around the room. "Are you sure it was an accident?"

"What, the car wreck?" Dr. Forsythe's head swiveled between the two men.

"Yeah, are you sure it was an accident?" Damien continued to pace.

Joe reached out and laid a hand on his friend's shoulder. "Doc, do you think we could see Laura?"

The fact Joe referred to the young woman by her first name told him this girl was special to them. "Alright. Follow me." Dr. Forsythe led them through the facility towards the cold storage room.

The heavy sliding door opened to a vacuum-like sound. Cool air smelling of stale cleaning solution and death hit Damien in the face. The rectangular room was lined with rows of drawers. Each one designed to hold a body for as long as needed. He walked to the far wall and pulled out a drawer.

The slab that held Laura pulled out on silent rollers. The locking clip that secured the drawer from extending all the way and flying across the room made an echoing boom like noise.

Damien stepped up to the body. Both Joe and Dr. Forsythe took a step back. Damien removed the sheet from her face. His breath hitched in his chest. The chill in the air burned the back of his throat. He'd seen worse, but he wasn't prepared for the bruising and disfigurement that now distorted Laura's once innocent face. He touched her forehead. Her cold skin seared his fingers. "I'm so sorry, Laura. I will catch him." He pulled the cover over her and slid her body back to her dark holding cell.

Damien turned to see Joe and Dr. Forsythe staring at him. He placed his hands on his hips. "Dr. Forsythe, is there any way this wasn't an accident?"

Dr. Forsythe crossed his arms. "Damien, do you know this young lady?"

Damien's head drooped. He trusted the Doc, no question. However, he didn't want to involve him.

"Damien, you seem to be struggling. Does she have something to do with the Rossdale case or is this more of a personal matter?"

Damien averted his gaze. "No, not personal. We spoke with her right before she died regarding the Rossdale case. Can you tell me what you know?"

"According to the report, she lost control of her car out on US-41. There is that outcropping of boulders, she lost control on one of the turns, and smacked into the rocks."

Damien lifted a single eyebrow. "No way that happened. Was there any evidence she had been forced off the road? Any proof of another vehicle involved in the accident?"

Dr. Forsythe frowned. "No. This was an unfortunate accident, Damien."

Damien walked back towards the drawer that held Laura. "There is no fucking way this was an accident," he said turning back to Dr. Forsythe. "She wouldn't have run into a fucking boulder after speaking with us about Senator Lockhart. There is no way this went down like this."

"Get a hold of yourself, Damien. It's not the doctor's fault." Joe said

"Damien, you can't be suggesting Senator Lockhart had anything to do with this girl's death?" Dr. Forsythe glanced between the two men.

"Maybe not him but someone close to him."

"Damien, there is no evidence linking Rossdale or this poor girl to the senator. You're going to find your ass in a sling if you go barking up that tree, son."

Damien turned on Dr. Forsythe. "Not you too. You worried about your ass getting caught in a sling?"

"What the hell are you talking about?" Dr. Forsythe recoiled swallowing hard. "I have never been worried about politics in this job. If I thought for one moment, this was anything more than a tragic car accident I wouldn't hesitate to state that on the record. But there is no evidence. Do you have any evidence there was someone else involved? If you do, tell me. I'll use that to change my ruling. Otherwise, these cases aren't related. You're grasping at straws."

"No, fuck no. I'm not grasping at anything because I don't have anything." He threw his arms up in the air. "But I know someone associated with Senator James Lockhart is involved. I have no fucking proof as to why or how, but I know it." Damien stopped and looked at his old friend. He tried to fight the emotions, but he had no control over them. The coolness of the room made the wetness on his cheeks chill his soul. "I know I'm right. I don't give a fuck what the evidence shows. That girl died for speaking to us. I will find who killed her and trust me when I say, you will not find this motherfucker's body."

Joe watched as Damien stormed from the room. He turned towards the Doc. "We got nothing but our guts. Something is going on in this case." Joe dragged a hand through his wavy red hair. "Listen Doc, don't tell anyone about this conversation. We are flying under the radar on this."

Dr. Forsythe laid a hand on his shoulder. "Listen, I won't say anything. If you guys get something that will help me change the status of this case, tell me. It doesn't matter where you find it, I will use it. There is a lot of pressure to shut the Rossdale case. I have no problem dragging the autopsy findings out. I will stall it at this end for as long as I can. But you need to keep an eye on Damien. It hasn't been a month since he was shot and had to deal with the last shitty case."

"I know you lost a good friend during that case," Joe said.

Dr. Forsythe pinched the bridge of his nose. The loss of his friend Father Mandahari weighed heavily on him. "Damien could get himself in trouble if he pursues this without concrete proof. Keep an eye on him. I don't want anything to happen to either of you."

"You love me more, though, right?" A wicked grin spread across Joe's face.

"Get the hell out of my lab." Dr. Forsythe shooed him out the door. He watched as two of his favorite men walked down the corridor. He worried Damien would let his emotions get the best of him. Dr. Forsythe thought if he was ever murdered, he hoped it would be Damien and Joe on his case. He knew they wouldn't rest until his killer was caught.

# CHAPTER TWENTY-THREE

Joe remained silent back to VCU. Only when they pulled into the Division Central parking garage did he speak. "Do you want me to come up with you to talk to the captain?"

Damien's brow wrinkled. "Fuck yeah. At least with you there, the captain won't try to say that I'm not psychologically ready for this case." Damien smacked the steering wheel. "Joe, I know Laura was murdered. There is no way she had an accident the minute she left our interview. How the hell are we going to prove this shit? We got *cazzo niente*. Fuck if I'm going to let this drop. I don't care if they fire my ass. Whoever is pulling the strings of the administration to close this case is in my crosshairs."

Damien's anger rolled off him in waves crashing into Joe full force. He knew enough to let his friend vent. For as long as Joe has known Damien, he recognized Damien's need to get it out to clear his head. After a few moments of silence, Joe spoke. "I agree with you. But we need to figure out why someone was watching Laura. If someone was watching her, it must be associated with the party. The one where she saw the confrontations. But to be honest, I'm not buying that."

***

They walked in silence to the elevator that would carry them up to the captain's office. The air seemed to crackle around them.

They entered the captain's outer office. Catherine, his watchdog, peered over her glasses at them. "Did you have an appointment to see the captain, Lieutenant?"

"No, Catherine we don't. But we need to speak to him about the Rossdale case. Could you ask him if he has time to speak with us?"

She picked up the receiver. "Captain, Lieutenant Kaine and Detective Joe Hagan are here and are asking for a moment with you. Yes, I will. Thank you, Sir." She replaced the receiver and pointed to his door. "He said to go on in."

Damien led Joe through the office door. He was always amazed at the stature and size of the captain, even sitting behind his massive desk. "Captain, thank you for seeing us."

"I always have time for my lieutenants. What's up, Damien?"

"I'll get right to the point. Are you aware of the wreck up on US-41?" Damien asked.

"Yeah, a poor college girl. It's a shame." The captain leaned back in his chair.

"No Sir, it wasn't a college girl. It was a young woman who worked in State Senator Lockhart's office."

The captain tapped a pen on his desk. He zeroed his gage on his lieutenant. "Damien, where are you going with this? That was an accident." The captain motioned for the two detectives to sit.

Damien closed his eyes for a few seconds gathering his thoughts. He wanted to tell the captain he and Joe had spoken with the girl before her death, but that would mean explaining the information they received from Amber Lockhart, and he wasn't ready to do that. Damien fixed his stare on his hands. Blowing out a breath he looked up. "Captain, I don't think the girl's death was an accident."

"Why would you think that? Because she worked for the senator?"

Damien rubbed his hands together. "There seem to be some coincidences that lead me to think that either Senator Lockhart or someone close to the senator is involved in these deaths."

Captain Mackey leaned forward on his elbows. He turned his attention to Joe. "Do you share your partner's beliefs in this case?"

"Yes, Sir. The evidence we have so far leads us to think there is a connection to Senator Lockhart or his office."

Captain Mackey frowned. "What evidence? I haven't seen any reports about any crucial evidence being found linking anything. Let alone these two cases. Can you tell me about this so-called evidence?"

Damien and Joe shared a sideways glance. "No, Sir," Damien said. "We don't have enough of anything to put in a report. But we both believe, our gut is telling us, these two cases are related, and they both point to the senator."

"You can't seriously think I'm going to entertain what your gut is telling you? Damien, I think you are one hell of an investigator, but I believe your last case has thrown you for a loop." Captain Mackey sighed. "Maybe it is too soon for you to come back to work, especially having to deal with this kind of case."

Damien's back straightened. "You can't take me off this case Sir. I'm perfectly capable of returning to work. I'm telling you we think Rossdale and this girl's death are related."

The captain leaned back in his chair and stared at his lieutenant. He had an impression there was another underlying cause for the dark circles under Damien's eyes, but he didn't want to press the issue. "Listen, I'm not going to take you off this case. Even though I think you are not quite ready to return, I will leave you in place for now. Unless you have some concrete evidence linking Rossdale to the senator or this young girl to the senator, I don't want to hear any more about it. Investigate Rossdale's murder as an independent case. And you need to leave the accident case alone."

"Sir," Damien stopped mid-sentence.

Captain Mackey held his hand in the air. "No. I don't want to hear it. I gave you a direct order. There are a lot of forces at work in this case, and a lot of things are out of our control. But unless you catch the senator red handed killing someone else, stay away from that idea of yours. There is a lot of pressure from up top wanting us to close this case. We will close the case when it's finished, but you will not associate Rossdale or the girl in the car wreck with the senator at all. Do I make myself clear?"

Damien's rigid body bristled at the captain's warning. "Yes Sir, you're loud and clear." He rose from his chair and stood sentry-like, waiting for the dismissal from the office. Joe stood next to him but didn't look at him.

"Go. If you do find something, I want it in a report to me. I will then tell you if you have anything substantial."

Damien nodded as he and Joe left the captain. Neither spoke until they reached Damien's office. Once inside with the door closed, Damien and Joe sat in silence for what seemed like an eternity.

Joe popped his last jelly bean into his mouth but didn't speak. He sat and waited. Damien's face tightened, and his lips pressed together. Joe knew enough to let the swirling emotions his partner and best friend was experiencing run its course. Joe had picked up on how the argument with Dillon hung on Damien's shoulders, and now not having the support of the captain was about all his friend could handle.

"Fuck! This is total bullshit."

Joe nodded as he grabbed a fistful of jelly beans. "Yes, it is. But you are going to need to calm down."

"The fuck if I will. Joe, do you think these two cases are connected?"

"Yes, I do. But we got nothing to prove our beliefs. We also now know the captain won't entertain anything shy of a bloodied knife in the senator's hand. So, until we get that kind of evidence, you and I are going to have to go at this alone."

Damien ran his hand through his hair. "I know if we had something, Captain Mackey would back us." He slanted his eyes at his partner. "I mean, you think he would back us, don't you? Or has he gone to the dark side too?"

Joe chuckled. "I think if we had anything substantial, he would back us. But because of the pressure from someone, he isn't going to entertain our notions."

"Who would have been watching Laura? It would have had to be someone from that party. She said the major players were the sitting senator's assistant, Rossdale, the senior senator, and some scary guy."

"Well the one thing we know is it wasn't Rossdale," Joe said with a sly grin.

Damien offered an amused smile. "Funny."

"Okay, all joking aside, how hard would it be to see what the assistant's plans for last night were?"

"Extremely. If we go over and ask where he was last night, one, the lawyers would eat us for lunch. Two, we would then have to divulge all the information that we have. I'm not ready to let what measly little information we have out. It's our one piece of leverage. No one knows where we are in this case. I want to keep it that way."

"What about the wife? Amber? She may be able to help us. We can use what we know about her and the assistant to see if she can tell us where the assistant was last night."

Damien placed his interlocked hands on his head. "I think we would be setting ourselves up to get into bed with the devil. But we will use that if we have no other option."

They sat in silence for a few minutes. Damien kept coming back to Laura being watched. It didn't seem plausible to him. "Listen, I can't explain this, but what if Laura wasn't being watched. What if it was a coincidence? Did someone happen to see her at the bar speaking with us? They made assumptions putting two and two together, then followed her from the bar."

Joe's mouth turned down on one side. "Maybe. But that's why I said what I said in the garage. I don't see it. We didn't notice anyone staring at us that night. Nah, I think there is something else."

"Okay, then someone had to see her give you the note. That led to her being followed and ultimately run off the road." Damien didn't believe his own words. It didn't make sense. Who was following her and why? What could she possibly have known? "It has to be something."

Joe's hand stopped midway to his mouth. "It could be us." He said before filling his mouth with jelly beans.

"Could be us what?"

"We could be the ones being watched."

Damien sat up straight. He squinted at his partner. "Who and why?"

Joe shrugged. "Whoever is trying to squash this case. Or someone associated with whoever is trying to squash this case."

"That means we are getting close to someone. If we were the ones being watched, we signed Laura's death warrant and didn't even know it." The statement hung heavily between them. "Hey, let's go to my house. Let's look at the book. Maybe we can find something in there that will lead us in a direction."

"I thought you already looked through the book?"

"I did, with you. The other day. But I didn't go through all of it." Damien's eyes lit up. "Oh, fuck me."

"No thank you."

"Shut the hell up. The letter."

"What letter?"

"The letter from Rossdale. I never read the letter." Damien stood and put on his jacket. "Go grab your coat. We are going to see if Mr. Rossdale wrote us anything in that letter that will help us."

"Then can we eat? I'm starving."

"Jesus man, you are always hungry," Damien said as they headed towards the stairwell.

"Hey what can I say? I'm a big boy. I need my nourishment to keep this body moving."

"Uh, you are going to be as big as a barn if you keep eating as you do. Then you'll need a fucking forklift to move that fat ass of yours."

Joe gave him the finger as they climbed into Damien's SUV.

# CHAPTER TWENTY-FOUR

Walking through the garage door into the condo, Coach didn't greet Damien at the door. Instead, he peered at him with one half-opened eye as he stayed snuggled on the sofa.

"Wow. He must be super mad at you. He won't even greet you at the door." Joe laughed as he headed for the kitchen.

Damien gave Coach an evil stare. "Yeah, well the fat ass forgets who saved him. He'll come around when Dillon is out of town, and he wants one of those cans of tuna he lives for." Damien watched as Joe grabbed two sodas from the refrigerator and a bag of chips off the counter. "Seriously, dude?"

"Hey, you wouldn't stop so now I'm eating your food." Joe threw one of the sodas to Damien as he walked towards him. Both headed into the office. "So, have you spoken to Dillon yet today?"

"You know damn well I haven't. Why are you even asking me that?"

"Why are you mad at me?"

"I'm not mad at you. I'm just mad." Damien opened the safe and pulled out the book with the letter. He sat at his desk and opened it.

Joe scooted the chair from Dillon's desk to the right of Damien's. "I hope there is some information in there. Otherwise, we are going to be chasing our tails for years to come on this Rossdale case." He took a big swig of his soda and smashed a handful of chips into his mouth. Joe munched all the while watching Damien, trying to gauge what the letter said based on his partner's reaction.

Damien looked up with wide eyes. "Holy fuck."

"What the hell is in the letter?" Joe scooted his chair closer abandoning his chips to Dillon's desk.

"Rossdale, he came across a story." Damien continued reading. When he finished the first page of the letter, he handed it to Joe. "He claims to have discovered that the Lockharts had something to do with Brock Avery leaving the Senate race. Ultimately helping James Lockhart get elected five years ago."

"That would be something to kill for. I mean c'mon, if it came out that Daddy did anything to sway an election, or James himself, there would go Jr.'s chances at getting into the governor's mansion."

"No shit. And that would explain the reason Mr. Bryce didn't want the senator talking to Rossdale."

Joe pointed at him. "You're assuming Bryce knew what Rossdale had. I don't think anyone but us knows what Rossdale had uncovered. I think there was only one person who knew what Rossdale knew besides us, and that was the killer."

"Well then, that means someone somewhere knows a lot of information. Unless the killer and the person pulling strings now is one and the same." Damien read through the letter some more. "Rossdale thinks Brock Avery was forced to leave the Senate race."

"Does he *say* who, how, and why?"

"Give me a few minutes to finish reading this."

"Shit, my blind grandmother could read faster than you," Joe said.

Damien continued to scan the letter. "No. Rossdale mentions at the time he wrote this note he hadn't gathered all the facts, names and such."

Joe sighed. "Well, I thought this letter was our Perry Mason moment. And we would have this case solved."

"You're real funny." Damien scanned the page. "Oh no."

"What?"

"Remember our first major case at the 17th? The Draper case, Kalvin Dale Draper."

Joe leaned forward placing his elbows on his knees. He hung his head before speaking. "That's the guy killed on the train platform?"

"Yeah," Damien watched as Coach waddled in and rubbed against Joe's leg. Joe picked him up and placed him on his lap. Coach turned and stared at Damien as he nestled into the big Irishman's lap.

Joe smiled as he watched Damien glare at the cat. "Hey, Coach, how are you doing?" Joe scratched the cat's head.

"I know what you're doing," Damien said to the cat. "He isn't going to be here to feed you. You just wait. Fatso." Damien read some more. "It looks like Rossdale stumbled onto that case when he started to investigate the Lockharts, and he thinks our murder victim from the platform was what forced Brock Avery to leave. But he doesn't say why."

"Okay, so the guy, Draper, I remember we were shot at when we entered his business office. And I remember that his home looked unlived in except for the stash of military grade weapons."

"Yeah, and Nicky could never find anything on him. I'm sure Kalvin Dale Draper was not his name, and without that information, we could never figure out who he was associated with or worked for. My father was sure he had his identity wiped. And for that to be done at the level it was, means this guy knew someone or had some skills." Damien took a swig of his soda. "When we interviewed Amber Lockhart, she said Brock Avery left the Senate race after someone close to him died. What if the dead guy from our case five years ago is that someone?"

Joe raised his eyebrows. "That would explain why Rossdale thought the Lockharts were involved. But that means they had our guy on the platform murdered and why would they do that?"

Damien held up his hand. "Wait, Rossdale mentions another case. Remember those two kids? Richie Green and Jeffrey McNichol who were on the platform at the time of the murder, they gave us that sketch. Rossdale thinks they were murdered to cover up that murder and the link to the Lockharts." Damien looked up. "I remember those two kids. Damn, to think they were killed because of the help they gave us."

"I remember Baxter telling us that those kids were shot outside of a club. He said the other detectives investigating it had been instructed to close it as an unfortunate drive by and that case was pulled from them," Joe said.

"For someone to pull that case and cover it up, pull our case, and get rid of all the evidence, that person has to have power. The problem is Rossdale doesn't mention who the person is that could've have pulled the cases."

Joe ran a hand through his hair. "I remember all the evidence went missing from the evidence locker too."

"Oh fuck, I forgot about that. Captain Franks had put in an inquiry to have a news story done about it, and within hours our case was yanked."

"Yeah, that weasel from internal came by and took all your files from your desk and told us not to talk to anyone." Joe smiled at his partner. "We shared a few beers at Mulligan's that night."

Damien laughed. "Yeah, you told me you tried to get a new partner, but the brass had shut you down."

"I never did that. I was only messing with you." Joe placed Coach on the floor. "It's a shame we couldn't get that picture the sketch artist provided us, based off those two kids' description, on the news before the case was yanked."

Damien guffawed at his partner. "Holy fucking shit."

"What the hell, man? Holy shit what?" Joe watched his partner move to his safe. "Um, what the heck are you doing?"

Damien almost laughed. "I can't believe I forgot I had this."

"Had what?" Joe rubbed his temple. "You are making me nuts. What the heck are you talking about?"

Damien reached into his safe and pulled out a manila folder. He turned around to see his partners glare. He couldn't stop the laughter from bubbling up. "Okay, remember when they took all our files from us that afternoon?"

"Yeah."

"Well, after they left, I was trying to get a folder out of my desk." Damien shuffled through the papers in the envelope. He chuckled as he continued to search for something. "When I finally got the folder out, a piece of paper came out with it." Damien stopped going through the envelope. A broad smile filled his face.

"Dude, do you have a naked picture in there or what? The smile on your face makes me think so."

"No, what I have is better than that." Damien held up a piece of paper that had once been folded into a small square. "Here."

Joe took the paper from his friend's outstretched hand. He squinted at him, tilting his head to the side. "If this isn't better than a naked girl, I'm punching you."

"Oh, it's better."

Joe looked at the paper. His jaw hung open. He glanced up from the paper to Damien and back again. "Get the fuck out."

"I know, right?"

"How the heck did you get this?"

"I must have put it in my desk, and it got stuck towards the back when that folder got caught. It never made it into the case file."

Joe stared at the picture. He remembered the boys had given such an excellent description of the man they saw next to their murder victim that day on the platform, that if they could have gotten it on the news, there would be someone who recognized this guy. "Man, the artist did such a good job of capturing this asshole's eyes. Those kids were scared shitless of this guy."

"Yeah, they kept saying 'his eyes were fucking scary.'" Damien was staring at his partner. Like a heat wave, the vision of Laura at Mulligan's the night she died smacked him in the face. He closed his eyes and could hear the conversation with her. She described the man at the party talking to the senior senator. Damien grabbed his notebook from his back pocket and flipped frantically to the page he was looking for.

Joe stared at his partner. "Dude, I think you have some problems."

Damien stood and shuffled his feet like an Irish jig. He shook his clenched fist in the air. "Yes! Listen, when we interviewed Laura, she kept referring to the man at the party as being scary. 'The man had these piercing, slate blue eyes, surrounded by a dark rim. Making them look black and empty like the devil's soul.' Basically, the same description the boys gave."

Joe looked at the picture then back at Damien. "Well, we got our answer."

Damien's brow wrinkled. "What answer?"

Joe placed the picture on the desk. "It isn't Laura being watched at all. It's us. The case five years ago," Joe pointed to the sketch artist rendering of their suspected murderer, "and our case now, both involve this guy. We have someone from our past cleaning house. And guess what?"

"What?" Damien used his phone to take a picture of the sketch.

"He's gonna want to make sure the two cops who have seen his face don't live to tell about it."

# CHAPTER TWENTY-FIVE

Dillon sat at the long conference table. AD Reynolds, SAC Marks, several other agents, and Director Sherman had been discussing a list of open cases. She should've been paying attention, but from the moment she left the house that morning, a black cloud followed her everywhere. It was the first time since she moved in with Damien she didn't want to go home. The thought of arguing with him left a sour taste in her mouth. It was times like this she wished she was being sent on a case.

However, with Senator Robert Lockhart calling out his dogs to force Damien to close the Rossdale case, the FBI wasn't about to send her anywhere. Which pissed her off even more. She knew the Bureau was using her to keep tabs on the investigation. The more she thought about that, the more she wanted to tell all these men to shove their dicks up their asses. Complicating issues, Dillon shared a special relationship with Director Sherman and his wife outside the confines of the FBI, and sometimes, separating the man and the director was a challenge.

Dillon spun around slowly in her chair as the AD droned on about a triple murder in Tennessee that the local authorities had asked for help with. Profiler Dennis McGee was already en route to the crime scene. Dillon had begged AD Reynolds to send her.

"Excuse me...Dillon? Hello?" AD Reynolds tapped on the table to get the profiler's attention. "Dillon!"

"Huh? What?" Dillon asked shaking her head to try to clear it. "What did I miss?"

"Where were you?" Director Sherman stared at her via the telecom connection.

Dillon shrugged. "What do you mean where was I? I'm sitting here in this fabulously informative meeting."

Director Sherman sighed as he stared at his favorite agent and profiler. "Agent McGrath, you seem awfully preoccupied. Is there anything you would like to discuss with us?"

Dillon's brow wrinkled together. "No."

"Well, do you think you could at least answer our question?" AD Reynolds asked.

"Um, what question was that?" Dillon glanced around the table.

SAC Marks tried not to smirk. "Do you know if Damien has come up with any new information on the Rossdale case?"

Dillon bristled. Her knee bounced under the table. Her eyes narrowed as she shifted her stare to her Director. "Do I now work for DC?"

Director Sherman tilted his head to the side. "What the hell do you mean by that?"

"Exactly what it says. How would I know if Damien has found any new information? He has been instructed to turn in reports that detail his findings. Why are you asking me?"

AD Reynolds leaned forward outstretching his arms. "Listen, Dillon, we aren't trying to put you in an awkward position, but this case warrants a modicum of respect for the Lockharts. It seems that Damien has a vendetta out for the senator."

Dillon sighed exaggeratedly. "A vendetta? What the hell do *you* mean by that?" Dillon glared at everyone at the table. SAC Marks sank into his seat as her eyes landed him. She brought her attention back to the man before her. "I'm waiting."

AD Reynolds recoiled when Dillon's glare remained on him. "I didn't mean that the way it came out."

"I'm not sure how else that statement could've been taken." Dillon leaned into the table. "I understand that Robert Lockhart is putting the screws to anyone and everyone to have this case distanced from his son. But I've wondered, why he is spending so much effort? Especially if Damien hasn't even come up with any leads pointing him in that direction."

"Oh hell, Dillon. You are not that stupid to think that Lieutenant Kaine doesn't have the sitting senator in his crosshairs." AD Reynolds leaned back in his chair. "He went and questioned him regarding Rossdale the same day the body was discovered."

Dillon's face flushed with heat as a wave of anger washed over her. "You're not suggesting that there was no reason for him to question the senator or that he did it to cast suspicion onto Lockhart deliberately?"

"Well, we have no idea, now do we? We haven't seen any recent reports on what his findings are. When I contacted Captain Mackey yesterday, he said the investigation was very slow going. He said when Kaine had any information, he would forward it to us," AD Reynolds said.

"Okay, back to my original question, why are you asking me?" Dillon wiped her palms on her jeans. The men looked at each other, but no one responded. "Oh, I see. Because I live with him and sleep with him, you figured I would have some inside scoop." Now her knee bounced at a frantic pace under the table.

Director Sherman cleared his throat. "Dillon, no one is asking you to break any confidence with Damien. We are, however, asking if you know anything that he hasn't reported on yet. Anything that may help us give Robert Lockhart some assurances, as well as those of us that are slightly concerned about the upcoming governor's election."

Dillon's head snapped around at the sound of Director Sherman's voice. She thought that maybe she misunderstood what he had said. Or maybe she hoped she misunderstood. "Did you just say we needed to report to the former Senator Lockhart on an ongoing case? Please tell me that is not what you just said."

AD Reynolds held up a hand. "Wait for a second, Dillon. You know damn well that the political powers that be have a lot of influence all the way up this chain of command. Director Sherman and I are being instructed to make sure this case doesn't affect the outcome of a highly political race. Especially if there is no basis."

"Well, hell. I had no idea we let politics play a role in murder cases now. Maybe I should call up Mr. Lockhart and ask him how I should proceed on my other open cases. I'm sure he can tell me what to look for and how to profile." Dillon's pulse pounded a beat in her head. The knot in her stomach coiled like a ribbon of molten steel.

"Agent McGrath, reel it in." Director Sherman glared at her through the monitor. "We are not asking for any compromises on any case. If evidence is brought forth that warrants Lieutenant Kaine's apparent suspicion, we will act accordingly."

"Yeah, right. But in the meantime, let's structure an ongoing open murder case to fit the current political parties' wishes." Dillon rose maintaining eye contact with her Director. "You know what I think?" She glanced around at the other men at the table then fixed her stare on Director Sherman. "I believe you guys don't have the balls to do what's right in this case. I think all of you and those above you are too afraid of an old, washed up senator who thinks because he has more money than God that he can pull the strings he wants and get a case to just poof.

"Well, gentlemen, I didn't sign up to work for former Senator Robert Lockhart or any other political asshole. I do a job, I find killers and put their asses away. And if it does turn out that the Lockharts or anyone associated with the Lockharts are responsible, I will personally put the cuffs on them."

She stepped back from the table. She directed her attention to everyone in the room. "Another thing, do not ask me to use my personal relationship with Lieutenant Kaine to further your agendas or anyone else's." Dillon grabbed her jacket and left the stunned and silenced room.

AD Reynolds stood to go after her.

"AD Reynolds, let her go." Director Sherman cursed as he threw a pen across the room. He stared at the remaining men around the table. "She was out of line, and I will deal with her." He sat quietly for a moment. "Agent McGrath is right. We often must let outside parties influence how a case is handled. Agent McGrath also has the luxury of not answering to those powers. I think if she had to sit in the office of the president and explain why shit didn't go the way it was expected, she may very well have a different view of this situation."

# CHAPTER TWENTY-SIX

Damien and Joe sat in silence in the condo office. Damien glanced up to find his partner staring at him. Damien's chest tightened, making it hard for him to take in a deep breath of air. "We're going to need help with this." He took a bottle of whiskey off the shelf. He grabbed two glasses and poured two shots. He handed a glass to Joe.

Joe took it without hesitation and downed it. "I'm pretty sure drinking on the job is against regulations, but I'm not sure how long we will have these jobs."

"No shit." Damien downed his shot and set the glass aside. "We are screwed. We can't trust anyone. We have no idea how far up the chain this goes. But someone had a helluva lot power over two precincts to pull ongoing cases and have them disappear. Not to mention cover up the murders of several people."

Joe's jaw clenched. He rubbed the back of his neck. "Well, I will agree with you, we are going to need help." He paused and looked around the room. His focused landed back on his partner. "You have to tell Dillon."

Damien tilted his head back. He closed his eyes and sat still. Sitting back up he glanced at his watch. "It's almost five. I have no idea when she is coming home. Fuck!" He tugged on the ends of his hair. "She may not even come home. She was pretty pissed at me."

"That shit doesn't matter. We know we can trust her. She would never do anything to jeopardize our safety. I have no doubt that she would back us and you do too."

"I know that. But that also puts her at risk. We are going to have to tell her everything about that case. We are going to have to tell her about this book and this letter. She is going to ask how we found out everything. That's how our argument started I told her about the senator's wife and Bryce having an affair."

"Yeah, but you didn't fill her in on anything, and you told her you thought she was covering her ass. She should've punched you."

Damien laughed. "She wanted to." At that moment, the garage alarm sounded. Damien raised an eyebrow. "You are staying while *we* tell her about this case."

"Are you afraid of your woman?" Joe roared with laughter.

"Hell yeah. You know she knows Krav Maga? She could kick both our asses."

*** 

Dillon pulled into the garage. She sat in her car for a few minutes. The silence engulfed her, surrounding her like a cocoon. The entryway that would lead her to her home loomed on the other side of her car door. When she left the meeting, she hadn't expected to get out of the building. She thought for sure the AD would have stopped her and relieved her of her weapon and badge. Dillon leaned her head on the steering wheel and sighed. "Good job, McGrath. You'll be lucky to have a job tomorrow."

She dragged herself out of her car. Her hand shook as she reached to open the house door. Upon entering, she smelled the familiar odor of home she had grown to love. Damien. A woodsy, outdoor masculine smell always hit her. She inhaled through her nose and immediately regretted her earlier thought that she didn't want to come home.

Removing her weapon, keys, and wallet, she placed them on the table near the front entryway. Her shoulder's drooped, and she turned to walk towards the voices in the office. Coach had run up to her and rubbed against her leg. He sat patiently at her feet, and when she failed to acknowledge him, he raised on his hind legs and pawed at her.

Dillon's expression softened as she gazed at the fat cat who had become one of her greatest loves. "Hey, sweetie." She picked him up and kissed Coach on his head. "I am so sorry. I shouldn't have ignored you like that. It's not your fault I had such a bad day." He snuggled against her chin. Dillon closed her eyes, the weight of the day crashed into her. She didn't let the tears fall, she held them at bay, but the heaviness was almost more than she could bear.

Walking towards the office, she heard Damien and Joe discussing something. She rounded the corner, still carrying the cat. Dillon lowered her head squinting at the two men. The conversation they were having stopped a little too abruptly. "Hey," she said. She shot glances between them. "Why are you two here?"

Damien glanced at Joe then turned his attention back to Dillon. "We were following up on a lead."

"A lead regarding this Rossdale case?" Dillon asked.

"Yes."

She placed the cat on the floor and leaned against her desk. She crossed her arms and sighed. "Is this a *real* lead or a gut feeling?"

Joe's arm hair stood on end. He noticed Damien's lips purse together. He jumped in before world war three broke out. "This is a real lead. There is something we need to discuss with you." Joe moved from her chair and pointed to it. "You want to sit or stand while we tell you about it?"

Dillon's eyes narrowed at the Irishman. She turned towards Damien, "I'll stand. What is it you have to tell me?"

Damien mentally ordered himself to calm down. He had to make sure that Dillon listened to all he and Joe had to say. "I haven't...there are some things...Fuck!" Damien pulled at his hair before letting his arms fall to his side.

Joe moved to lean against his partner's desk. "Listen, Dillon, we are about to tell you some things that Damien hasn't put in any report."

Dillon stiffened. Her back went rigid. "You were supposed to keep the FBI as well as your captain up to date on everything. Why the hell haven't you put it in a report?"

Damien's eyes narrowed at her. "Not everything should go in a damn report."

"Yes, it should. What the hell are you doing holding shit back? How the hell are we supposed to run this investigation without your fucking reports?"

"Excuse me? Run this investigation? Last I knew I didn't work for you or the FBI." Damien took one step towards her.

Joe reached out both hands in their directions. "Okay, I have had enough of both of you." Joe turned towards Damien. "You need to take a fucking chill pill." He spun around towards Dillon. "And you need to pull that stick out of your ass. I understand both of you are raw from your previous fight, but Dillon there are some things you don't know. We are about to tell you those things, and hopefully, you will understand why we haven't shared anything."

He leaned back against the desk. "Now, I need you to listen to what we have to tell you." He focused on Damien. "Can you explain it, or do I need to?"

Damien nodded. "Yeah, I got it." Damien moved to lean against the desk as well. "Okay, I need to start with a case from five years ago." Damien proceeded to explain the case he and Joe had while at the 17th precinct.

Dillon frowned as he told the story. "I don't see what that case has to do with now."

"I'm getting to that. Do you think you can give me five fucking minutes to finish?"

"What the fuck? Finish your damn story already."

Damien breathed in through his nose and out his mouth. His body tensed and as his stomach knotted into a tight coil. *Why the hell is this so hard?*

# CHAPTER TWENTY-SEVEN

Damien ogled Dillon, taking in her beauty. He loved her more than he thought loving someone was possible, but at this moment, he wanted to walk away. To say fuck it. His lips pinched together. Sighing exaggeratedly, he continued. "When we first spoke with Rossdale's assistant, she gave us something. I never entered it into evidence, and I don't plan on doing so."

He reached around his back and grabbed the book. "It was this book. It has information on all kinds of people. Nothing horrible, but it was evident that Rossdale was good at finding secrets. Along with that book was a letter. I have read the..."

She pointed at him. "You have evidence that you haven't turned in yet? Are you fucking out of your mind?" Dillon stood and stomped around the room. "I can't believe I'm hearing this. What the hell is wrong with you men? I can't believe you have withheld information that could help solve this case. It would go far in keeping the fucking Lockharts off my ass."

"Are you serious right now? You're worried about your ass?" Damien seethed.

Joe's skin tingled as the air crackled with tension. "Okay, that's it. What the hell is wrong with you two?" He moved to stand between them. "You," he pointed towards Dillon, "I need you to calm the fuck down. Leave Agent McGrath at the door. We need Dillon." He turned towards Damien. "You, shut the hell up. I'll tell the damn story."

Joe proceeded to explain the letter and all that was in it. At some point during the conversation, he could see the shift on Dillon's face. Amazing what a little clarity can do for a situation. "So, now you should have a better understanding of what we are up against."

Damien now spoke calmly. "We aren't sure how far this goes up the chain. Someone five years ago had the power to cover up murders, make evidence disappear, and keep people quiet. The letter goes on to say that Rossdale thought he had a lead on something that would explain how the senior senator may have helped his son get his current legislative position. However, he doesn't go into it, or he didn't have enough to put it in this letter."

Damien searched for the letter in the papers on his desk.

Joe nodded at Dillon. "Here's the thing," he handed the sketch of the murderer to Dillon. This guy is the one who was seen at the train station, and the boys who gave us this sketch were killed shortly after this. Damien and I think this guy is cleaning house. Whatever went down five years ago, is playing a huge roll in shit now.

"Rossdale was murdered because of something he found out about the Lockharts. The problem is we aren't sure what exactly that is. Not to mention we don't know who the fuck is pulling strings. Is it Robert Lockhart, or is he looking out for his kid? Is it whoever had these cases pulled five years ago, or is it this fucker?" Joe pointed to the sketch.

Dillon stood between the two men. "Okay, okay. I get it now. I'm sorry. I get it. But that doesn't explain why you kept it from me." She glared at Damien. "You and I will need to have that discussion later. As for this case, don't put any of this in a report. I don't know what you are going to report but don't use any of this. Whoever is at the center of this has pull all the way up the chain of command. And when I say all the way up, I mean to the top."

Joe glanced between Damien and Dillon. "You mean like the president?"

Dillon nodded. "Yeah. I get the feeling the FBI, including Director Sherman, are being told this better not get close to the junior Lockhart. Some heavy hitters have a lot riding on this election."

Damien crossed his arms across his chest. "Who the fuck can we trust? I know the captain is being pressured. So, whoever it is, has power in DC as well."

The three stood there in silence. Dillon finally spoke. "Alright. Here is a plan. First, get rid of that letter. Take it and the book out to your family. Have them hold it out there. I know you give them stuff all the time to hide in that fortress of theirs. Do that with this. No one can know about either of those items."

Damien moved to the safe with the book and letter in his hand. Standing in front of it, he looked at Joe and Dillon. "When we no longer need to reference this for this case," he held the book up, "I will take it to my Dad's house."

Dillon sighed as she leaned against her desk. "I need to smooth over something at work, then I need to get a meeting with the senior senator. That may give us some inside information. If anything, maybe I can get a fix on Robert Lockhart and see if he is protecting his kid or if he is orchestrating this whole thing."

Joe raised an eyebrow. "Smooth something over at work?"

Dillon smiled. "Yeah, if I still have a job in the morning, that is."

Damien opened his mouth to say something but thought better of it. "Do you believe that we can trust the captain? We need his help."

Joe rubbed his temples. "Yeah, I think we can trust him. He has never given us reason not to. And the last case proved he always has our back. I think the smart thing would be to bring him in on it. But we can't discuss this anywhere near DC."

Damien nodded in agreement. "No, that conversation needs to take place in my SUV. It's the one place I can be sure no one will have eyes or ears."

"Tomorrow, you need to tell Mackey everything. I will arrange the meeting with Mr. Robert Lockhart. I bet I can get that in the next day or so. I need to have that happen at his house though. Where he thinks he is in control of the situation." Dillon pulled her hair out of her usual ponytail. That alone eased a headache that was beginning at the back of her head.

Damien glanced at his watch. "It's almost six. Joe, why don't you take my truck and come back here and pick me up in the morning?"

Joe stood up and stretched. "I can do that. I'll text Taylor and let her know. I can see what she wants for dinner." Joe grabbed the keys from Damien's outstretched hand. "Seven thirty?"

"Yeah, that sounds good." Damien watched Joe head out. He heard the garage door open and close a short time later. He stood in the quiet room with Dillon still leaning against her desk. Neither one spoke nor made a move to clear the air between them. He hated this feeling of unsettledness.

"Listen, Dillon, I didn't keep this from you because I don't trust you. I wasn't sure what to do with all this information."

Dillon glowered at him. Damn if his sapphire blue eyes didn't make her insides melt. But she refused to let this go. "Damien, you seem to withhold information from me regularly. Yet, if I don't tell you something, you say I need to trust you more. I don't get the double standard."

"What the hell are you talking about? I don't have a double standard. Sometimes I want you to leave the agent behind and just be Dillon."

"Are you kidding me? What about you? Do you ever leave Lieutenant Kaine at the door? Hell no."

Damien took a few steps towards her. "You're right. I don't leave my job at the door. This case has engulfed me."

"The problem, Damien, is that all your cases engulf you."

"Now who is calling the kettle black? Like you don't live and breathe these killers you chase. I remember not too long ago you neglected to tell me about the exact nature of your interview with Jason, that bastard murderer. What was your excuse then? And at least I don't walk away and not speak to you all fucking day."

Dillon's lips tightened into a thin line. Her chest rose and fell at a rapid pace. Her eyes narrowed into thin slits as she rose from the edge of the desk. "I don't have to tell you everything. You don't own me. And I don't have to call and check in with you either."

"Now who has the double standard?" Damien's eyes squinted together.

"Fuck you, Lieutenant Kaine."

Damien grabbed her by the shirt. He heard her gasp as he ripped open the blouse. Buttons flew in every direction. He broke the hook on her front clasp bra and pushed both shirt and bra off her shoulders locking her arms in place by her side.

He watched as her whiskey-colored eyes burned an amber flame. Damien spun her around and bent her over the desk. He reached around and undid her pants and pulled them down low enough where he could then use his foot to push them to her feet. Damien leaned forward and bit her exposed shoulder. Dillon's bodied shuddered, and a moan escaped her lips. He unzipped his pants and pushed her wet panties to the side. Entering her slowly from behind, he was instantly sheathed in a velvety cocoon of warm flesh.

Fueled by anger, lust, and desire, Damien moved slowly in and out of her at first. Dillon's arms and hands still locked in place by the shirt and bra keeping her pinned against the desk. Damien bent against her and reached underneath her upper body lifting her up slightly, so her back was against his chest. He held tightly to one breast while his other hand grasped her waist.

Dillon's body trembled against him as her moan rumbled up her throat before it escaped. She whispered his name, and that was all he needed. He slammed into her at a frantic pace. A bead of sweat formed on his back. Her moans filled the room as her body shook from her impending orgasm. Damien followed her over the edge, grunting as he emptied himself into her. When finished, he stayed in her for a few minutes. Both of them were unable to speak.

When Damien did extricate himself from her vice-like grip, he rested his head against her back. "I'm sorry about last night and today. I've been all messed up over our argument. I'm sorry I didn't trust you. Please forgive me."

Dillon turned around Damien helped pull her shirt back up onto her shoulders. She reached out and touched his cheek and kissed him sweetly on the lips. "I didn't like the way our argument bothered me either. All day this cloud followed me around. I'm sorry too. I love you, Damien. I will always love you."

Damien pulled her into his chest. "I love you so fucking much. You have no idea what you mean to me."

She smiled at him. "I think I have a pretty good understanding. Unless this is how you make up with everyone you have an argument with."

# CHAPTER TWENTY-EIGHT

*Sitting in his truck in the driveway of a nearby vacant residence, David watched the sexy brunette go into the Irish cop's house an hour earlier. He had a few ideas about what he would like to do to that woman. But he wasn't into raping women, and there was no time to form a relationship with her or any woman for that matter. However, she would be fuel for a few of his fantasies.*

*He glanced at his watch. He had wanted to hang out at the other detective's house, but he thought the Italian posed more of a threat than this guy since he lived with the FBI bitch. As much as David wanted to take care of her and her cop boyfriend, he didn't want to mess with that situation yet. If he killed her now, it would bring way too much heat on him. However, he knew the time would come, giving him his chance to make her pay for the shit storm she caused in his life all those years ago. Of course, he could also thank the bitch. Had it not been for her, he never would have found his true calling in life.*

*The Irish cop pulled up to his house the same time David's cell phone buzzed on the seat next to him. Glancing at the screen, he was expecting this call.* "Yeah?"

"There are some extra loose ends I need you to take care of."

"What kind of extra loose ends?"

"A couple of people that may pose a threat to my plans."

"Well, if you had let me do my job five years ago, you wouldn't be in this mess now."

"You are in this mess with me, buddy. Not just me."

"You have that wrong, my friend. I am merely the hired hand. If anyone learns of my identity, I will know it came from you. And you and your family will then disappear. Now tell me who you want me to take care of."

*The caller on the other end of the line remained quiet for a moment.* "Two people, Officer Thadd Lynn and Brock Avery."

"Why Lynn now? He did his job, he doesn't know anything, and I thought Avery was taken care of when he received the money for his business?"

"Thadd may be able to figure out who gave the command to remove the file from the evidence locker. And as for Avery, I did take care of him, but I don't trust him to keep his mouth shut. Once the governorship is secure, I *have a feeling he may come back to get a bigger piece of the pie."*

*"You should have let me take care of him when I silenced that overrated bodyguard of his. I would have one less mess to fix, and you wouldn't be out so much more money. Which by the way, my fee is double, and I want it in my account before I take care of your problems."*

*"Double? What the hell, you can't double it."*

*"Yes, I can. I don't think you can find someone else on such short notice let alone get someone to touch the cluster fuck you've created."*

*"Fine. The money will be there. It's not my money, anyway. I want this taken care of ASAP. Before the big fundraiser gala."*

*"I'm going to suggest, again, that you take care of the last player who knows everything. He removed those cases from evidence as well as shut down any investigation into those two kids. I'm telling you it's a mistake letting him hang around."*

*"You just let me worry about him. He is so wrapped up in his position and his wife's new restaurant that he wouldn't want anything to jeopardize that."*

*"Okay. Whatever you say." David disconnected the call as the detective exited his vehicle. He watched the Irish cop enter his apartment, wondering if he should take care of him now. He decided against it and thought it might be better to strike up a conversation with the brunette at her favorite deli.*

# CHAPTER TWENTY-NINE

Friday morning

Joe pulled in front of Damien's garage. He entered the code, and as he waited for the door to open fully, he received a picture from Taylor. She stood in a pair of blue panties and bra.

*Too bad you had to leave early. xoxoxo*

Joe instantly got a hard-on. "Damn, that woman is a tease." He adjusted his jeans walking into Damien's living room. "Yo, you guys dressed? I don't want to walk in on you two having sex or something." Joe chuckled to himself as he shut the door. Right then, the front doorbell rang. Joe frowned as he looked at his watch. Seven-fifteen, who the hell is this? Joe thought. Quickly looking at the security screen a big smile spread across his face.

He opened the door to a little short, gray-haired woman. Joe took her in his arms and lifted her off the ground. "Hey, Mrs. C. Haven't seen you since the Kainetorri Christmas gala."

"Oh my," she giggled as Joe spun her around. "You're going to make me drop my cake."

"Cake? What kind of cake?" Joe narrowed in on the round cake container.

"Mrs. C.," Damien said, "is everything okay?" He gave her a hug and a kiss.

Dillon came up next to Damien and hugged her as well. She arched an eyebrow. "Hi, Mrs. C. What you got there?"

"I brought you guys a cake. I'm going to be going out of town with a friend, Marsha, and I wanted to make sure you knew to keep an eye on my place." She handed over the cake to Dillon. "Now, Dillon baby, you make sure you eat a piece of that. You need more meat on your bones. But I imagine being around these two men you don't get a morsel of food." She squinted at Damien. "Do you feed her?"

Damien nodded his head. "Yes, Mrs. C. I feed her when I let her out of her cage to go to the bathroom."

That got him a smack from both Dillon and Mrs. C.

Mrs. C. gave Dillon another hug. "I don't know how you put up with these two. Where is my baby? I don't see him."

"Coach is in the kitchen, eating, again," Damien said as he gave Dillon the evil eye. "Dillon likes to feed him two breakfasts. The cat is going to weigh fifty pounds soon."

Mrs. C. made her way past the trio. She returned with the fat cat snuggled against her chest.

Coach gave everyone a sly look, as he rubbed against Mrs. C.'s chin. Essentially saying *ha-ha look at me.*

"This is who I really wanted to see. How's my big baby?" She kissed Coach's nose, making him purr wildly in her arms.

"You never hug me like that," Damien said as he pouted.

"Me neither," Joe followed with a big pouty smile.

"Neither of you are as sweet and cute as my baby." She placed Coach on the floor. "If you need me, send me a text or call me." She reached for the door. "Do not eat all the cake. I'm supposed to have dinner with your parents, Damien, when I get back. Maybe you and Dillon can join us. I will mention it to your mom and dad." With that, she left Damien's condo.

"I want a piece of cake." Joe reached for the container in Dillon's hand.

She twisted away, keeping the cake out of reach. "Uh-uh. I will cut you a piece, one piece. Not the whole cake. Didn't you eat breakfast, Joe?" She led the boys to the kitchen. Coach dashed in front of her, almost tripping her. "Damn, Coach, are you trying to kill me?"

"Yes, Dillon, dear. I ate breakfast. But you are holding one of Mrs. C.'s famous cakes. I need a piece of it," Joe said.

"You need a diet," Dillon mumbled.

"I heard that, woman."

Damien giggled at the conversation. "Okay, you two. Dillon, give the big man a piece of cake before he passes out from low blood sugar."

"Boy, you two are so funny, aren't you?" Joe greedily took the piece of cake from Dillon. He winked at her as he dove in.

"What is our plan of attack? Dillon, what are you going to be doing today?" Damien asked.

"Is your dad still calling you about the case?" Joe asked.

"Not really," Damien said.

Dillon's brow wrinkled. "What about your dad?" Dillon sat at the table. Poured orange juice in the three glasses before her.

Damien sighed. "My dad called me the other day before I came home and we had our argument."

Dillon sat back. Her eyes narrowed. "What did he want?"

Damien held his empty fork in his hand. His mouth watered at the untouched cake before him. "He had gotten a call from Robert Lockhart, and my dad wanted to tell me to drop the case. He said he and the Lockharts were good friends and I was barking up the wrong tree. Going after James Lockhart."

"Well now, that explains a hell of a lot about that day." Dillon leaned into the table. "As for my plans this morning, I'm going to go in and grovel to AD Reynolds. I will proudly blame Damien for my actions yesterday." She smiled at Damien across the table.

Joe sniggered. "Look for her to throw your ass under the bus."

Dillon hit Joe in the arm. "You know I would never do that unless I had to." She winked at Damien. "I'm going to explain that I was frustrated and took what they said personally. And I have a new plan. I will suggest the AD set up a meeting with Robert Lockhart at his home. Oh, damn!"

"Oh damn, what?" Damien asked. "Oh, shit this is the best cake ever. I think we should tie Mrs. C. to the stove and make her bake us fifty of these."

Joe nodded. "I second that motion."

"I just realized I have to call Director Sherman and apologize. I'll explain that my emotions got the best of me." Dillon glanced at her watch. "I better get going. I want to make that call from my car." She stood and placed her plate in the sink, after scraping a few of the cake morsels into Coach's bowl.

"Seriously? Cake? That fat ass won't be able to move without the assistance of the same crane we will have to use on Joe's ass."

Dillon bent over and kissed Damien, more passionately than she intended. "Mmm, cake. I like that taste on you." She winked at Joe. "I will call you sometime today. Get the captain involved. We're going to need his help."

Damien turned towards Joe. "Got a plan on how to tell the captain?"

Joe guffawed. "Me? W.T.F? You're the lieutenant. You're supposed to come up with a plan."

They placed their empty plates in the sink and headed towards the front door. Coach had sprawled himself out on the sofa, fat and full of his many breakfasts that morning. Damien scratched his belly. "You are so fucking spoiled. You are a king among peasants."

Coach stretched his front legs over his head inviting Damien to rub his whole belly.

*\*\**

Once on the road, Damien glanced over at Joe. "Well?"

"Well, what?"

"What's our plan?"

"What fucking plan?"

"How are we going to get the captain to help us? And not have him boot my ass for withholding evidence."

Joe sat quietly for a moment. "How about you call up Captain Mackey, tell him you need to speak with him about the case, but you want to do it away from DC?"

Damien sized up his partner. "That's what you got?"

"Yeah. Just ask him to lunch or something. Easy, it doesn't have to be elaborate."

Damien pulled into the DC parking garage. "Since when have we ever asked the captain to lunch?"

Joe shrugged. "Explain that you want to discuss some new evidence before you put it in the report. That should pique his interest. Then we will tell him everything. And I will sit in the back seat so he can't reach me after he punches you." Joe smiled as he exited the SUV.

Damien laughed. "I have no doubt you mean that."

*\*\**

At eight a.m. DC was a bustle of activity. Damien made his way to his office, stopping long enough to talk to his other detectives and check on their open cases. At his desk, he shuffled through papers, mail, and phone messages. He put off calling the captain as long as he could. After exhausting every excuse, he reached for his phone.

"Captain Mackey's office, how may I help you?"

"Catherine, it's Lieutenant Kaine, may I speak with the captain?"

"One moment, Lieutenant."

Damien waited on the line. He ran his hand through his hair. Breathing in through his nose and out his mouth, wanting to calm himself. His heart raced. *What the hell, he thought, I'm just talking to the captain.*

"Captain Mackey."

Damien exhaled, gathering his thoughts. "Hey, Captain. Do you have plans for lunch?"

"Excuse me?"

"Yeah, do you have plans for lunch? Joe and I would like to discuss the Rossdale case with you."

"Damien, why can't you discuss the case with me up in my office? Or better yet, send me that damn report I have been waiting for."

"Well, that's kind of the problem. Before I put some things into my report, I would like to discuss them with you. They are of a sensitive nature." Damien held his hand up as Joe entered his office.

"Why do I get the feeling there is more to this than just lunch?" The captain sighed. "It's almost eleven. Let's head out at eleven thirty."

"That's great. I will pick you up on the lower level of the garage. Thanks, Captain." Damien hung up before Captain Mackey could ask why the hell he wanted to do that. He nodded at Joe. "We leave in thirty."

# CHAPTER THIRTY

Damien pulled up to the doorway on the ground floor of DC's garage. The captain stood there waiting.

Joe opened the front passenger side door and jumped out. "Hey, Captain. You can have the front seat."

The captain looked quizzically at Damien as he climbed up in the SUV. Glancing over his shoulder at Joe, he turned his attention back to Damien. "So why the hell did you want me away from my office? What is it we need to discuss that we can't discuss in my office? And what is up with all the cloak and dagger shit?"

Damien recoiled at the captain's questions. He maneuvered through the mid-day traffic. "I haven't told you all the evidence in the Rossdale case. But for a good reason. After we interviewed Senator Lockhart and his assistant, we found out, via a few informants, that things weren't peachy keen when it came to the senator and those who surround him.

"First, we found out that the assistant is having an affair with Senator Lockhart's wife. We used that information to get Amber Lockhart to tell us about her father-in-law, Robert Lockhart. We had a secret interview with a young woman from Lockhart's office."

Captain Mackey turned in his seat to face Damien. "Let me guess, that was the young girl killed in the car wreck?"

"Yeah. She had just left a meeting with us when she had that wreck." Damien looked at Joe in the rearview mirror. "Both Joe and I think that someone knew she spoke with us."

Captain Mackey glanced over his shoulder at Joe. "You guys obviously think someone followed her."

Damien grimaced. "Not exactly. See, she slipped Joe a note when we were leaving the State Building. No one would have seen that. We called her and set up a meeting at Mulligan's. We think someone was watching us."

The captain frowned. "Why in the hell would someone be watching you? Damien, do you think you might be reaching for straws here?"

Joe leaned forward. "Listen, Captain, there is more that will make this a little clearer. Go on Damien, tell him about the letter."

Damien turned the SUV onto Lakeshore Drive. He opened the can of diet soda he had left that morning in the drink carrier between the seats. With the frigid temperatures, he didn't have to worry about it being hot. "Alright, first a little background." Damien took a long sip before he filled Captain Mackey in on the case from five years ago. "When we went to see Rossdale's assistant, she gave us a letter from him. He had explained to her if anything ever happened to him, to give me the letter."

"Why you?" Captain Mackey asked.

"He was familiar with Belgosa from the last case." Damien took another sip of his soda. "The letter stated that Rossdale had come into some information about Senator Robert Lockhart and his son."

"Wait for a second, what did Rossdale find out about the senators, former and current?"

Damien sighed. "I know you are a big supporter of the Lockharts."

"Yes, I am. Now tell me what he found."

"Alright, it ties into our case from the 17th precinct. First, Rossdale believed the Lockharts facilitated Brock Avery leaving the Senate race. Rossdale figured out that our case and the one regarding the murder of the two boys were removed from the system and all evidence removed from the evidence locker."

"I don't understand the connection," Captain Mackey said.

"Rossdale thought that the Lockharts forced Brock Avery to leave the race. When we spoke with Amber Lockhart, she explained that Brock Avery left the race after someone close to him died. Rossdale didn't have all the pieces yet. But he believed that the dead guy on the train platform was what forced Avery to give up his Senate seat."

Captain Mackey lifted a single eyebrow.

"Wait, hear me out," Damien continued.

Captain Mackey stared straight ahead. He exhaled, nodding.

"Alright. Rossdale tied our case from the 17th to the Lockharts and winning the election. He knew someone ordered all the evidence in the cases to be removed. He was aware that it had to be someone with a lot of pull to get that done. Couple that with the fact that Robert Lockhart is pushing for this case to be closed makes me wonder why."

"Damien, what you are suggesting is ludicrous," Captain Mackey said.

"Here's the deal. When we interviewed Laura, the girl from the car wreck, she told us at a party she attended for the junior Lockhart, she witnessed a man talking to Robert Lockhart. She doesn't know what they spoke about, but she described the man. The man she described fits the sketch we were given by the two kids in our case from five years ago."

Captain Mackey held up his hand. "How do you know this is the same man if the evidence from that case was taken?"

Damien peered over at the captain. "I held onto the sketch. After all the evidence was taken from us, I found the sketch stuck in my desk drawer."

"Okay, if I'm following you, you think this is the guy who killed Laura?"

"Yes." Damien looked at Captain Mackey. "There is some more. The guy who was killed at the train station, we never found out who he was. Now, knowing what Rossdale uncovered, I don't think it's a stretch that the dead man on the platform is directly related to Brock Avery. If we can establish who he was, that would tell us why he was killed and how it helped get Avery out of the way for James Lockhart to win the election."

The captain stared out the window at the lake as they continued their drive around the city. He turned back to his lieutenant. "Damien, this is a hell of a mess. Have you thought about what you are implying?" he paused. "You're suggesting that the Lockharts had your train station victim murdered to get Avery to leave the race. Thus, allowing for James to get his current position."

Damien nodded. "Yeah."

"Are you fucking nuts?" Captain Mackey's stomach clenched. "Oh, fucking hell." The captain sat back in the seat.

"If we can find out the identity of the man on the platform, and who pulled all the cases, we can find the link to Avery, and we can prove the Lockharts had something to do with it. That would also explain why Rossdale was murdered."

"How the fuck are you going to do that?"

"I don't know yet. Dillon is working on her end to try and see if she can get anything from Robert Lockhart that may lead us in a direction. Rossdale's assumptions, Amber Lockhart telling us that Brock Avery left the race after someone close to him died, our dead guy on the platform, and all the evidence taken away is all we have to go on. Amber Lockhart explained that Dad always gets what he wants and that if something stands in his way, he removes the obstacle. I think if we go back to her, she may be able to give us some information regarding the events leading up to her husband being elected."

Captain Mackey cursed. "Alright. I don't want any of this in any report. Let's keep this between us." He pulled a card from his wallet. "This is my private number. Contact me via this with any information on this case. As a matter of fact, send me a report letting me know you have no current leads on the Rossdale case. I'm going to hold a quick news conference stating that there is no ongoing investigation into the senator's association with the Rossdale case. That should take the heat off and make Robert Lockhart think he is getting what he wants."

Damien pulled onto the street leading to the DC parking garage. "Captain, I hate putting you in this position, but you and Dillon are the two people Joe and I can trust. Someone from our past is cleaning house. Joe and I think we are on that list. Our killer is highly skilled, evident by the way he killed our guy five years ago."

"Explain that to me," Captain Mackey said.

"Our victim from five years ago had his subclavian vein cut. The killer jabbed a sharp instrument into our victim's shoulder-neck area and used a lever like motion to sever the vein. The poor guy bled out internally. Because of our involvement then and now, that puts us on the top of his list."

Damien drove through the parking garage and stopped, adjacent to the doorway.

Captain Mackey started to open his car door and stopped, turning towards Damien. "This is a fucking mess. I don't want anyone but you, Joe, me, and Dillon knowing these assumptions. I don't want to put somebody in a compromising position until we know if these assumptions are even accurate. Keep your asses covered. I don't want either one of you being shot. Too much damn paperwork." Captain Mackey slammed the car door and headed into the building.

Damien pulled around into a parking spot. He and Joe sat in silence. "Well, at least he didn't laugh us out on our asses and take our jobs."

"No. But at this moment, I think I am ready to quit this fucking job. I'm telling you, we need to start our own bar. Get the hell out of this rat race."

# CHAPTER THIRTY-ONE

*The picture of Officer Thadd Lynn sat on the counter. David had done his research and found out that the poor guy was highly allergic to almost everything, but mostly peanuts. He walked to the hall closet and took out the suitcase he stored there. Placing it on the counter, he pulled out a wig and mustache set and the small lighted mirror. This set had adhesive already built into the mustache, so he wouldn't need to do any extra prep work.*

*Putting the wig on and adhering the mustache to his upper lip, he admired his new face in the mirror. "Not too bad," he said, twisting his head from side to side. He combed the wig a little, adjusting it one last time.*

*He grabbed the button up shirt and tie from the hanger he had placed on the doorknob of the pantry. After tucking it into his casual khaki pants, he admired himself one last time. "I think I could pass as a junior lawyer from Arthur and Arthur."*

*Glancing at the clock on the wall, he had roughly an hour before he needed to head out to the 17th precinct. David knew the shift change of the officers would occur at three p.m. and he wanted to be there about thirty minutes before, to carry out his plan.*

*He grabbed a plastic sandwich bag and a handful of paper towels and stuffed them into the bag. Earlier that morning he had purchased peanut oil from the organic health food store. David opened the baggy and poured the oil in. He used enough oil to make sure the paper towels were coated but not soaked through. His employer had wanted every death to look like an accident and even though sometimes that was impossible to do, this one was going to be easy.*

*David chuckled at the thought of killing one of their own right under their noses. By the time they realized how Officer Lynn had died and what exactly happened he figured this job would be near completion if not over, and he would be long gone.*

*Moving to the table, he opened his laptop, accessed the Tor browser, and searched the Chicago Crime Lab employee roster. "Ah, there you are." The Irishman's girlfriend took quite the sexy photo. He pulled up her apartment on his satellite feed and mapped out exactly where he needed to go. Kaufman's deli wasn't too far from her place of work, but he'd wanted to check out her apartment as well and see how tight security was in case he wanted a more personal meeting with the sexy brunette.*

# CHAPTER THIRTY-TWO

Dillon sat at her desk. The phone call that morning with Director Sherman had gone better than expected. He gave her a pass but told her she had to smooth things over with the AD. He also said he understood her frustrations, but until she commanded an entire division of agents and had to deal with the political powers that be, she had no right to assume he or the AD was not doing their job. Or that they were listening to a civilian, no matter how rich and powerful he may be.

Fortunately for her, AD Reynolds was not in the office and hadn't been all morning. Dillon scanned through stories about the Lockharts dating back ten plus years. "I can't believe there aren't more scandals surrounding this family. No one can be in the spotlight this much and have nothing but glitter on them. There has to be some rust somewhere." She mumbled to herself. She jumped ahead in time to around the young Senator Lockhart's election. She scanned through newspapers accounts of all the celebratory galas held during the period. The family regularly boasted throughout the election of its philanthropic accomplishments and altruistic ways.

"McGrath, in my office now." AD Reynolds barked as he walked past her desk.

Dillon stood and rolled her shoulders. She adjusted the light cardigan sweater she wore and made her way to the AD's office. Each step she took caused her morning meal to sour even more. She reached the open door and hesitated before entering.

AD Reynolds looked up from his desk. "Come in, close the door, and have a seat." His eyes narrowed as she took one of the chairs. "Are you in a better mood today, Agent?"

A wry smile formed on her face. "Mostly."

AD Reynolds mouth twisted downward to one side. "Mostly? That's the best you got?"

Dillon studied her folded hands in her lap. She closed her eyes and settled her desire to say a sarcastic comment. Meeting her AD's stare, she spoke, "I am truly sorry for my outburst yesterday. I had no right to speak to any of you the way I did. It is no excuse, but I had an argument with Damien, oddly enough about the Rossdale case the night before and being interrogated by you guys didn't sit well with me. And even though that is no excuse for my insubordinate behavior, I thought it might at least help you understand my reaction."

AD Reynolds remained stoic for about forty-five seconds before breaking out into laughter. "Holy shit. That had to be the hardest thing you have ever had to do." He chuckled some more as he silenced the phone call that tried to interrupt their conversation. "Oh, Dillon, you are by far one of my favorite agents. I am often amazed at your black and white view of everything. As an agent, especially one in your position, you will need to learn to operate in the gray. You can't let the things you can't control take over and dictate.

"I have no doubt you will get the hang of that. I'm not now, nor will I ever, use your relationship with Damien to put you in an uncomfortable spot. However, in the confines of this case, I decided it was warranted to ask you what I did. I am sorry if I put undue stress on you. Not my intention at all. Now tell me where we stand with this case."

"Damien is at a loss for evidence. He just sent me an update saying he had no new leads in the case. He said he would be sending Captain Mackey a detailed report this morning. There is something, though, I was wondering. I would like to have a meet with Robert Lockhart if that is at all possible," Dillon said.

"I don't understand why you want to speak with him if there isn't anything leading the investigation to the Lockharts."

"I guess it's my profiler mind, but I am curious as to why he wanted the case closed down so fast. I thought that maybe I could use my position as the liaison to DC to smooth over any hard feelings that might put DC or this office in a contentious position with the future governor."

AD Reynolds beamed a smile at her. "Now you're thinking. I believe I can call him and arrange a meeting. I can get him to come down here..."

"No. I would rather go to him, at his home if possible. That way we are on his turf. Asking him for forgiveness at his house will make it seem like we are at his mercy."

"Sometimes the way you think is a little scary. I know you have the capabilities to manipulate situations." AD Reynolds paused, leaning forward, placing his elbows on his desk. "I have listened to that interview with Jason several times. You did a fantastic job of needling him and getting him to talk at the same time. That interview is being used in some of the cadet training."

Dillon shrugged. "Yeah, I have to give a training session next month about interview techniques. Should be interesting, but I hate staying in those damn barracks."

AD Reynolds smiled at her. He pulled out a small phone book. "Hello, Senator Lockhart. This is AD Reynolds...Yes, Sir, it looks that way...Well, I was wondering if you had some time for myself and Agent McGrath to come by your residence...No Sir, there is nothing wrong. We were hoping to get an opportunity to speak to you in person."

Dillon sat and listened to the one-sided conversation. She hoped she could get an appointment as quickly as possible, but she didn't get her hopes up.

AD Reynolds eyebrows arched. "Okay, yes Senator. Agent McGrath is the profiler assigned to DC...Yes, I agree. She is one of our best profilers...Thank you, Senator. I don't think that will be a problem at all...Yes, Sir, we can be there by two p.m....I am sure Agent McGrath will be more than willing to explain that to you...Okay, we will see you shortly. Thank you again, Senator, for your time."

Dillon peered at her AD. "What exactly will I be more than willing to do? I draw the line at sexual favors. The FBI doesn't pay me enough."

AD Reynolds chuckled. "No, we definitely don't pay you enough for that. The senator wants to see us this afternoon."

"Are you serious? This quick? I thought for sure he would make us wait."

"Nope. When he found out you were coming to the meeting, he seemed anxious to meet you in person. Evidently, he is a big fan of yours. Specifically, he wants to know about Jason and your family."

Dillon's posture stiffened. Her eyes squinted at her assistant director. "What the hell does he want to know about my family?"

"I think he wants to meet the girl who suffered such a tragedy and now is one of the most sought-after profilers. You don't have to tell him anything about your family. That is yours to tell when and who you want. That is something the FBI will back you one hundred percent on."

The breath she held burned her lungs. Exhaling slowly, Dillon relaxed back into her seat. "I don't like sharing that part of my life. I know reporters get a hold of my information, that I can't stop, but I don't want to share it readily."

"And I don't blame you." AD Reynolds looked at his watch. "We have about ninety minutes to get to his estate. We better leave now."

They both stood at the same time.

"I'll go get my jacket and meet you at the elevator." Dillon turned on her heels and headed out.

# CHAPTER THIRTY-THREE

Dillon rode with the AD. She tried to suggest they take her car. That suggestion garnered a wry smile and shake of AD Reynolds' head. He vowed never to ride with her again after their last excursion. Dillon chuckled. Who knew a rugged FBI Assistant Director was afraid of a little speed?

Dillon sat in silence, fiddling with her phone. AD Reynolds took several calls as they made the ninety-minute drive to the former senator's sprawling estate.

Pulling onto the narrow drive, they stopped at a manned security gate. The security guard leaned out of his troll-like doorway. Dillon tried not to laugh, but the guard was large and looked disproportionate to the size of the hut.

"What is your business?"

"Robert Lockhart is expecting us. I'm AD Reynolds with the FBI, and this is Agent McGrath."

"Oh, yes. Mr. Lockhart is expecting you. Follow the drive. Have a good day."

Dillon gasped in awe at the rows of Northern White Cedars lining the winding driveway. As the AD's vehicle entered a clearing, her heart damn near stopped. "Wow, so this is how the super-rich live?"

The residence of the former senator looked as if it had been picked off the shores of Scotland and dropped here. It resembled an eighteenth-century castle with walls made of alabaster stone. The front of the home had several steps leading up to a grand uncovered porch. Off to the left-hand side, facing the home, there was a large archway that led back to what Dillon assumed was another small residence. Or a large garage that held the family's transportation, although she couldn't see anyone from this home driving themselves anywhere.

At the opposite end, the building had been designed to look like a giant turret. Dillon smiled and wondered if the former senator housed those who disagreed with him at the top of the structure, locked away for good.

At the top of the steps stood a grand entrance. The arched doorway held two of the largest wooden doors Dillon had ever seen. As she got closer, she could see the detail of an ancient battle. Men on horseback and suited in armor rode stood ready to crush the opposing forces. She glanced back over her shoulder. The view of the estate was breathtaking, and yet, she wouldn't be caught dead living in a such a house.

One of the massive oak doors opened. A young lady, dressed in all black, stood back and gestured to them. "Please come in. Mr. Lockhart is expecting you."

Dillon once again was in awe. The entryway was something out of a Hollywood movie. Two spiraling staircases flanked either side of the massive room. The entire floor was made of Italian marble. An intricate design had been inlaid making it look as if a Monet had been hand painted on the floor. A double chandelier hung from the twenty-foot ceiling. The crystals gave the effects of a brilliantly lit weeping willow hanging above her head.

They followed the young woman. She led them through a corridor that had been paneled in a dark, rich cherry cedar wood. The entire passage was arched giving it more of the castle illusion. The young servant led them through a doorway that entered what looked like a staging room. The walls were lined with paintings from the sixteenth century to the nineteenth century. The room had robust chairs and end tables but lacked anything else. The young lady disappeared behind a large set of pocket doors leaving Dillon and her AD to wait for permission to enter.

Within minutes, the pocket doors slid open, and they were gestured in. Once inside, the young lady disappeared, leaving them in the presence of the owner of the manor. Robert Lockhart stood before them. His salt and pepper hair slicked back, revealing a receding hairline that, on most men, would make them look old. Yet, on Mr. Lockhart, it added to his good looks.

His eyes sparkled at Dillon as he narrowed in on her, but it was his smile that rocked her back on her heels. The former senator had perfect white teeth and slightly plump pink lips that seemed better fit on a man of a younger age. When he smiled, his cheeks pushed up, and Dillon could instantly see the older man transformed into a younger version of himself.

Robert Lockhart came around his desk and shook the AD's hand. "AD Reynolds, pleased to meet you. I had dinner with the Director of the FBI last week on Capitol Hill." He turned to Dillon and beamed a smile at her. "You must be Agent McGrath. Your reputation proceeds you, young lady. I'm impressed with your credentials."

Dillon extended her hand. The senator's warm palm engulfed hers. She was surprised at the urge to wipe her hand on her jeans. She quickly stuffed both hands into her pockets. "Thank you for taking the time to see us, Mr. Lockhart."

"Please, Agent, call me Robert. May I call you Dillon? I have wanted to meet you since you were transferred here. I hope the Chicago office has proven to be a good change for you."

Dillon understood what Robert Lockhart was up to. His reference to her as a young lady and now removing her title of agent set the stage for her to know she was nothing more than a woman, who had no place being in a man's position of authority. However, that would work in Dillon's favor. "Of course, Robert. You can call me Dillon." She glanced around the room. The office had a study-like appeal with the undertones of a manly library. Books of all kinds, dealing with everything from politics to war, lined one wall. On the other wall, personal photos of the senator filled almost every space.

Dillon moved to the far wall that held the photos. Her skin tingled as the Senator's eyes followed her. She didn't turn around to look at Robert Lockhart. "Are all these pictures of you Senator? I mean Robert."

He moved to stand closer to her. "Yes. They are."

"You were very handsome as a young senator." Dillon turned to acknowledge him. "And you seemed to get better with age, like whiskey in a barrel."

Robert Lockhart laughed heartily. "My, that is a nice analogy. Thank you for the compliment. Yeah, these pictures span my college days and my time in service in the Congress." He continued to admire his pictures of himself before turning towards the AD.

"AD Reynolds, I am surprised Dillon hasn't taken your position. With her gracious charm and ability to command a room, she would do well to lead this group."

AD Reynolds eyeballed the old snake. "Agent McGrath would be very capable of commanding an FBI unit."

Robert Lockhart turned his attention to the stunning agent. She was prettier in person than he had expected and found himself drawn to her.

Age wasn't a factor. If he wanted something, he got it, and he was wondering if Dillon should go onto that list of things he wanted.

Dillon turned to see Robert staring at her. She smiled and leaned slightly into him. "Tell me who all these people are." She pointed to the picture of one guy. "He is in most of your photos, is he a good friend or family member?"

"Oh hell, that is Gage. He and I go way back. I'm a couple of years older, but he was in my fraternity. I helped him, years ago, get his current position. He's practically family."

Dillon continued to study the pictures. She kept coming back to Gage. In all of them, he almost had a look of admiration for the senator. But something niggled deep in her gut. The pictures seemed forced. Almost staged, especially the more recent ones. "You have a lot of friends." She eased her way along the entire wall of photos. Studying each picture. "I don't think I have ever had that many friends in my life."

Robert Lockhart stayed next to Dillon. Her vanilla citrus scent engulfed him. Very subtle, yet the smell lingered in her path. "I find that hard to believe. Someone as smart as you I'm sure had no problem making friends."

She placed her fingertips on his forearm. "Some of us aren't all they seem to be. I may look like I make friends easily, but I find that hard to do." Dillon smiled at him. She started to pull her hand away when Robert patted it.

"Sometimes you need a push in the right direction." He winked at her.

Dillon's blood curdled. She had an intuitive feeling that something wasn't right with this man. Damien's suspicions were right on target. Robert Lockhart took what he wanted, when he wanted, and how he wanted. Of that she was certain. "I see this picture, is it from your swearing in or your son's?"

A proud smile filled the senior Lockhart's face. "That was at James'. I was very proud of him that day."

"Did he always want to follow in his father's footsteps?" Dillon turned to see the AD sitting and watching her. She nodded subtly at him. His lips formed a slight grin as he raised his eyebrows at her.

"James had no aspirations of being in politics. I had to give him a little nudge in that direction." Robert turned and led her back to his desk.

"What did he want to be?" She asked.

"A lawyer. We have enough of those." Robert laughed.

"Can you tell me about being in politics? I would imagine the two of you are a force to be reckoned with." Dillon took the seat adjacent to her AD. She focused on the senior Lockhart.

Robert Lockhart leaned against his high-backed Italian leather chair. He adjusted the ring on his middle finger and stared intensely at her. Dillon watched as he seemed to struggle with the statement.

"Unfortunately for my son, he has yet to master the skills of authority. His position in the political realm gives him that, but he doesn't know how to wield it." He sighed. "I can teach my son how to walk, run, and drive. But some things you either have, or you don't. I have had to help him realize his potential."

Dillon tilted her head. "He is lucky to have a father who helped blaze a trail for him to follow. He was very young when he ran for the Senate seat he currently holds. Your position must have helped him with that."

He nodded. "I was happy to help him get the position." Robert Lockhart immediately regretted his statement. He focused on the beautiful FBI agent before him. "So, I know you two didn't drive all this way to ask me questions about my son and my college days."

AD Reynolds shifted in his seat. "Senator, we wanted to assure you that in no way have we found any evidence linking your son to the grisly murder of Glenn Rossdale. Unfortunately, due to his death and who he was, we must investigate everyone who had contact with Rossdale. The FBI is truly sorry for any inconvenience that may have been brought upon your family."

Dillon folded her hands in her lap. "As the liaison for Division Central, and as an agent in the FBI, I too would like to assure you that the detectives assigned to the case were merely doing their jobs. I would think if you had a family member who had been murdered, you would want the police to leave no stone unturned. All Lieutenant Kaine and Detective Hagan were doing was their job."

Dillon watched as Robert Lockhart's lips formed a thin line and the veins bulged under the skin of his neck. She smiled on the outside, all the while she reveled in the discomfort the mere mention of Kaine's name caused the man.

"I appreciate the candor of your statement. Can you tell me where the investigation lies now?" Robert leaned forward on his elbows and waited for an answer.

AD Reynolds crossed his legs. "I do apologize, but we can't discuss an ongoing investigation. I can tell you that your son is not a suspect."

The senior Lockhart adjusted his button-down shirt as he cleared his throat. "I understand your position. I do hope that you will keep me in the loop." He rose and stepped around his desk gesturing towards the pocket doors they had initially come through. "I have a late afternoon meeting that I need to get ready for. We are planning the gala for next Thursday, and there is a lot to do until then. I do hope you understand."

Dillon followed AD Reynolds towards the door. She took a last look at the man referred to as Gage and burned his picture into her brain. She looked up to find Robert Lockhart's pleasant demeanor now gone, replaced by a hard edge.

Before she exited the room, she turned towards the senator. "Thank you for your time, Robert. I think I have a perfect understanding of your role in the political world."

He bristled but maintained his outward pleasantness. "It was my pleasure, Agent. I hope that one day we can get to know more about each other. I would be fascinated to hear about those years after your family was murdered."

Dillon noticed the twitch at the corners of his mouth. His attempt to rattle her using her family was misguided. "What's to learn? They were murdered, I wasn't. Went to live with my grandparents. And now I use that experience to pay a little more attention to my surroundings and those in it. Thank you again for your time."

At the outer office, the young girl waited to escort them from the residence. Once in the car, AD Reynolds smirked at Dillon. "Well now, he was in love with you for the first twenty minutes of that interview. Then I think he was plotting your death towards the end. You want to explain to me why you and he were having a weird mind fuck session?"

Dillon chuckled at his comment. "You know, if you had asked me three days ago if I thought Damien's claims that the Lockharts, or someone associated with the Lockharts, was involved in Rossdale's murder, I would have laughed at you. But after that interview, I think Robert Lockhart not only knows what happened to Rossdale and why, I think he played a part in it."

# CHAPTER THIRTY-FOUR

After the secret meeting with the captain, Damien had a lot of paperwork to catch up on. Captain Mackey wanted a report outlining his non-progress in the Rossdale case. He made sure to make it seem like there was no evidence linking the Rossdale murder to Senator Lockhart. This report, of course, was for show. It would go into the official report log for anyone to see later.

The captain also wanted it posted before the statement from DC was given to the press regarding the progress of the Rossdale murder. Damien finished typing the report and reread it before he hit the send button. "One thing done," he said, looking at the mound of notes and phone call messages to return, "only ninety-nine more things to do."

He grabbed the first piece of mail to open when his cell buzzed next to him. The display lit up with someone he never tired of talking to. "Yo, Nicky, whatcha up to bro?"

"Damien, man you've got to do something about this Rossdale case."

Damien sat up in his chair. "What the heck do you mean by that?"

"Look, *fratello*, Dad is driving me fucking crazy. All he is doing is complaining about you and the fact that you are trying to link the Lockharts to this murder. He has me planning a dinner for the Lockharts here at the house."

Damien leaned back and closed his eyes. "Nicky, I already told Dad that I had to investigate anything and anyone that may have a reason to kill Rossdale. Dad of all people should understand how being a detective works."

Nicky laughed. "He understands, he thinks you have lost your mind, though. Don't believe you understand how much this is bothering him. Can't you call him up and reassure him, tell him that you have moved on or that you have other suspects. Shit, man, I'm not a party planner, you have to help me. Please."

Damien giggled at the frantic quiver in his brother's voice. "I get that Dad is a loyal friend and that he sticks up for his buddies. He is a ride or die guy. I get it. But I can't tell any of you anything that is going on in an open investigation..."

"I'm not asking you for that kind of information. I want you to tell him not to worry and to leave me alone."

Damien laughed. "I told you to move off the property a long time ago. But you had to stay near Mom and Dad so they could watch the bambinos. Now, look what it's gotten you."

Nicky roared on the phone. "Ha! Wait 'til you and Dillon have kids. I'm willing to bet you and her will be building on the far side of the estate for that very same reason. And you know he has the plot of land already being prepared, right? They are expecting it, like any day."

"Not going to happen, big brother. Not in this lifetime. I may want them to babysit, but I am never living basically right next door." Damien pinched the bridge of his nose. "Okay, listen I can't tell you anything, but tell Dad that DC will be making an announcement regarding the Rossdale case. That should help alleviate your stress. I'm not sure what the statement will say, but Dad will be happy. That's all I can tell you now. Okay?"

"Yeah, that's great. Anything to get him off my back. Man, I will owe you for that. Listen I think they're going to be planning a big family dinner this Sunday. Look for a text from one of us with the time. Being able to tell Dad about the news may make my weekend not suck so much. Your ass better be at the dinner, though, or I will kick it all over Chicago."

"You and what fucking army? Your ass can't whip my ass. I've been beating you up ever since we were kids."

"Whatever. Just make sure your ass is here on Sunday. Love you brother."

"Love you too, Nicky." The line went dead. Damien hoped the news about Lockhart and the Rossdale case would help get his dad off his back. But more than that, he hoped it would make the Lockharts or whoever was working with the Lockharts think they were home free.

# CHAPTER THIRTY-FIVE

*David Allen Parker walked into the 17th precinct. He winked at the girl behind the desk as he walked to the elevators. The lobby bustled with activity, allowing him to move with ease past the police officers milling about waiting for roll call and shift change.*

*Exiting the elevator, David turned towards the evidence locker. He smiled as he pulled his wallet from his jacket pocket ready to show it to Officer Thadd Lynn.*

*David had placed the bag with the paper towels and peanut oil in his right-hand coat pocket. Leaving the bag open for easy access. He gave the man behind the counter a friendly grin. "Hey there, I need to examine some evidence in a case."*

*"Okay. I'm going to need to see the paperwork and your ID. But if you can go ahead and tell me the case number, I can look that up," Officer Lynn said.*

*"I'm with Arthur and Arthur Litigations, that case number is QR 1900-45NOLA." He reached his hand into the baggy and grabbed the paper towels making sure to get peanut oil on every fingertip and on the palm of his hand.*

*Officer Lynn typed the number into the computer. His forehead wrinkled. "Are you sure that is the right case number? I'm not showing anything in our system."*

*"Gosh, I'm pretty sure that's it. I started at this firm a few weeks back."*

*"Hey man, I understand working in a new place. Where did you come from?"*

*"Oh, I'm a transplant from Indiana." He leaned forward. "I had to get out of the farmlands, man." He laughed at his joke. "I couldn't take the country anymore."*

*"Are you liking Chicago?" Officer Lynn sat on his stool. He rarely had anyone visit and talk to him. The break from the monotonous routine was a welcome change.*

*"I am. I need to find a good place to get a beer." David kept his oil covered hand below the counter.*

*"Yeah, Mulligan's is a great place."*

*"Thanks for that. Okay regarding this case number, I was told to go to*

the 15ᵗʰ precinct..."

"Well, no wonder I can't find it. You are at the 17ᵗʰ."

"Oh, hell no. I'm so stupid. Listen, I'm so sorry I took up your time. I appreciate your help." David reached his right hand over the counter waiting for Officer Thadd Lynn's hand. His chest ceased all movement as he waited for Officer Lynn to accept it.

Officer Lynn reached out and took the man's hand. "Hey, no problem man. Thanks for the few minutes of distraction. Head over to Mulligan's sometime. Maybe I will see you around."

David stepped away from the window. "I sure will." He waved to the man as he headed down the hallway. As he entered the elevator, he heard Officer Lynn coughing.

# CHAPTER THIRTY-SIX

Sunday

Damien was pinned under the weight of Dillon's leg as she rolled over and sprawled across him. Her hair fanned out across the bed, and he could hear her lightly snoring. He was beginning to doze off again when Coach jumped up and perched himself on his chest. Damien half opened one eye and peered at the enormous cat whose face was mere inches from his.

"Seriously? Why do you have to do this? I never see you jump onto Dillon's chest. I never see you wake her ass up to feed you. Why is that, hmm?" Damien reached out and scratched the cat's head. His purring a few moments ago was a soft rumble, now it sounded like an outboard engine. He reached his big paw out and touched Damien's chin.

Damien laid there, deciding if he should move or be crushed slowly by the weight of his cat. Before he could decide on his own either way, his phone rang on the stand beside him. He fumbled for it with his left hand. Not even looking at the caller ID he answered. "Kaine."

"Lieutenant Kaine, this is Sandra. Rossdale's assistant, do you re-member me?"

Damien pushed Coach off his chest and sat up in bed. "Yeah, Sandra, of course I do. What's going on, is something the matter?" Dillon stirred next to him. He didn't want to wake her if he didn't have to, so he gently rubbed her back with his hand.

"I'm so sorry to call you this early. But I think someone is after me."

Damien swung his legs off the side of the bed. "Tell me." The bed moved, and he turned to see Dillon awake and staring at him.

"Okay. Over the last couple of days, I saw this man. He has been eve-rywhere it seems like. I see him at my favorite coffee shop, I saw him on the corner of the street as I entered Glenn's apartment building, now *my* apartment building. I moved in two days ago."

There was a long pause. "Are you still there, Sandra?"

"Yeah, I'm still here. That was hard to say. Okay, so this guy has been around everywhere. Lieutenant Kaine, I'm scared."

Damien fiddled with his phone. He pulled up the photo sketch of the man they thought was their killer. "Sandra, I'm texting you a picture of a man. I want you to tell me if that is the guy you keep seeing around."

"Oh, sure. Wait, here it is. Hang on." Silence filled the line.

Damien heard a soft gasp. "Sandra, are you okay?"

"Oh my gosh, that's the man. How do you have a picture of the man following me around? I'm terrified now."

"Sandra, I need you to listen to me. I want you to pack a bag. Do you have any pets?"

"Umm, no. No, I don't have any pets."

"Sandra, I want you to pack a bag. Are you at the residence now?"

"Yes."

"Good. Stay there. I will be over to get you. I want you to pack for a lengthy stay. Bring whatever you need. Do you understand?"

"Yes, Lieutenant. How long will it take you to get here?"

"Thirty minutes. Listen to me. Do not open the door to anyone. Do you hear me? If it isn't me at the door, do not open it. Do you understand? Not even to the doorman or a neighbor. No one." Silence filled the line. "Sandra? Damn it, do you hear me?"

"Yes. No one. I won't open the door to anyone. Please hurry. I'm scared."

"Hang up, go pack. Don't text anyone or call anyone else. I'm on my way, Sandra."

"Thank you."

Damien disconnected the call.

Dillon was already out of bed and in the closet getting clothes. "What's going on?"

"That was Sandra. Rossdale's assistant. She identified the man in our sketch as a guy she has seen following her. I'm going to pick her up and take her to my Dad's compound. I know she will be safe there."

Dillon reached out and grabbed his arm. "We will take her to your Dad's place."

Damien pulled her into his chest. "Fuck, Dillon. I caused the death of Laura, I will not to let another girl die."

"Whoa, you didn't do anything to cause Laura's death. I don't want to hear you blaming yourself."

Damien breathed deep through his nose, inhaling the citrus scent of her hair. He had told himself repeatedly Laura's death wasn't his fault, but he hadn't come to believe it yet.

Dillon pushed him back and stared at his blue eyes. They now bordered on indigo color. "We won't let anything happen to Sandra. You got that?"

"Yeah. I got it." He kissed her forehead and finished getting dressed, Within minutes, they were en route to Sandra's home.

# CHAPTER THIRTY-SEVEN

They had picked up Sandra, and now they were on their way to Damien's Dad's house. Dillon glanced in the back seat to see Sandra gripping tightly to a weird stuffed elephant. "Who is that, Sandra?"

Sandra frowned and eyed Dillon. "I'm sorry?"

Dillon pointed to the creature she held in a death grip.

Sandra followed the pointed finger and chuckled. "Oh, I must look like a stupid little girl. This was one of the last things Glenn gave me. I guess I should act my age and bring this out at night. When no one is around."

"No. It is perfectly normal behavior. Especially after suffering the kind of loss you have experienced." Dillon turned towards Damien. "Do you need to give your parents a heads up?"

Damien grabbed his phone from the Bluetooth cradle, he didn't want the entire conversation to be heard. "Good idea." He dialed the number. "Hey, Dad. I know it's early, but I need a favor. I'm bringing someone over that needs protection...Yeah, it's someone involved in the Rossdale case."

Dillon listened to the call. He was speaking in Italian which meant he didn't want Sandra to hear the details. For a moment, she missed part of it when Damien passed a station wagon with parents and what looked like fifty kids. She didn't understand what possessed someone to have that many kids. *What the hell were they thinking,* she thought to herself.

Dillon typed out a text to AD Reynolds letting him know what was happening and explaining she would fill him in on more details when she had them.

"Okay, I love you too, Dad."

Dillon watched Damien place his phone back in the charging cradle. She grinned and leaned into him. "Secret conversation, huh?"

Damien nodded. "Something like that." He nodded towards the back. Dillon winked at him.

"I don't want to be a bother, Lieutenant," Sandra whispered from the backseat.

Damien peered at her in the mirror. "You aren't a bother at all, Sandra. This is the kind of work my dad specializes in."

Dillon turned her attention to Sandra. She spun around to face her. "Sandra, I'm sure that Damien and his father will tell you this again. But I need you to pay attention. You can't tell anyone where you are. Not your friends, family, or coworkers. Do you understand?"

Sandra nodded before speaking. "Yeah, I get it. My dad was a cop. It's not like I have a lot of people to tell anyway."

Dillon let that go. She knew what the young lady was experiencing. They were close in age, Dillon was a few years older. Dillon understood what it was like to have no one to talk to. She had lived most of her life that way.

# CHAPTER THIRTY-EIGHT

Damien entered the code to get through the security gate. The driveway was a long meandering single-lane road with several camera checkpoints along the way. As he pulled up in front of the house, the front doors opened and the greeting squad surrounded the vehicle.

Damien looked over at Dillon, exchanging a knowing look with her. She barely hid her chuckle.

Sandra saw everyone come out of the house and immediately wished she had bunkered down in her own apartment, Glenn's apartment. "Oh, Lieutenant, just take me home. This is such an inconvenience."

Dillon smiled and her expression softened as she turned towards Sandra. "This family lives for this kind of stuff. They will treat you like one of their own. You have nothing to worry about."

Damien's lips curved upward at the comment and took Dillon's hand, kissing it before he opened his door.

Angelina Kainetorri grabbed her son in a big hug. "Damien, my *dolce bambino.*"

"Hey, mama. Seriously, do you have to strangle me?"

"Si. That's what mamas do."

Sandra exited and stood against the vehicle. She cringed as a woman swarmed her. Sandra stiffened as arms wrapped around her. The woman looked close to her own age. However, her long dark hair, creamy olive colored skin, and rich mahogany brown eyes made it hard for Sandra not to stare in awe at her exotic beauty.

"Hi, I'm Catherine, Nicky's wife." She grabbed her in a hug.

"Catherine, give her some room to breathe." Damien took Sandra's bags from the back of the SUV.

Nicky grabbed one and hugged Dillon at the same time. "Hey there, gorgeous. How is the FBI treating you?"

"Like shit. But it's a government agency. Would you expect anything less?" Dillon smiled at him. She had loved Nicky and his wife from the moment she met them.

Catherine led Sandra into the house. Damien's mother, Nicky, and Dillon followed them.

Giovanni Kainetorri put his arm around Damien's shoulder. "Is she

Glenn's assistant?"

Damien nodded. "Yeah. She was very close to him. He treated her like his daughter. Left his estate to her."

"Glenn was a very generous man. I heard him speak of her, but I had never met her. She is a lovely young woman. Tell me what is going on," Giovanni said.

They walked into the foyer to find Nicky and Dillon waiting for them. Damien glanced around. "Where is Sandra?"

Nicky pointed to the kitchen. "Feeding her. Like she was a lost puppy."

"Where is Daniella?" Damien asked his father.

"She had to go with William to San Francisco. They are expected back in a few days. Now, tell me about what is going on."

Damien sighed.

Dillon took his hand. "Tell them everything, Damien. You can trust them."

"Five years ago, Joe and I had a case when we were at the 17th precinct. The case was ultimately pulled from us along with all the witness statements. I retained a copy of a sketch of who we think was our killer. Sandra called me and said someone was following her. She identified the man from the sketch." Damien moved around the foyer. "A girl recently died, and everyone thinks it was an accident. But Dillon, Captain Mackey, Joe, and I know that this guy is killing people. He killed this girl, and I am not about to let someone else associated with this damn case lose their life."

Giovanni reached out and grabbed his son's shoulder. "Damien, what else is troubling you? Tell me. Above everything else, you can trust me."

"Dad, it has nothing to do with not trusting you. I know how much you think the Lockharts aren't involved in this. But something is going on, and it centers around James Lockhart and when he was first elected five years ago."

Giovanni zeroed in on Dillon. "What does the FBI think of his theories?"

Dillon looked at all three men. "I can't speak for the FBI, but AD Reynolds and I recently met with Robert Lockhart, and after that meeting, I believe the man is capable of using every means possible to get what he wants."

"I find it so hard to believe. I have known the Lockharts for many, many years. I know Robert Lockhart to go after what he wants, but I can't believe he would sanction the murder of anyone for his gain," Giovanni said.

"Dad can you tell me anything you remember from five years ago. Precisely centered around James Lockhart and his election?"

Giovanni led them into the sunken living room. He went to the bar and poured four shots of whiskey. He handed one to each of them. "Tell me about the case from five years ago first."

Damien and Dillon sat on the sofa. Nicky and Giovanni sat across from them. Damien placed his empty glass on the table. "Joe and I hadn't been detectives very long at the 17th precinct. We got a call about a guy killed on a train platform."

Nicky interrupted. "Was that the case you had me search that guy's identity?"

Damien nodded. "Yeah. We have never been able to identify him. Don't know who he was or who he worked for. We found guns at his apartment, and his office was ransacked. We were shot at when we got to his office. The guy got away from us."

Giovanni sat silently for a moment. "James Lockhart was not a shoo-in to win his seat. He was going up against Brock Avery, who had held that position for two terms. I remember hearing that a few months before the election Avery pulled out. Resigned his seat and ultimately gave the win to Lockhart."

Damien leaned forward, placing his elbows on his knees. "I remember hearing about that, but the news didn't make a big deal about it."

"No. Not much was said about it. But some of the whispers suggested that Avery didn't think he could win, so he bowed out. Something about the Lockharts just had too much pull and power. I think I remember hearing about him opening a restaurant out near the DC area." Giovanni went to the bar and poured four more shots of whiskey.

Damien leaned back with his head against the sofa. "That really doesn't help me. I need to know who that guy was. The one who was murdered on the train platform."

Nicky looked at his dad. "Hey, didn't Avery have a personal body-guard?"

Giovanni nodded. "Yeah, he had a long-time bodyguard. I think I remember hearing he was a friend of his from college, and Avery hired him when he first became a senator. I don't know if that helps you. I can't remember his name, though."

Damien's mother came into the room followed by Sandra and Catherine. "There you all are. We were wondering where you had gotten off to."

Damien stood and gave his seat to Sandra. "Dad, I figured Sandra could stay in one of the bungalows."

"No. Certainly not." Damien's mother went and stood next to her husband. She placed her hand on his shoulder. "Sandra will stay in this house. She can have Nana's suite."

"Yes. She needs to stay here," Giovanni said.

Sandra's eyes widened. "Oh no. I couldn't possibly do that. I'm a burden already." Her eyes filled with tears. "I couldn't ask that of you all."

Angelina noticed the bunched skin around Sandra's eyes. The young woman's pained stare broke her heart. "Nonsense. You are not going to stay in a bungalow by yourself. You need family around you in a time like this. We are your family. At least for the time being. You shall stay here." Angelina Kainetorri was not going to take no for an answer.

Sandra's shoulders curled. She brought a shaky hand to her forehead. After the loss of her parents, she hadn't had anyone care for her until Glenn came into her life. Now, with him gone and no one else, Sandra tried to speak but her voice was choked by the tears. Her hands covered her face as she cried.

Angelina Kainetorri moved to the sofa and scooted Sandra down. She sat next to the young woman and took her in a hug, pulling her close to her. "There now. You have us now. I can't imagine what you are going through." Angelina took Sandra's chin in her hand and lifted it. "We are here for you. Damien brought you here to keep you safe. We will protect you and comfort you."

Sandra wrapped her arms around Angelina's waist and buried her head in her shoulder.

# CHAPTER THIRTY-NINE

*Monday Morning*

*Taylor stood in line at Kaufman's deli. She had fallen in love with this place, and every Monday she came in to get a fresh bagel and some muffins for the office. She frowned as she glanced around the room. Glancing at her watch, she gasped. "Oh man, I'm going to be late." Taylor glanced at her watch again, tapping her foot on the floor.*

*"Are you waiting for someone?"*

*Taylor turned at the sound of the deep voice. A very handsome man with a set of brooding, scary eyes stood before her. Had it not been for his sweet smile she would've been frightened of him. "No. I can't afford to be late to work."*

*"You look like you run the company. I would've thought you were the boss." He winked at her.*

*"Hmm, I wish. Although I run the lab, I still have to answer to my bosses." Taylor stepped up to the counter and placed her order. The handsome man stepped up next to her and held out cash. "What are you doing?"*

*"I'm paying for your breakfast. If I thought I had a chance, I would ask you to dinner." He gave her a wickedly sexy smile.*

*Taylor tilted her head down. "I'm flattered. I can't thank you enough for buying my breakfast. Maybe I can do it for you one day."*

*"I travel a lot. But if I'm ever back this way I'll make sure to look you up." He took his order from the lady behind the counter. "Can you tell me your name?"*

*"I guess I forgot to introduce myself. I'm Taylor. Pleased to meet you...?" she asked holding out her hand.*

*He took her hand and lightly kissed the back of it. "I will save my name for the next time we meet. It was truly my pleasure to meet you, Taylor. Enjoy your day."*

*Taylor watched the man leave. He was handsome. However, something seemed unsettling about him. She chalked it up to feeling like she cheated on Joe for flirting with a handsome man at the deli.*

# CHAPTER FORTY

Joe sat at his desk. He and Taylor had a great weekend. There were no calls, and they spent the entire weekend eating and sightseeing. Taylor had suggested they go to all the touristy sights. At first, he didn't want to go. But after spending a few hours with her on Saturday, he ended up having fun being a tourist.

Damien walked into the VCU when Joe's cell phone rang. "Hagan here."

"Hey Joe, it's Baxter. You got a minute?"

Joe and Damien had worked with Baxter at the 17th. Joe noticed Damien nodded at him and headed towards his office. He gave his partner a thumb's up and went back to his phone call. "Yeah, Bax man, what's up?"

"You remember Officer Lynn, Thadd Lynn?"

Joe's lips puckered. "I think so." Joe placed his feet on his desk.

"Well, I got some bad news. He died over the weekend."

"Get the hell out. How?"

"It looks like he died Friday after encountering some peanuts or something with peanut oil. He had an allergic reaction to it."

Joe's tone flattened. "Man, that is a shame. How is his partner taking it?"

"Oh, no dude. He didn't have a partner. Don't you remember him at all?"

"I thought I did. But I must be thinking of someone else. Fill me in. Who was he?"

"The evidence officer. Been in that damn evidence room for like eight fucking years. We always joked that he would go batshit crazy before he ever retired."

Joe's feet came flying off the desk as he stood. "Baxter, are you telling me the same evidence cop from when Damien and I were at the 17th is the one who died?"

"Yeah, dude. Anyway, the funeral is going to be sometime this week."

"Great, Bax man. Keep me posted. I gotta run. Let's get together for drinks soon. I miss you, man."

"You too, you big ugly Irishman."

The line went dead the same time Joe ran to Damien's office. "You'll never believe what happened."

"I got some news for you, too," Damien said.

Joe held up his hand. "Me, first. Baxter called me. Officer Thadd Lynn died over the weekend. Apparently from an allergic reaction to peanuts."

"Okay. That is sad. But who the hell is Officer Lynn?"

"The evidence officer from the 17th."

Damien gaped at his partner. "Why the hell do I...holy shit! You're telling me our evidence guy from that platform case is now dead?"

"Yeah, and Baxter said it looks like an unfortunate accident."

Damien picked up his desk phone. "Hey, Travis. I need you to do something. Can you get the video for, hang on," Damien snapped his fingers to get Joe's attention, who seemed to be enthralled with his phone.

Joe looked up, "What?"

"When did the guy die?"

"I think Friday. Yeah, it was Friday afternoon," Joe said.

"Travis, can you pull the video from the 17th evidence locker. Say, from one p.m. until four p.m.?"

"Sure, Kaine no problem at all. Let me get into the system, and I will pull the video. Shouldn't take me but twenty minutes," Detective Travis said.

Damien hung up the phone and looked fixedly at his partner. "What the heck are you so fascinated with?"

"I'm trying to see if there were any obscure newspaper stories from five years ago. About the time that platform case took place. Man, we need to figure out who that fucker on the platform was." Joe stopped and looked up. "You understand that Officer Lynn didn't die of an accidental allergic reaction, right?"

"Hell, yeah. I know that and you know that. Can we convince anyone else? Fuck if I know."

"You said you had news too. What is it?"

"Huh?" Damien's eyebrow squished together. "Oh, yeah. Over the weekend I had to take Sandra Kirkland, Rossdale's assistant, out to my parents' house. She called me early Sunday and said she thought someone was following her. I sent her the photo of our suspected killer, she said that was the man she had seen following her over the last few days."

Joe's mouth hung open. "Holy shit. Why does this guy want her out of the picture? She wouldn't have any information. Unless he thinks she knows something or has something."

Damien shrugged his shoulders. "I don't know. I really don't. But let's go off the assumption he is cleaning house, maybe he doesn't want anyone left that has a tie to his victims. Sandra has a direct link to Glenn. Maybe our killer thinks he needs to take any threat to his identity away."

"I could see that. The killer may think by the nature of her relationship with Glenn Rossdale, that she knows something that may lead to who he is," Joe said.

"Okay, I got more," Damien said. "I asked my dad if he remembered anything about James Lockhart's election. He said a few months before the election, Senator Brock Avery resigned his seat. That is the current position James Lockhart holds. He also mentioned that Avery had a bodyguard, someone, he hired outside the Senate. But my dad had no other information."

Damien adjusted his watch, then peered out his door before continuing. "Here's a theory. What if the guy at the train station was Avery's bodyguard? And what if that death was what caused him to give up his seat?"

Joe sighed, rubbing the back of his neck. "If that is even remotely true, that means that someone not only set in motion the events to get James Lockhart elected, but signed the death warrants for anyone who helped with those events."

Detective Travis walked into Damien's office. "Hey, Kaine, I got what you wanted. I looked through it, but I don't see anyone or anything suspicious." Detective Travis handed him a tablet. "Just hit play."

Damien placed the tablet on the desk where he and Joe could both view the video.

"I put it on a faster speed. But it can be slowed by double tapping the screen," Detective Travis explained while he grabbed a handful of jelly beans.

"Okay," Damien said. He and Joe watched the video. "Wait," Damien reversed the video. He hit play then double tapped the screen to slow the film down. "There." Damien pointed to a man who approached the counter. "Watch."

Joe leaned closer to the tablet.

Detective Travis peered over their shoulders at it. "I've watched this a couple of times. I don't see anything out of the ordinary."

Damien and Joe remained glued to the screen. The man in question reached out and shook Officer Lynn's hand before he left. Within minutes Officer Lynn started to cough. He grabbed at his throat gasping for air and collapsed behind the counter. Damien stopped the video. He squinted at Travis. "Can you send me the clip of that man as he comes to the counter and then leaves, continuing until Lynn collapses behind the counter?"

"Sure." Detective Travis grabbed the tablet. Fiddled with it a few minutes then looked at Damien. "There. I sent it to your email. You need anything else?"

"No. Thank you. I appreciate your help," Damien said.

"Anything for you, Kaine." Detective Travis chuckled at the frown he received from his favorite lieutenant.

When the detective was out of earshot, Damien looked over at Joe. "I need to call the captain." Damien pulled his phone from his pocket and hit a button to his Captain's private number.

"What's up, Kaine?"

"Hey, we have some information about what we discussed the other day." Damien tapped a pen on the desk.

"I'm not at Division Central. I won't be available until tomorrow. Let's meet at Mulligan's at eleven for lunch."

The line went dead.

Damien sat in his chair.

Joe grabbed a handful of jelly beans. "Well, what did Mackey say, dude? Don't leave me hanging."

"Not a hell of a lot. He isn't available until tomorrow at eleven. He wants to meet at Mulligan's."

"Speaking of food, I'm getting hungry."

Damien leaned back in his chair and closed his eyes. Without opening them, he spoke. "How about you and Taylor come over for Chinese tonight? I'll call Dillon and let her know. You can message Taylor."

Joe smiled a Cheshire cat-like grin. "Oh, yeah, now you're talking." Joe texted Taylor to meet at Damien and Dillon's house after work.

Damien also messaged Dillon when his desk phone rang. "Kaine. Okay, I will be there."

"What you got?" Joe asked

"Lieutenant shit I got to do. Listen, don't go for lieutenant. The paperwork and all the other shit you have to do doesn't make it worth it."

Joe laughed as he stood. "You don't have to tell me twice."

"You going to ride with me or do you want to take your vehicle?"

"I'll follow you."

They stood at Damien's open door for a few minutes.

Joe finished the last of his jelly beans. "You think Captain Mackey will believe our findings?"

Damien thumbed his ear. "I don't know. We are going to tell him that an officer was killed by a man using peanut oil, in order to make it look like an accidental death. We are going to tell him, that same man is stalking Sandra and that we believe Lockhart hired him." Damien sighed. "He may believe us or he may boot our asses into the psych ward.

# CHAPTER FORTY-ONE

*Monday Afternoon*

*David sat in the backseat of the hired car. He closed his eyes and inhaled through his nose. The leather seats and new car smell helped him relax. He didn't usually let jobs get to him, but he had spent too much time here this go around, and he was ready to head to a new location.*

*His pant pocket vibrated, breaking his one solace moment.* "Yeah?"

"The plane is ready. Where are you?"

"ETA is ten minutes."

"Are you sure you can pull this one off?"

"Do I ask you if you can do your job?"

"I'm paying you enough to buy a small island, I can ask you whatever the hell I want. I want to make sure this goes down without any screw-ups."

*He opened and closed his fist. Breathing deep through his nose he slowed his breathing. David reminded himself he was being paid a pretty penny, and until he had all his money in hand, he couldn't take care of this pompous ass.* "Have I let you down yet? Maybe you should remember who you're speaking to."

"No, you haven't let me down. This target has information that can screw up my plans for the governorship. I spent a lot of time putting this shit together. I don't want this fucker from years ago getting a conscience."

"By this time tomorrow, he will no longer be a problem."

"Listen, I thought about what you said, about the last loose end. I want you to take care of him. He is going to be in Chicago tomorrow too."

"I'm not going to mess with this one looking like an accident. I don't have time to set that up. I'm going to take him out of my way."

"I don't give a shit how you kill him. I know he has plans to visit The Fig and Duck. I don't know when, but you can figure that out."

"I can take care of him."

*The car pulled up to the plane. David exited grabbing his bag from the seat. This wasn't an overnight trip, but he still needed a few things.* "I'm at the plane. Did you arrange for me to have a car for the duration in Virginia?"

"Yes. It will be there waiting. Don't screw this up."

*The line went dead. David nodded at the beautiful flight attendant as he boarded the jet. Once seated, his thoughts came back to the asshole who'd hung up on him. He may have to set something up to rock this fucker's world, and stopping his political plans just might be the best punishment of all.*

# CHAPTER FORTY-TWO

Damien pulled down his drive followed by Joe in his monster-size truck. Damien saw Taylor's vehicle parked out front of the condo. He keyed in the code for the garage door and pulled in. Joe exited his truck and followed him into the garage before Damien shut it.

"Mrs. C. still gone?" Joe asked.

"Yeah, she will be gone a few more days." Damien laughed. "You were hoping she would make some more cake?"

"Hell yeah. That woman makes the best damn cakes I have ever had." Joe patted his stomach at the same time he licked his lips.

They entered the living room to laughter coming from the kitchen. The aroma of Chinese food filled the entire house. "They must have bought the whole menu from the restaurant," Damien said.

"Damn, I hope so. I did paperwork the entire afternoon. I'm weak from thinking too much." Joe placed the back of his hand against his forehead.

"No, you're weak from carrying your fat ass around."

Joe smacked Damien on the back as they entered the kitchen. "Oh damn. Seriously? You two are so mean."

Taylor looked up and smiled. "He loves it."

"I don't think so." Damien stood and stared at his poor cat. "Dillon, you have to quit feeding him. That Superman costume looks like it is strangling him. Damn, can he breathe?" Damien snorted.

Joe smiled as he looked at his partner. "I know this is one Superman that can't fly. His ass weighs too much."

Taylor and Dillon extricated the plump cat from his fabric prison. Dillon placed him on the floor and filled his bowl with his favorite prime kibbles. "He loves it, getting all this attention and we feed him too."

"Man, you got enough food." Damien peered in the containers. "Shit, this looks like a thousand dollars' worth of Chinese food."

Dillon frowned. "A mere five hundred bucks is all. I wanted to make sure I got enough so Taylor and Joe could take some home."

Taylor did a happy dance. "I will make me a container to take for lunch. Oh boy."

They started to sit when Damien remembered something. He

squeezed Dillon's shoulder. "Hey, I'm going to go get the file off my desk containing what we have on the Rossdale case. Our unofficial file, anyway." Within minutes Damien was back at the table.

"You know I got a weird call today regarding this case." Taylor spooned shrimp fried rice onto her plate.

Joe took a long sip of his tea. "What kind of call?"

"Some guy called about the Rossdale case. Wanted to know where the investigation stood. Wanted to know if Senator Lockhart was still under any kind of suspicion regarding Rossdale." Taylor took a bite of her egg roll. "I think he said he was with one of the magazines. I directed him to the press office for the lab."

Damien gave Joe a sideways glance. "Maybe someone was testing to see what information they could get after that announcement came out."

Joe shrugged. "Maybe."

Dillon poured more tea into Damien and Joe's glasses. "I saw that release. Very good. I guess Captain Mackey is at least giving you a chance to see where your theories go."

Damien swallowed his bite of food. "I don't know. He hasn't said I'm off base, but I get the feeling he isn't a hundred percent convinced. But he also hasn't kicked my ass out on a 5150 charge, either."

They all ate in silence for a few minutes. Damien opened the folder and thumbed through it. "I wish I had a little more information. If I had the right piece of information, I could link all my theories together."

Taylor peered over at the open folder. Something caught her eye. She reached over and moved the paper obscuring her view of what interested her. "Hey, I know this guy."

Both Damien and Joe stopped what they were doing and eyeballed her.

"What do you mean you know this guy?" Joe asked.

"Every Monday morning, sometimes other days too, I go to Kaufman's. I met him there this morning." She took a bite of her noodles. Taylor looked back up to see the men and Dillon staring at her. "What? What's wrong?"

Joe calmly put his fork on the side of his plate and turned towards her. "Taylor, I need you to think about everything that happened this morning. Tell us everything from the moment you got to Kaufman's. I need you to try and remember every detail."

Taylor glanced around the table. "Okay. Let's see. I got to the deli, and the line was outrageous. I stood there and thought I was going to be late, and I thought I should just leave. But I had to have my bagel and my muffins. Mondays at the lab are bad enough, they would be miserable if I didn't have my bagel and my muffins.

"As I waited in line, this guy came up behind me. He asked me if I was waiting for someone. I told him no that I didn't want to be late to work. He said he thought I was the boss, and then bought my breakfast."

Joe's eyes narrowed. "There's more. What else?"

Taylor squinted at him. "I dunno. That's it." She lifted her fork to her mouth then stopped. "Well, when he bought my food, he said he traveled a lot, but if he had the chance, he would prefer to take me to dinner. I asked him his name, but he wouldn't tell me. He said he would save that for next time."

Joe nodded at Damien. "He's fucking with us. He must have seen her with me or at my house. Which means he has been watching you and me for a while now."

Taylor shrugged. "He seemed like a nice guy. Except for his eyes. If his smile hadn't been so charming, his eyes would have scared me. I wouldn't have spoken to him. Who exactly is he?"

Joe took her hand. "When we leave here, we will go to your place. Get some clothes and that hundred-year-old cat, and you two will be staying with me until this case is over. Or until I think it is safe for you to be alone at your place."

"Joe, I will not be coming to your house. I have a gun, and I can protect myself." Taylor smugly rolled her eyes at him.

"Taylor, I don't doubt you can take care of yourself. But this guy killed a trained high-level bodyguard. He would eat you for dinner."

"Wait, this guy is your killer?" Her eyes darted around the table.

"Yeah, Taylor," Damien said. "That is why we were so interested in what he said.

At that moment, it dawned on Taylor. "OMG that means he knows who I am and my schedule. He knows what I like to eat, and that means he more than likely knows where I live."

Joe remained calm on the outside but inside his heartbeat pounded at an abnormally fast rate. They all pitched in and cleared the food. Dillon packed up a bunch for Taylor and Joe. They hugged at the door.

Damien put his hand on Joe's shoulder. "Listen, you call me if anything suspicious happens. If you want to take her to work, then meet at the station, we can go from there to meet the captain."

Joe nodded. "I will let you know if anything looks fishy."

Damien closed the door and followed Dillon into the office. She carried the fat cat and placed him on her desk. He rolled his eyes at her display of affection. "What do you think about that?" Damien asked her as he turned on his computer.

"I think that guy has been keeping tabs on you two, long before Rossdale's murder. I also think he will always be one step ahead until you catch him."

"Fuck. This case is one big fucking black hole." Damien sat behind his desk. "Tell me about your visit with Robert Lockhart."

Dillon sat on the corner of his desk. "He likes to play head games. He called me Dillon and referred to me as a young lady. The way he looked at me made my skin crawl. But I played along with him. Complimented him when I could. Stepped inside his personal space. However, when I started to ask questions, he pulled away."

She pulled her hair from the ponytail holder. "Oh man, that feels so much better. Where was I...he had a shit ton of photos of himself. They covered this one wall in his study."

"Pictures of himself?" Damien poured two glasses of red wine.

"No. Him and all his numerous cronies. Some I recognized from having to deal with different branches of government. There was this one guy, though. He was in a bunch of them. I asked him who he was. At first, he said he was his frat brother, then he made it sound like he was more like family."

Damien's ears perked up. "Who was the guy?"

"Some guy named Gage. That was all he would tell me."

"That doesn't tell me anything. See, I think whoever is the link to the evidence being taken is our link to the whole case. That would tell me who wanted that evidence and why."

"Well, I didn't get the information for you."

"If I pull a few photos of Robert will you look at them and see if you recognize that one guy?"

"Sure, babe. Put it up on the big screen, and I can sit in my chair and drink my wine." Dillon removed her boots, picked up the cat, and pulled her chair around to sit next to Damien's desk. She set the cat in her lap and picked up her glass of wine.

Damien typed away on his computer. "Okay, let me pull up a bunch of the senator from roughly five years ago, and you see if you see anyone that looks like Gage." Damien continued typing, and a series of photos came up on the screen.

"None of those are Gage. But they were in some of his photos." Dillon sipped her wine.

Another series of pictures came up.

"Nope. Not him."

The next grouping flashed on the screen, and there he was. "Wait that's him."

Damien glanced at one of the photos. "Which one?"

Dillon pointed to the middle picture. "Him."

Damien's brow wrinkled. "That's the former police commissioner. Reginald Price. Not Gage."

"All I know is that's who he called Gage. Never once did he call him Reginald."

Damien frowned. "Something doesn't make sense. I think he left the commissioner's position a year or so before James became a senator."

"All I know is that guy was his fraternity brother. Robert said he helped him get the position he has now and that was it. As a matter of fact, old Robert went from wanting to do me in the servant's quarters to wanting to kill me and bury me in the backyard."

Damien laughed at that. "So basically, you mind fucked him, and he figured it out and didn't like you being smarter than him?"

She shrugged. "Something like that. I'm going to take a long bath." She headed towards the stairs. "You know, you could always join me."

"Yes, yes I can." Damien jumped up and grabbed the bottle of wine and their two glasses and ran up the stairs after her.

# CHAPTER FORTY-THREE

Joe turned into his driveway and Taylor followed him. She got out with Muffin's crate, and he grabbed her two massive bags. He was sure he threw a disk out loading them into his truck. "Taylor, you live less than ten minutes away. We can go back to your house for things as we need them. You didn't have to bring everything you own."

"I need all this stuff. I have to do my hair, put on makeup, and I need all those outfits."

Joe lugged the bags up the stairs. "Fuck. Did you take out life insurance on me and this is your attempt to kill me? How many fucking pairs of shoes does one woman need? You have two fucking feet, Taylor. Two."

Taylor rolled her eyes at him. "Seriously, you with your eighteen pairs of the same athletic shoe? I don't think you have any room to talk."

"Yeah, that may be true, but I still only take one pair with me at a time." He pointed to his feet. "Again, I have two feet." Joe placed everything in the bedroom then fell onto the bed.

Taylor let Muffin out of her portable prison cell.

Joe watched in awe as the old blind cat made her way around the apartment. After one or two crashes into a wall, her dementia cleared enough for her to remember the layout of his apartment. The cat never ceased to amaze him. The mere fact she was still alive was a feat unto itself.

Joe raised up on his elbows and focused on Taylor unpacking her things. His walk-in closet was huge, and there was plenty of room for her stuff. Even with the thousand pairs of shoes she had him carry. She hummed while she placed her things on the shelves. He had broached the subject of her moving in with him several months back, but she wanted to make sure it was something he wanted. Taylor had worried he was asking her out of a sense of obligation to move their relationship to the next level. That was so far from the truth. Joe loved it when Taylor stayed all night and the sense of loss that surrounded him in the empty apartment when she left to go home was overwhelming at times.

Joe smiled at Taylor when she poked her head out of the closet. "How are you doing, babe?" he asked her.

"I'm okay. I'm a little frazzled about being attracted to a hired hit-man only hours earlier, but I'm more frazzled that he knows where I live and my habits. That's a little scary."

Joe sat up on the edge of the bed. "You were attracted to him?"

Taylor chuckled at his expression. "He is a charming man. His eyes are terrifying and intense, but his smile throws off any warning signs you may be picking up. It's like your body says 'oh my,' but your head says 'run, get the hell out of there.'"

Joe's eyes narrowed. "Hmm, you may need to be punished for that later."

She winked at him. "Why do you think I told you?"

Joe laughed. "You are such an evil woman."

"So, do you think he has been keeping tabs on you and Damien all this time?"

Joe laid back on the bed and stared at the ceiling. "I don't know. I don't think he had been in this area since our murder case five years ago. I believe he has been traveling like he told you. I do think he has kept tabs on us and that he has a regular place here that he considers his home base."

"Do you think you guys can figure out who he is?"

"Damn if I know. But, when Damien gets a bone, he is relentless to let it go. And right now, he is pissed at this guy for killing our witnesses, especially Laura, and leading us around by the nose."

"Well, I know that Roger Newberry is working on every piece of evidence collected. He said he is determined to find out who is behind these murders." She leaned out the closet door. "He was a big fan of Glenn Rossdale."

Joe sighed. "Are you almost done?" He waited for her to answer. "Taylor?" He sat back on the edge of the bed. He looked up to find Taylor wearing a pink furry teddy. Two holes allow for each breast to protrude out. The lace body continued down to a pair of garter belts that hooked onto thigh high stockings. She wore no panties. "Holy shit! Wow!"

"I figured we could stop with the shop talk and maybe you could punish me. I was a naughty girl today." Taylor pouted at him.

Joe stood. "I definitely think you should be punished. Get on your knees and undo my pants."

Taylor did what he said. She undid the button of his jeans and slid them down his legs. She glanced up to see the amusement had left his face. His usually sparkling emerald eyes were now darkened by a smoldering look of desire.

Taylor removed his boxer briefs, and he sprang free from the constraints, his dick level with her mouth. She knew better than to touch it without permission, but she couldn't wait. Taylor touched the tip of it with her tongue. Her hands moved slowly up his thighs. She stopped and looked up at him through hooded eyelids. Waiting for the okay to continue, hoping her aggressiveness and desire may be rewarded with another punishment.

"I didn't tell you to touch it. But I sure as hell didn't tell you to stop. I'm beginning to wonder what your motive is, Taylor. I think you need a few discipline lessons."

Taylor took him into her mouth and sucked on the tip. Her tongue gently caressed the outer rim of the head then she licked the length of him. Her hand wrapped around his large girth. Joe grabbed the side of her head. Taylor's body reacted with a flood of moisture between her legs.

He guided her at the speed he needed. With every movement, his dick went further into her mouth. One hand reached between his legs and lightly squeezed his balls. She used her fingernail to scrape the sensitive skin surrounding the area. Joe's body shuddered under her gentle touch.

Joe grabbed Taylor by her arms and lifted her up off the floor. He pulled her towards his chest. "Fuck, woman, I love it when you do that. I can't wait, though." He kissed her neck, moving down her body he took one of her breasts in his mouth. His tongue circled the hard nub. Joe heard the sharp intake of air. He pulled back. "Get on your knees on the bed."

Taylor again complied. He followed behind her and positioned his knees between hers. She leaned back against him. Joe reached around with one hand and grabbed her breast while the other reached between her legs. His finger slid in easily, coated by her wetness. "Oh baby, you are so wet."

Taylor moaned at his touch.

Joe grabbed her underneath her chin and tilted her head back so he could kiss her. She whimpered at the momentary loss of his finger inside her. He pushed her down onto the mattress. Her ass stuck up in the air. Joe smacked it once then rubbed the red flesh. He smacked it again, this time Taylor moaned. "Ahh, that's my girl," Joe said. He teased her opening with the tip of his dick.

Immediately Taylor pushed against him.

"Ah ah ah, not so fast." Joe heard the almost wounded sound escape her lips.

"Please, Joe. Don't make me wait. Please fuck me now."

Joe entered her. A velvety warmth engulfed him. He closed his eyes to concentrate on not losing it, but the pure ecstasy surrounding him made it an almost impossible feat. He wasn't going to last long. He moved in and out, the friction of her body driving him to madness. Faster and faster he thrust. Taylor's cries for more drew him closer to the edge.

Joe gripped her waist and thrust harder and faster. Taylor's body trembled. Her thighs quivered against him. Within moments, the rush of warmth and wetness coated him. He moved in and out of her with ease now. Her body's reaction paved the way for him to devour her.

His climax came full force and rocked him back. He exploded inside her with the force of a cannon. Her panting in rhythm with his, Taylor fell forward, and Joe fell beside her.

"Hey, baby. You doing okay?" He nuzzled her neck.

"Mmhmm. Yes, I needed this. I needed you. Oh, Joe," Taylor whispered. "I love you."

Joe didn't speak. He reached over and caressed her. His fingers tingled as they slid down her back. His mouth moistened. It was so much more than sex with this woman. His body craved Taylor's touch, and his breath quickened every time he was with her.

Joe rose and pulled the sheets and cover back. Taylor was almost asleep, and she was easily moved around the bed. Joe didn't bother removing the pink teddy. He liked it on her. He turned off all the lights, grabbed Muffin, and climbed into bed behind Taylor. He placed the nearly fossilized cat next to Taylor and snuggled in behind her. She wiggled her butt against him and was sound asleep.

"I love you, Taylor. More than I ever thought possible." He drifted off, wondering if she would accept his offer and make this her home.

# CHAPTER FORTY-FOUR

Tuesday mid-day

Damien and Joe walked into Mulligan's ten minutes before the scheduled meet with Captain Mackey. They snagged a booth in the corner.

"Hey, guys, what can I get you two?"

"How about two diet sodas," Damien said, turning his attention to Joe.

"Coming right up. Here are some menus. I'll be right back with those drinks."

Joe kept his head down and glanced around the room. "How are you going to approach this with the captain?"

"I'm going to tell him everything since our last conversation. I am especially," Damien trailed off. He nodded to towards the door. "Showtime." He stood and moved to sit next to Joe. "Hey, Captain. How was your trip?"

"Horrible. Had to spend the day with my mother-in-law. I keep thinking she is going to die one of these days. But, knowing my luck, she is going to live until I die." Captain Mackey ordered an iced tea when the waitress brought Damien and Joe's drinks. "Now. I'm assuming you have some new information," he said adding sugar and lemon to his tea.

"Yes. Officer Thadd Lynn was the evidence officer at the 17th precinct when Joe and I had that case. He died over the weekend." Damien pulled his phone from his pocket and cued up the video. "Watch from this point."

Captain Mackey watched the video. "Okay. There's a guy, and then the officer starts to cough. What does this have to do with anything?"

Damien took a moment. "Officer Lynn was allergic to peanuts. He died after encountering peanuts or peanut oil. The guy in the video is seen pulling out his hand from his coat pocket and then shaking the officer's hand."

"That's a stretch. What else?" Captain Mackey asked.

"Over the weekend I had to take Sandra, Glenn Rossdale's assistant, out to my parents' house. She called me and said that someone was following her. She positively identified the guy from our sketch."

The captain took a drink of his tea. "This isn't much, Damien."

"There is more. Our killer contacted Taylor Monday morning at the deli she goes to."

"Kaufman's?" The captain asked.

Damien nodded.

"Damn, they have the best bagels. Go on," the captain said.

Joe nodded. "Yeah, she goes every Monday morning. Which tells us he has been watching her, along with us."

"She wasn't influenced by seeing the picture at your place?"

"No. The sketch was hidden. Taylor saw it and said she knew the guy, that she had met him that morning."

Captain Mackey sat back in the booth.

Damien shifted his gaze between Joe and the captain. "When I took Sandra out to my Dad's, I asked him specifically about Brock Avery. Now, we still don't know who the man on the platform was, but my dad said that Brock Avery had a bodyguard for a long time that he hired outside the security pool for the Senate members. I think that was our guy on the platform. Then we have Rossdale, Laura, and now Officer Lynn dead."

"Damien, you can't be suggesting that Robert or James Lockhart arranged for the death of all these people to push their political agenda and aspirations? You have got to be fucking kidding me."

Damien dragged a hand through his hair, tugging on the ends. He bit his bottom lip before he spoke. "Captain, look at everything going back five years ago. Those two cases, the evidence guy, Rossdale, Taylor, Sandra, Laura, even one of the security guards from the State Building took an extended vacation because he spoke with us and questioned his safety. Couple that with what Dillon experienced when she went to Robert Lockhart's house and what James' own wife said about Robert Lockhart. Who else could be behind it?"

"What did Dillon find out?"

"She and the AD went out there. She said he was very affectionate to start, then as she asked questions about the election of James, he changed on a dime. She believes he is more than capable of doing what he needs to do to get what he wants.

"Look, how about if you give me a day to travel out to Virginia and talk to Brock Avery. At least give me the opportunity to speak with him." Damien turned towards one of the TV's when something caught his eye. "Hey," he motioned to the waitress, "would you turn that up?" He pointed to the TV.

The volume came up, and Damien heard the mid-day news.

*"Again, if you are just tuning in, a horrible accident has happened at the residence of former Illinois Senator Brock Avery. Preliminary reports have stated, that his Virginia home had a gas leak and has exploded. According to on-scene reporting, everyone in the family perished in this horrible accident."*

Damien turned to Captain Mackey. "There is no fucking way you can tell me that is a coincidence. This fucker took him out."

Joe reached over and put a hand on Damien's forearm. "Captain, C'mon. You have to see the connection to all these deaths."

Damien slowed his breathing. "Okay, when Dillon was over at Robert Lockhart's house, she saw a picture of a guy who was in a bunch of photos with Mr. Lockhart. Robert referred to him as Gage. But when she saw pictures of him, she pointed out the former Police Commissioner, Reginald Price. Do you know anything about him?"

Captain Mackey nodded. "His nickname is Gage. I have met him a few times. He never goes by Reginald, always introduces himself as Gage Price." The captain pulled his phone from his pocket, typed out something, and placed it on the table.

"What does he do now?"

"Gage Price now works for the Secretary of State. I remember hearing he got a high-level position that has him in line to be one of the sub-cabinet members. It isn't an actual working position, more of a bragging right. However, it does put him in the company of some top-level executives. His former position as Police Commissioner gave him an unusual insight into things, and he had a lot of people in high places back in the day. That's about all I know."

"Fuck, that explains a lot. See, Dillon, said that before the senior senator clammed up and kicked them out of his house, he mentioned that he helped him get his current position. I'm afraid I didn't keep up with politics or the Police Commissioner, so it didn't register with me."

Now it was the captain's turn to curse. "Oh, fuck this is a mess." Captain Mackey couldn't believe what he was hearing. "You think that Robert Lockhart had all these people under his thumb, got them to do things that ensured his son's election, and now he has paid someone to get rid of everyone?"

"Yeah, I do." Damien leaned into the table. "And I think Gage Price is the last of the witnesses. He is the last one who knows everything. Think about it. As Police Commissioner, he would have the ability to pull the files. Even if he left office. He still may have had the pull. Either way, he used his position to cover up the deaths of those kids. He hid all the evidence and let that fucker Lockhart do what the hell he wanted all to get his pansy ass kid into a Senate seat."

"Oh hell. I can't fathom that a man I supported, has paid for someone to kill all these people. Brock Avery's entire family was just blown up. Fuck!" Captain Mackey breathed in slowly through his nose, out through his mouth. "Damien, you realize this is going to put a bullseye on your back from here on out?"

"I don't care about that. This fucker Robert did all this shit to get his son elected, possibly to get the governorship, and the presidency. He has had men and women killed, and now fucking kids. I may not be able to get the killer, but I sure as hell am going to make that arrogant fucker pay."

"How do you plan on doing that?" the captain asked.

"Well, I was hoping you could get me a phone call with Mr. Price," Damien said.

"Somehow I knew you were going to ask me that." The captain glanced between Damien and Joe. "You guys have to be sure. By talking to Gage Price, you're going to have to tip your hand to him. If you're wrong, he will go back to Robert Lockhart and tell him everything. Are you ready for that?"

Damien looked over at Joe. "Joe? What do you think?"

"I believe that's a risk we need to take. We have no other options," Joe said.

"Can you help us, Captain?" Damien asked.

Captain Mackey picked up his phone off the table and hit a few buttons. He heard Damien's phone vibrate. "That's Gage Price's number. Tell him you know about what he did five years ago, with Brock Avery being murdered you need to speak with him immediately."

Damien glanced at the phone but remained still.

"Call him now." The captain sat back.

"Right now?"

"Yeah." Captain Mackey nodded.

Damien frowned at Joe who shrugged.

Joe turned towards the captain. "Who did you have to get the number from?"

The captain smiled. "You don't need to know that. I hope you two are right. Or I have a lot of explaining to do later."

Damien held up his hand. "Mr. Price, Gage Price?"

"Yes, this is Gage Price."

"This is Lieutenant Damien Kaine, with Captain Mackey's Vicious Crimes Unit. I was wondering if I could speak with you, in person, regarding the murder of Glenn Rossdale."

"I don't think I can help you with that, Lieutenant."

"I think you can. I have come into some information regarding Robert Lockhart and a case my partner and I were working on five years ago out of the 17th precinct. I also have information regarding Brock Avery. I think you know what I am referring to."

There was a long pause on the phone. "Mr. Price, are you still there?"

Gage Price finally spoke. "I'm in town today. I need to meet you at my wife's restaurant, The Fig and Duck. Be there in an hour."

"Thank you." Before Damien finished the sentiment, the line went dead.

Captain Mackey nodded. "Does he want to see you?"

"Yeah, in one hour." Damien turned to Joe. "We are going to The Fig and Duck." Damien looked at the captain, "that's his wife's restaurant."

The captain stood. "You call me as soon as this meeting is over. Be careful. Both of you."

# CHAPTER FORTY-FIVE

Damien and Joe entered The Fig and Duck. A late afternoon lunch crowd of men in suits and women in pencil skirts lined the bar and filled the tables. Damien made his way to the hostess stand.

"Hi, we're here to meet with Gage Price." Damien leaned on the podium.

"Yes, Lieutenant Kaine, follow me, please." She led them through a doorway along a short hallway and into a private dining room.

Gage Price looked up from a ledger. He stood and held out his hand to the detectives. "Lieutenant Kaine?"

"Yes. I'm Kaine, and this is my partner, Detective Joe Hagan. I can't thank you enough. I think you can help me with this case."

Both Joe and Damien joined Mr. Price at the table. Damien noticed the man didn't look well rested. He had to wonder if his conscience was weighing on him.

"I didn't have much choice."

"We all have choices, Mr. Price," Joe said.

Gage Price nodded. His face tensed. "Ah, that may be true, but it isn't as simple as that."

Damien pulled his notepad from his pocket. "Mr. Price, do you know why Brock Avery left the Senate race?"

Gage rubbed his hands on his pants. He reached for a glass of water, spilling it on the pristine white tablecloth. "Robert Lockhart got me this position in the State Department. It was a huge jump in pay, let alone prestige. This job provided all kinds of opportunities for this restaurant to be opened." Gage looked between the two detectives. "It was like a magic wand had been waved."

Damien rubbed his temples. "That doesn't tell me why Brock Avery left the race."

"I'm getting to that." Gage took another drink of water. "About six weeks before the election, Robert had me over for drinks. I had been at my new job for maybe five months."

Damien squinted at the man across the table from him. "Did the Lockharts ask you to make those cases disappear?"

Gage's head hung as he nodded. "I didn't understand at first, or maybe I wanted to be blind to it, but those cases happened a few weeks before Brock Avery left." Gage sighed. "I didn't put the two together."

"Why?" Damien's tone deepened. "Why would you help hide murder cases?"

"You have to understand something. Robert Lockhart approached me. He said that there may be something associated with those two cases that may tarnish his son's chances to get elected. He stated that it wasn't the murders themselves, but people involved in it. He wanted to make sure that nothing blew back on James. He reminded me of my new position and that a lot of the things I had received because of the job, would disappear."

Joe noticed the vein in Damien's neck pulse. He reached out and touched his partner's arm. "Mr. Price, did you not think that was suspicious?"

"Yes, but Robert and I had been friends since college. I went over the case files. The two boys had been randomly shot outside a club and that guy killed at the station, well, we couldn't even identify him. I didn't think it would do any harm to stick two cases that would never be solved in a place they would never be found."

Damien squinted at the man. "If you weren't the police commissioner, how did you pull the files?"

Gage Price lifted his palms. "I can't tell you that. I never told Robert how I did it, and I'm not telling you, either."

A loud crash echoed from the kitchen. Gage jumped in his seat banging against the side of the table.

"Mr. Price, why are you so jumpy?" Joe's body posture perked up.

Gage's eyes darted from the detectives to the doorway. "I saw the news of what happened to Brock Avery and his family. It doesn't take a genius to figure out what Lockhart is up to." Gage Price scooted closer to the table. "When James was in college, he got a girl pregnant. He went to his dad, and Robert paid the girl off."

"We heard about that from Amber Lockhart. She said that Robert sent the girl away, and when she came back there was no baby," Damien said.

"That isn't the end of it, though. The young woman was threatened with the release of a sex tape of her and James if she didn't have an abortion. She was also told that it would be made to look like she was blackmailing James. She, of course, had the abortion. Robert later set her up in business to keep her silent."

"How do you know this?" Damien asked.

"I knew someone who knew the parents. I heard about it from a confidential source when I took my position with the State Department." Gage studied his hands. "It was then I realized I'd made a deal with the devil."

Gage reached into his pocket and pulled out a jump drive. He held it in his fingers staring at it. When he looked up, his eyes were moist. "A few things have happened since I destroyed those case files. After about a year or so, Lockhart approached me. He said if I keep my mouth closed, I would be rewarded. If not, I wouldn't come home one evening to my family."

Gage held up the jump drive. "It was after that incident that I decided it would be in my best interest to record everything. Anytime I was around the Lockharts, I recorded the conversations. Any text or email I got, I kept. I used my position in the State Department to do a little research. I found out that Lockhart had funneled tons of money from the family estate into private accounts."

Damien rubbed his forehead. "Depending on where you were when you made those recordings will determine whether they are admissible."

Gage nodded. "The ones recorded while I was in DC are permitted. There are some that I recorded here in Illinois. Those won't be. I purposely recorded as many as I could in DC because of the One-Party Recording law."

"What else did you learn about the Lockharts these last few years?" Damien asked.

"When Glenn Rossdale came up dead, I knew Lockhart was behind it. I had spoken to Rossdale about three or four weeks before his murder. He phoned me and told me that he knew about the role I played in the files coming up missing from your case five years ago. Glenn said he had found out that the man on the platform was Avery's bodyguard, Zach Franklin."

Damien sighed. "We have suspected our train station victim was Avery's bodyguard, we just didn't have a name. But how did Rossdale come up with that?"

"Rossdale told me, he wasn't after me, he wanted the Lockharts. He wouldn't say how, but he found out that Lockhart hired a hit man to kill Brock's bodyguard, Zach."

"Why did Zach have to be killed?" Damien asked in an uncertain tone.

"Lockhart used Zach's death to force Avery out. Essentially threatening him that if he didn't drop out of the race, his family would be killed. Lockhart couldn't kill Avery. If a sitting senator dies, the sitting governor can fill that seat. Lockhart couldn't afford for someone to win the election on a sympathy vote over him."

"Who wiped Franklin's identity? His prints came back to a Kalvin Dale Draper, who did that?" Damien asked.

"The guy Lockhart hired. He had the ability to do it. Rossdale learned from Brock Avery that Lockhart bragged that the police would never discover Zach's real identity."

"Okay," Damien dragged a hand through his hair. "So, when we investigated the murder on the platform and interviewed those two kids and got information from them, Lockhart got scared and had them killed too?"

"Yes. When they gave you that description of the killer, Lockhart knew he was going to have to get rid of those kids." Gage now stood and walked around the room. "Listen to me, I spoke with Brock Avery right after Rossdale was murdered. I asked him about that time during the election. He said that Lockhart came to him and told him that Zach's killer was skilled at killing and making it look like an accident. He bragged about how easy those kids were to kill. Lockhart told him if he dropped out of the race at a certain point, that he would be set up with everything he needed to start that restaurant."

Joe's shoulder's sagged. "Bloody hell, tell me you recorded the fucking conversation?"

Gage nodded stopping next to the table. "I did. There is one problem, though. Besides that conversation, every other conversation with Lockhart is carefully guarded. The man always watched what he said."

Now it was Damien's turn to pace. "Fuck. You mean to tell me that Robert Lockhart covered his ass enough so that we can't even pin this shit on him?"

"What?" Gage asked him. "Why are you concerned with Robert? All the evidence you have will point right to Robert. You should be able to arrest him, not only on collusion to fix the election, but all the money that was used for payoffs came from his accounts. That will go a long way to keeping him in prison."

Damien pinched the bridge of his nose. "I don't understand, you said all the conversations were guarded? That he seemed to protect himself."

"Oh, fuck, you haven't figured it out, have you?"

"Figured out what?" Damien's brow wrinkled. "I'm not sure what you are referring to."

"It isn't Robert that has sanctioned all these killings, it was James." Gage waved his hand dismissively. "But you will never touch James."

"Wait a second. James did all this?" Damien couldn't believe what he heard.

"Not only did he do all this, but he set his dad up. Everything will point back to Robert. On this jump drive, you will find the last thing I found. I just downloaded the information. I can't tell where I got it, but a plane was rented in Robert's name and paid for with Robert's account. A vehicle was also rented at the Virginia municipal airport, again in Robert's name. The trip took place yesterday, Avery's house blew up sometime during the night."

Silence filled the room. Damien realized he'd only been half right about the Lockharts. He stared at Gage. "Why now? Why have you given us everything now?"

"When Rossdale was murdered, I knew that Lockhart was cleaning house. It's only a matter of time before this hitman comes after me. Rossdale was my friend. I messed up years ago. By giving you this jump drive, I hope I can atone for my sins."

Damien took the drive from Gage's outstretched hand. "I don't know how to proceed. It sounds like we will be able to get Robert for a shit ton of things that his son committed. It doesn't seem like justice will be fully served."

Joe stood. "I'm going to go to the restroom. Be right back."

Damien watched Joe leave.

"Lieutenant Kaine? There is something else. But you can't share this with anyone. Not even your partner, Joe. Do you understand?" Gage looked over Damien's shoulder towards the door.

"No. I don't think I do. What are you talking about?"

"After the last time I spoke with Rossdale, he said he was overnighting something to me. He said if anything happened to him, to give this to you. He never told me how he got this information. He said he came across it when he was piecing together that Lockhart hired a hitman." Gage held up another jump drive. "This may help you figure out the identity of this killer. I know he has messed up a lot of lives. Knowing what I know of you, you won't rest until you catch him. Be prepared, though, that you may not like what's on here."

Damien's brow wrinkled as he took a small step back. "I still don't understand."

Gage's shoulders sagged. "Rossdale said his research on the Lockharts led him to another name. Someone that this killer is associated with. At the time he gave this to me, he still wasn't exactly sure of the name of the killer, but he found something that may lead you to him." He held out the drive. "Rossdale was still trying to figure out the connection when he was murdered. Which may have helped get him murdered in the first place, if the hired hitman realized what he knew. Remember, don't tell anyone. You can't trust anyone with what is on here."

Damien stuck the jump drive in the pocket of his jeans as Joe entered the room. "We can't thank you enough for all this information. I hope we can use it to get James. But at this point, I will take Robert." Damien sighed. "You know there will be an investigation into what you did five years ago. You have to know that."

"I do. I will be available when that time comes. I won't stand in your way or put up any roadblocks. All I ask is you give me some time to get my family in order."

Damien nodded. "I think I can swing that."

They all gathered their things. Gage led the way outside to the curbside sitting area. Damien inhaled the cool, crisp January air. The sun was trying to warm the temperature, but the cold winter wasn't quite ready to relent.

Damien turned to speak to Gage when the first shot of a high-powered rifle echoed in the air. By then the bullet had found its target. Blood splattered on Damien. Gage fell backward, with half his head missing. Damien scrambled for coverage when the second shot echoed. Not sure who the intended target was, he dove, knocking Joe behind a pillar. He looked up to see blood pouring from a wound on Joe. "Fuck, Joe, are you all right? Talk to me, buddy."

# CHAPTER FORTY-SIX

Joe was slow to respond. His movements fumbled as he tried to push himself to a sitting position. "Seriously, what the fuck just happened?" He grimaced as he managed to sit upright behind a short concrete pillar. A searing pain radiated throughout his entire arm. "Fuck, it feels like someone is using a blowtorch on my fucking arm."

Damien crouched in front of Joe. He ripped the sleeve of his shirt and inspected the wound. "It looks like a through and through. It's in the fleshy part but it's mangled pretty well." Damien used the piece of material to tie around the arm and stymy the flow of blood.

Joe peered over Damien's shoulder. "Fuck, you need to cover Gage Price. Half his head is gone. That was a perfect shot."

Damien turned around. A large pool of blood flowed around Gage Price. He crawled over to a table, grabbed its tablecloth, and covered the man's body. The area was in chaos. A few tables had been overturned. Planters and floral vases shattered all along the sidewalk. Because of the chilly air, no one was seated outside, helping to keep casualties down. However, at the sound of gunshots several people going into the restaurant ran for cover.

Crouching back behind the pillar, Damien pulled his phone out and dialed 911. "This is Lieutenant Damien Kaine, I need immediate assistance at The Fig and Duck. Shots fired. One dead and one injured. Roll me over to Captain Mackey." He waited on the line for Mackey to pick up.

"Damien, what the hell is going on over there? I'm getting reports of a shooting."

"Yeah, we came out of the restaurant, and our killer shot Gage Price. Joe was also shot, and as soon as I get someone here to be in charge, I'm bringing him to the hospital."

"Where was he shot? Is he alright?"

"I think so. He was shot in his upper arm; the wound looks like a through and through. Listen, meet us at General. I will text you when I'm en route."

"Alright, Damien, get your ass there as quickly as possible."

The line went dead.

Five patrol cars and SWAT pulled along the curb. Damien turned to Joe. "I think our shooter is gone. He intended to kill Gage and warn us. If he wanted you or me dead, we would be." Damien stood and went to the SWAT leader. Several news crew vans pulled onto the street. A few patrol officers impeded their progress, but they were still within camera view.

Joe stood on wobbly legs. A wave of dizziness and nausea hit him. He grabbed onto the pillar for support.

Damien stepped up alongside Joe. "Hang on, buddy. If you fall, you're going to damage the sidewalk." Damien held onto Joe's good arm and led him to the SUV. "I spoke to the SWAT leader, and he will have his team check out the building across the street. Looking at the angle Price was shot, I'm not seeing any other place on this block that would work for that shot. I told him this was in connection with our ongoing investigation, and I told him not to tell the press anything."

"What about our statements? They're going to need that."

"I told him I informed Captain Mackey we were leaving the scene. There isn't much here. Our killer is long gone. Once he killed Price, he didn't need to hang around. I told him we would give our statements later at DC." As Damien led Joe towards the vehicle, he heard a howl like scream. He glanced over his shoulder; Mrs. Price collapsed in the arms of a patrol officer. Damien hated what Gage Price did regarding the cases, but he didn't want Mrs. Price to pay any more than she already had to for the sins of her husband. He also knew over the next few days, Mrs. Price would learn some things that would only put salt in the wound.

Joe climbed up in the SUV. He reached up with his wounded arm and grabbed the overhead handle and yelled out in pain. "Fuck that hurts."

"Duh, don't use that arm, dumbass."

# CHAPTER FORTY-SEVEN

Damien texted the captain and told him they were on their way to the hospital. He glanced over at Joe, who rested his head against the seat. His color had paled, and he had a bead of sweat along his brow. "You want me to call Taylor, so she doesn't hear about it on the news?" Damien hit the lights and siren as he pulled away from the curb.

Joe nodded. "Yeah, that is probably a good idea. I'm sure she will hear about it."

Damien dialed Taylor's number. "Hey Taylor, it's Damien."

"Hi, Damien, what's up?"

"Look, Joe was shot. He..."

"What? Oh my gosh! Is he okay? Where was he shot? Oh my gosh, tell me where you are!"

"Taylor," Damien lowered his tone. "Taylor, he's okay. He was shot in the arm. We are on our way to General. I wanted to call you so that you wouldn't hear about it on the news. I am sure he's going to need several stitches."

"Okay. Okay. I'm going to leave the office and meet you there."

Taylor hung up. Damien was about to call Dillon when his phone rang. "Hey, babe."

"Holy shit, tell me that wasn't you at The Fig and Duck? The news is saying two detectives investigating the Rossdale murder were on scene and one was wounded."

"Dillon, we had a meet with Gage Price, the former Police Commissioner. That was his wife's restaurant."

"Who was shot?" Dillon asked.

"Joe. Meet us at General. I'll explain everything. Joe is going to be okay. He was shot in his upper arm."

"I'm heading there now."

The line went dead. Damien looked at Joe. "You better not be bleeding all over my car."

Joe didn't answer.

Damien turned down the street the hospital was on. "Joe, c'mon buddy, wake up." Damien reached over and smacked his shoulder. Joe barely mumbled. Damien stepped on the gas and swerved across the lanes of traffic. "Fuck, I should've driven faster. Fuck!" He shouldn't have assumed it was a flesh wound. "C'mon buddy, hang on. You stupid Irishman."

Damien screeched to a halt at the doors of the ER.

A security guard came out waving his hand in the air. "You can't park..." his voice trailed off when he saw Damien's badge on his belt. "What happened?" The security guard asked.

"My partner was shot in the arm. Get me some help."

The guard signaled for a medic team. Within a minute a doctor and another physician came out.

Damien opened the door and saw the blood-soaked bandage dripping onto his partner's lap. "Fuck, he's bleeding pretty bad."

The ER doctor looked at Damien. "When was he shot?"

"About an hour, maybe less. I left there and drove here, but I thought it was just a through and through." Damien's voice flattened.

The ER doctor and the other physician already had Joe on the stretcher. He spoke in a soothing tone. "That tourniquet you put on probably saved his life." He turned towards the other medic. "Let's get him to OR. We need to get a look at the brachial artery. I bet it has been nicked." Looking back at Damien the ER doctor smiled. "Don't think the worst. I'll be out with an update as quickly as I can." The man disappeared behind the OR doors.

Damien inspected his shirt and jeans. He was covered in Joe's blood, and some of Price's as well. He waited in the OR waiting room. He called Joe's parents.

***

The captain and Chief Rosenthal walked into the ER. Captain Mackey saw all the blood on Damien's clothes and the look on his face. "What the hell? You said it was a flesh wound." The captain said.

"I thought that was all it was. Fuck, I didn't drive like a bat out of hell, either. I figured it was just a flesh wound, nothing more." Damien kicked the chair in front of him.

The captain placed his hand on his lieutenant's shoulder and squeezed. "Damien, you had no idea it was a more severe injury. Let the doctor's deal with it. Quit blaming yourself."

Taylor and Dillon ran through the doors.

"Where is he?" Taylor asked as she barreled past others in the waiting room. She saw the blood on Damien's clothes. "What is going on, Damien? You told me he would be fine."

Moisture seeped into Damien's eyes. "He was all right. Then on the way here, he lost consciousness. I didn't think it was more than a flesh wound."

Taylor came to Damien and wrapped her arms around his waist. "It's not your fault. He's as strong as an ox. Yeah?" She glanced at Dillon, tilted her head to the side. "Right, right, Dillon? He's going to be okay, right?"

Dillon moved to embrace them both. "Yeah, guys, c'mon. This is Joe. He's going to be fine."

Joe's family burst through the door. Damien got a text from his parents saying they were on their way.

They waited for some word to come from the OR.

An hour later, the ER doctor emerged. He found Damien in the little OR waiting room in a sea of people. The doctor pointed at Damien as he approached the group. "Umm, Lieutenant, right?"

"Yeah, I'm his partner, and that's his family." Damien pointed to his left.

"Well, your partner is going to be okay. The gunshot nicked the brachial artery, just as I thought, but it was a minimal injury. I had that repaired quickly. The arm itself was a mangled mess. I wanted to take the time to fix that up. He should heal fine in a few days."

An audible gasp erupted at the same time from officers and detectives that had filtered in the minute they heard one of their own was shot.

Damien's guilt eased slightly. Dillon squeezed his hand. Joe's family hugged everyone and spoke at length with the doctor. Taylor sat with them and Damien's parents.

Captain Mackey nodded to Damien. "How about you and Dillon step out with the chief and me. I want you to fill me in on what the fuck happened."

The four of them walked out into the parking lot. The late afternoon sun was dimming fast. Damien leaned against the wall. First, he gave a rundown of the shooting.

"You're sure it was your killer?"

"Yes, Captain." He pulled the jump drive from his jacket pocket. "Before he was shot, Gage Price gave me this. Everything we need is on here." Damien proceeded to tell the chief and the captain about all the details Gage Price gave to him before he lost his life.

The captain's mouth slacked, and his eyes widened. "You have got to be fucking kidding me. That little fucker is the one behind all of the deaths?"

"Yeah." Damien handed the jump drive to the captain. "I think you should review this. Have Detective Travis pull the conversations that will help us the most. There is one that is between Brock Avery and Gage Price. It will put the most pressure on James."

Dillon glanced between all the men. "Listen, give me a copy of that drive. I know when I tell AD Reynolds about this, he and Director Sherman are going to shit themselves."

Chief Rosenthal lowered his head and released a heavy sigh. "I can't believe that all these years I supported Robert Lockhart and his son. The fallout from this is going to be far and wide. However, the Lockharts have a lot of lawyers working for them."

"I know this is going to be a hard case to prove. But I know there is enough to get an arrest warrant. I have an idea. They have the gala for the governor's election this Thursday, two days from now. Let's get the arrest warrants and let's execute them the night of the gala," Damien said.

Captain Mackey and Chief Rosenthal exchanged glances.

Chief Rosenthal rubbed his chin. "I think I know of a judge that will do this. Not too many are going to want to touch this. We need to have a meeting between all of us. Dillon, AD Reynolds, you Kaine, Mackey. We have no time to waste. We need those warrants by Thursday. Dillon, do you think AD Reynolds will support us on this arrest?"

"I can't speak for him, but knowing what I know, I believe he will support this. I know after our meeting with Robert Lockhart his opinion had shifted. I think when presented with the information on the drive this operation will have the full support of the FBI. At least this office, anyway."

Chief Rosenthal nodded. "Good, let's get out of here, Mackey. We got a lot of shit to do. Damien, stay here with Joe, keep me posted on his progress. You are going to have to give a debriefing about what happened at the restaurant, but that can wait until tomorrow."

"Dillon, I will email you the contents of this jump drive. Within the next few hours at the longest. Damien, I want to be updated ASAP about Joe. The chief and I need to get the warrants lined up. Chief, let's go," Captain Mackey said.

Damien watched them leave before turning to Dillon. He reached out and took her in his arms. "Now I understand what you guys went through when I got shot. I can't forgive myself for not thinking it was more than a flesh wound. I could've killed him."

Dillon tightened her hold on his waist. "Baby, you had no idea the shot was worse than it was. You can't beat yourself up over this. Joe is going to be okay. He should be released by tomorrow and knowing Joe, he will want to participate in the arrests."

He chuckled. "Yeah, I can see him wanting to put the cuffs on these fuckers." Damien kissed her. "Let's go in and talk to everyone and find out how Joe is doing."

# CHAPTER FORTY-EIGHT

Damien walked back into the hospital. Joe's parents and Taylor were gone. Only Damien's parents sat there.

"Damien," his mother said, "Joe is going to be okay. He has been moved to a room. He will spend one night here if there are no complications." She patted his cheek. "You didn't do anything wrong. Si?"

Damien nodded. "Yeah, mom. I'm trying to convince myself of that."

Angelina Kainetorri grabbed Dillon in a big hug. "We don't see you enough. You need to come back to the house for another dinner." She moved towards Giovanni and wrapped her arms around him.

Giovanni kissed the top of his wife's head and hugged her. "Joe's parents are going to stay a while longer. I think Taylor said she would stay the night with him. We were waiting to make sure you were okay."

"Yeah, Dad, I'm fine. Or at least I will be all right." Damien looked around the almost empty room. He smiled at his parents. "How is Sandra?"

"Oh, she is doing fine. She has been working some and resting a lot. The poor girl has no one." Damien's mom looked up at her husband. "I have told your father we need to adopt her."

"Angelina, she isn't an orphan child." Giovanni smiled at Dillon and Damien.

"I'm sure she needs you guys right now. Thank you for looking after her."

Giovanni hugged them both. "No worries, Damien. We will see you two soon at the house."

Damien waved as they walked out the door. "Are you staying or heading out?" he asked Dillon.

"I want to go tell AD Reynolds what is on that jump drive. I will call you in a little bit." She held him tight and kissed him. "No worrying. Okay?"

"Yeah, no worrying. I won't stay long. Too much to do."

"You should stay as long as you want to. Stay as long as you need to."

***

Damien found out what room Joe had been moved to. He knocked before he entered. Sticking his head through the door, he saw Joe sitting up in bed, his parents on one side, Taylor on the other. "Well, damn. Don't you look chipper?"

Joe grinned. "I've been given some great drugs. So, I'm in an excellent mood." He giggled.

Damien laughed. "Did anyone record him?"

"Yeah, I did. I will use it for blackmail material later." Taylor walked to Damien and gave him a hug. "Have you quit beating yourself up over this? You know nothing was your fault. It's the damn guy who shot him." She squeezed him. "He loves you, Damien he would never hold this against you. You shouldn't hold it against *you*."

Joe's mother hugged Damien next. "You are more than just Joe's partner to us." She held his face in her hands. "The surgeon told us that the nick in the artery was small, but without that tourniquet, he would have bled out." She kissed him like a mother kisses a son. "Thank you."

Damien fought the tears, but they welled over anyway. It hit him all at once what they had been through earlier in the day, and he held on tight to Mrs. Hagan. He gathered himself and moved to the bed. "You are a dork. You know that?" He said to Joe.

A goofy grin spread across Joe's face. "You love me." He made a smoochie face. "Give me a kissy."

Damien roared with laughter. He glanced at Taylor and Joe's parents. "As you as my witnesses, I will never let him live this down." He turned back to Joe. "They say you're going to get out of here by tomorrow. Taylor will pick you up and take you home. If you feel up to coming into the VCU, I will pick you up Thursday morning. We're going to have a briefing before we arrest the Lockharts."

Joe's eyes cleared and his body stiffened. "Can we just shoot those fuckers?"

"It would save taxpayers, now wouldn't it?" Damien asked.

Joe laid his head back and snored lightly.

Damien patted his arm. "I'm going to go and let him rest. Taylor will you call me and let me know when they are going to release him?"

"Sure, Damien. No problem." Taylor took the seat next to Joe's bed and held his hand.

Joe's mom sat on the other side of the bed across from Taylor. Taking Joe's other hand, she hummed an old Irish tune. Joe's father sat and read the paper.

Damien stood at the edge of the room, away from the others. He fidgeted with his blood-stained clothes. Smoothing them down. He quietly exited the room. Walking towards the elevators, his mind filled with thoughts of the killer. He could've killed them both, but instead, he chose to warn them. The killer wanted to let them know he could take them anytime. Until Damien could hunt him down, both he and Joe had a target on their backs.

Damien reached his hand into the front pocket of his jeans. A tingling sensation spread throughout his hand as he rolled the second thumb drive in his fingertips. Damien needed to know what was so important that Rossdale would give Gage Price a secret jump drive.

# CHAPTER FORTY-NINE

*Tuesday Evening*

He packed the few suitcases he had. The furniture came with the rental house making moving on easy. David had already disinfected and wiped every surface. Next time he would need a more secluded place. The plans he had for the next visit to Chicago would require a little more privacy.

He scanned each room making sure nothing had been left behind. David sat at the table and opened his secure computer. His travel documents were all in order. Next stop, Spain. A high-paying job had come through. However, it required a lengthy stay in Europe. His phone rang. Glancing at the burner phone's screen, his jaw and facial muscles tightened. He'd been waiting for this call. He hit record. "Yeah?"

"What the fuck were you thinking?"

"What do you mean?"

"You fucking know what I mean. You couldn't come up with another way to take out Price?"

"Hey, I told you I wasn't going to waste my time making it look like an accident. Don't worry, no one can trace anything back to you or me." David attached his burner phone to his computer.

"Listen, I paid you a lot of money. I expected you to do the job right. I can pull my money back out of your account. I have that ability, you know?"

David rubbed his temples and sighed. "First of all. You paid me because you are too fucking stupid to pull any of these jobs off on your own. That is evident by the many fucking messes I had to clean up. Second, that account was closed the minute you put the final payment into it."

He grabbed the bottle of water off the table and took a long swallow. "Now, I really don't like to be threatened. You, my friend, are in no position to threaten me. I know where you live and I have recorded all our voice conversations. I also know all your secrets."

"If you think of blackmailing me, I will tell the authorities who you are." His former employer had a slight quiver in his voice.

"Again, with the threats. Tsk tsk tsk. Let me explain something to you. I know everything about you. I know you have that sweet little redhead on the side. I know you have accounts stashed all over the place. I know that you *are a fucking idiot and couldn't find your way out of a brown paper sack. I also know that I won't hesitate to kill you. In the most painful way I can come up with. After I make you watch me kill your family."*

*Silence.*

*"Don't ever threaten me again. You need to figure out a way to keep your ass out of jail. I think shit is about to hit the fan where you are concerned."*
*David took another swallow of water.*

*"Nothing is going to happen to me. I covered my tracks well. I think it would be best if you didn't come back to Chicago."*

*David roared with laughter. "You think you are way more powerful than you are. I wouldn't be too sure of things, James."*

*He disconnected the call. Using software on his computer, he transferred the voice recording. Once complete, David made another call. "Havier, listen, it's me."*

*"Ah, my friend. Where are you?"*

*"Listen, plans have changed. I need to take care of our contract at a later date."*

*"In the many years I have known you, David, you would not cancel a job unless something much more pressing came about. What is it, my friend? Do you need my help?"*

*"No. And I am not canceling the job. I am merely postponing it. I need to take care of a nuisance and a long overdue payback."*

*Laughter bellowed from the other end of the line. "Revenge is often sweet but can lead to your downfall. Be careful, my friend."*

*The line went dead. He loaded his bags into the backseat of his truck. Once in the driver's seat, he pulled up a photo on his new burner phone, he had only one picture on it. The girl had grown up into a beautiful woman. Her slender figure had the perfect curves, and her eyes made you crave a glass of whiskey. The fact remained, Dillon McGrath had fucked up his world. David Allen Parker had vowed that day, long ago, to make her pay. Now was as good a time as any. A tight smile pressed his lips together. Making sure the cocky fucker James never saw the outside of a prison cell was going to be a sweet reward. However, teaching Dillon McGrath a lesson about fucking with someone's family seemed like a perfect way to end his time in Chicago.*

# CHAPTER FIFTY

Damien didn't bother returning to DC. The conversation earlier with Captain Mackey had made it clear he didn't need to. The captain had explained he and the chief were planning their approach with the judge on Wednesday. Mackey had told Damien to make sure he got the incident report filled out, and what time his debriefing meeting with the Fatality Incident Manager was on Wednesday as well.

He pulled into the garage. He sat in the car for a few moments. The day slammed into him. He dragged himself inside. Damien needed to shower. The stench of dried blood wafted with every movement. A constant reminder of how close he came to losing his best friend. His phone pinged, Dillon.

*Hey, baby. I'm gonna be late. The shit on this jump drive is unfuckingbe-lievable. AD Reynolds and Director Sherman are pissed they ever supported this family. The blowback may knock some people off their perch. Gotta go, love you.*

Damien entered the house. Coach came to him and rubbed against Damien's leg and pawed at him for him to pick him up. Damien picked him up and grunted. "Damn cat, you need to exercise or lay off the kibbles." Coach, oblivious to the fat joke, snuggled under his chin. Damien carried the cat up the stairs, placed him on the bed and stripped off the stiff, blood covered clothes, leaving them in a heap on the floor.

The 101-degree water temp flowed out of the twenty jets pulsing against his body. The events of the day slowly lost their hold on him. Damien closed his eyes, letting the guilt wash off and run down the drain. He took solace in the words of the surgeon that his tourniquet saved Joe's life. Damien gladly took his words and ran with them.

Lathering the rich, creamy shampoo, he washed his hair and body. The shower filled with a woodsy, aromatic scent, clearing his head of the fog it had when he stepped in. Turning off the water he let the steam swirl around him. Damien exited the shower grabbed a pair of loose-fitting sweats, and carried his clothes to the washer. Throwing everything in, he went to the fridge grabbed two pieces of cold pizza and a beer and headed to the office.

Coach followed and perched himself on the desk, waiting for Damien to share. "Fine. Here." Damien broke off several pieces of pepperoni and placed them next to Coach. He wolfed them down like he hadn't a meal in days. "Jesus, Coach, did you inhale those?"

Damien searched his desk. "Where the fuck did I put it?" He shuffled papers and his laptop and still couldn't find it. "Where the fuck...oh shit." He took off running to the washing machine. He hit the pause button. "C'mon you fucking door, unlock already." Tapping his foot, he pulled on his hair. The loud sound of the click echoed. "Fuck." Damien grabbed his pants and searched the front pocket. At first, he didn't find it, and his heart beat in his throat. His fingers finally grasped the small prize.

He ran to the kitchen grabbed a small plastic container and some rice. He threw the jump drive Gage Price had given him into the container. Remembering Gage's words not to tell anyone, Damien put the container into the safe in the office. "Merda. I can't fucking believe I did that." Damien threw the pizza in the trash, his appetite gone. He guzzled the beer.

He dragged himself to the couch and flopped on it. He wondered what Rossdale had uncovered and why he thought it was so important to give it to him. He rolled over onto his side. Coach meandered in and jumped up. "Hey, buddy. You gonna keep me company until your true love comes home?"

Coach head-butted him and snuggled sweetly into his chest. Damien wrapped his arm around the cat and sighed. Closing his eyes, he let the sound of Coach's purring lull him into oblivion.

# CHAPTER FIFTY-ONE

Dillon rolled into the house around ten thirty. They had secured several federal warrants against the Lockharts for the things committed during the election. They were ready to move on them, but she convinced them to allow Damien and Joe and the VCU to arrest them at the gala. Both AD Reynolds and Director Sherman, after consideration, decided the karma justice gods would be well served.

Having a State Department employee with the connections Gage Price had being shot in an open bistro, had the press working overtime. AD Reynolds gave a press conference letting the vultures know there was no terrorist connection and more information would be released in the coming days.

Dillon entered the house to see Coach and Damien asleep on the couch. She removed her gun and credentials, placing them in the bowl on the little entry table. This habit had become so regular, that she often forgot she had even done it hours later, looking for her weapon before she crawled into bed.

She knelt beside the sofa and scratched the cat's head. His purring increased and he extricated himself from Damien's grip. "Hey there, Coach. How's my baby?"

"Seriously? You snuggle him before you kiss me?" Damien peeped at her through hooded lids.

"Well, he is so soft and furry. I love him." She kissed the cat's head and gently placed him on the floor. She removed her boots, pants, and jacket and scooted in next to Damien. She put her butt next to him and snuggled under his arm.

"What you're saying is if I get obese and hairy, you'll love me more than the cat?"

"I wouldn't go that far."

# CHAPTER FIFTY-TWO

Wednesday morning

Damien walked out of the Fatality Incident office. He glanced at his watch. "Three fucking hours of my life I can't get back." He walked to his office. The VCU was a mess. Desks were piled with papers, and empty coffee cups and soda cans littered almost every surface. Most of his detectives sat at their desks, working on open cases. "Alright, this place is a pig sty. Before you all leave, clean this shit up."

Several detectives had incredulous stares on their faces.

"What are you talking about?" asked Detective Jenkins. "This is lived in."

"Hey, Lieutenant. How did the interview go?" asked Detective Jamal Harris.

His partner, Detective Mike Cooper, nodded at Damien. "I think someone is a tad bit pissy." His cheeks pushed up high by his smile.

"I wouldn't be in a pissy mood if I didn't have to babysit a bunch of slobs." Damien grabbed two empty soda cans off Cooper's desk. "How fucking hard is it to throw your trash away?"

Detective Cooper gave Damien an evil eye. "Yeah, well, I was attached to those cans."

Damien snickered. "I'll attach those cans to your ass if you want. I mean if you are that attached to them."

"I think that is police brutality," Detective Harris chimed in.

Damien squinted at his detective. "I'll show you some brutality." He threw a wadded-up piece of paper at the man.

"Hey Lieutenant, how's Joe?" Detective Hall asked.

A thin smiled pulled at Damien's lips. "He gets out today. Probably after lunch."

"Don't worry, Damien. We will all work with you to find the guy who shot Joe. We all decided if you ever need extra help on that, we are all here for you," Detective Hall said.

Damien smiled. "You guys are too good to me." Damien headed into his office. "Clean that pen up before any of you guys leave. Rosy cleans the area, but she isn't responsible for all your crap."

Walking into his office his phone pinged a message from Taylor.

*Joe is being released in an hour. He wants to come in, I told him no. Knowing him, he will be there in the morning.*

He messaged back. *Tell him I will pick him up around seven thirty.*

Damien sat in his seat. While he completed the incident interview, the mail and message fairy delivered a stack of stuff. Damien gawked at the pile. He wondered what the other lieutenants of DC got in their daily mail. Surely, he wasn't the only one to get this much crap.

Thirty minutes later, Damien was sure the pile kept replicating itself. His desk phone rang. "Kaine."

"Get up to my office," Captain Mackey said.

***

Damien smiled at Catherine.

She waved him right in. "They are waiting for you."

Damien's stomach knotted. He wanted to ask who *they* were, but in less than fifteen seconds he would find out. Upon entering the office, he saw his favorite thing in the world. Dillon. She winked at him.

"Damien, come in." Captain Mackey gestured to him. In the chairs sat Chief Rosenthal, AD Reynolds, and SAC Marks stood next to Dillon. "As you can see, we are having a meeting. We are missing Joe. How is he? I called the hospital. They weren't sure, but they thought he would be released sometime today."

"Yes, Sir. He is getting sprung in about an hour. He wanted to come in, but I told him I would pick him up in the morning." Damien moved to stand on the other side of Chief Rosenthal.

"He needs to be cleared before he can work," Captain Mackey said.

"I understand. But I know he will want to be a part of the arrest team tomorrow. Will he at least be able to be there for that?" Damien glanced at his captain and the chief.

The chief nodded at Captain Mackey. The captain turned and stared at Damien. "He can be part of it."

AD Reynolds looked at Damien. "That jump drive was a damn gold mine. There is enough to hang them on. Now does that mean we can get them for the murders, I'm not sure. But there is a ton of circumstantial that links both men to the deaths of Officer Lynn, the two teenagers, Zach Franklin, and Brock Avery."

Damien looked around the room. "I haven't seen anything on that drive yet, but in my conversation with Gage Price, he indicated that

James set up his dad to take the fall for everything, leaving him to look like the innocent victim. Did you see anything to the contrary?"

AD Reynolds smiled. "We caught on pretty quick to that scheme. James alluded to his plans in several conversations that Price recorded. And taken at face value, that is what you might assume happened. However, one of the files that Price put on there had to do with the plane rented that the killer used to get to Virginia and kill Brock Avery.

"When he rented the plane, James used an account that ties back to the Lockharts' Foundation. We traced that payment. All amounts larger than ten thousand dollars are tracked through the Foundation. They flagged it and automatically put a tracer on it. If it had pinged back to an unknown source, the Foundation would have blocked the payment."

AD Reynolds nodded to SAC Marks. "Agent Marks can explain the rest."

"The foundation implemented this software that was designed specifically to track fraud. For anyone to even transfer funds for any payment, they have to have one—a certain clearance level, and two—a specific code. When James put in his code, it tracked it back to his computer at the State Building."

SAC Marks beamed a giant smile at them. "This software was implemented without anyone knowing its full scope. James would have put in the code thinking it tracked back to the Foundation itself. He would have had no clue about the tracking."

"That is a helluva break. That ties James Lockhart directly to the payment for the plane," Damien said.

"It does. However, let's not forget that anyone can use that computer at the State Building. So, we need to show it was him and not someone else. We will have to interview everyone involved in that flight and see if anyone can give us a description of the passenger," AD Reynolds said.

Captain Mackey glanced at Damien and nodded.

Damien cleared his throat. "I may be able to help with that, but I don't know how you will want to proceed."

AD Reynolds scrutinized Damien. "What do you have?"

"When my case five years ago was taken, I found the sketch that the kids had given us. I only recently remembered that I had it," Damien said.

AD Reynolds shifted in his seat and looked at Dillon. "Did you know anything about this?"

Dillon looked at Damien and, before she could answer, Damien spoke up.

"She didn't know. I haven't told anyone about it." Damien lowered his gaze. "I apologize. I should've turned it over immediately."

Chief Rosenthal let out a long sigh. "Mackey, we will have to discuss this later."

"The problem, no case goes with this sketch. Lockhart's lawyer would have a field day with it," Damien said.

Dillon stepped forward. "Why don't you use the sketch to question people around the Lockharts and the flight crew to see if anyone recognizes him. We can always say he is a person of interest. And we don't release it to the news."

AD Reynolds nodded. "That's not a bad idea. We don't want this picture out. It would drive the killer underground, and right now he thinks we don't know anything about him. That gives us an upper hand."

SAC Marks looked at Damien. "Get me a copy of that sketch."

"I will get that to you by the end of the day," Damien said.

Chief Rosenthal tapped the arm of his chair. "Alright, let's get down to business. AD Reynolds, I know you have federal warrants, and I managed to convince Judge Willows to give us our warrants on murder for hire, conspiracy to commit murder, and for being an all-around douche bag."

Captain Mackey looked at Damien. "The Lockharts have the gala at the Ritz. I know the head of security there, and I can count on him to keep everything in confidence. I spoke with him about security and entry into the event. His group will be at the door. He said when we show up, he will let us in, no need for SWAT or sharpshooters."

Captain Mackey spoke to AD Reynolds. "I'm assuming you guys are going to be present as well?"

"Are you really asking me that? I figure Joe and Damien would like the honors of putting on the handcuffs. They can read off the charges you guys have. Then one of us," he motioned to Dillon and SAC Marks, "can read them the federal charges."

AD Reynolds smiled at Dillon. "I think you should read off Mr. Robert Lockhart's charges. I want to watch his face when you do it." He turned towards Chief Rosenthal and Captain Mackey. "He was disrespectful and belittling towards Agent McGrath when we interviewed him."

"If I'm being honest, I say that will be a gratifying experience," Dillon said.

"What time are we looking at? Let's say, we will gather here, in the VCU conference room by six p.m. The gala is set to start at seven. I want them having a good time before we arrest them. If we are lucky, we can time it to coincide with their speeches, and we can arrest them in front of everyone." Captain Mackey leaned back. He nodded towards the chief. "Don't you have a ticket?"

Chief Rosenthal smiled. "I sure do. And I would appreciate it if you didn't mess up the food table storming around. Because, no matter what happens, I will fill my thousand-dollar plate full of goodies." He chuckled. "I can text you when the speeches are about to begin. That way you can be right outside and ready."

Captain Mackey's lips tightened into a thin line. "I think that will give us plenty of time to get over there and be at the ready for the chief's call."

Damien's smile filled his face. "I can't wait for that. I know that Senator Lockhart will be defiant and smug. I hope he does something that allows me to at least punch his ass."

"As much as I would love to see that," AD Reynolds said, "I can't stress enough to be on your best behavior. We don't want to give their attorneys anything to squawk on."

Captain Mackey addressed the room. "Under no circumstances is any of this to get out. I want full confidentiality."

"You know the Lockharts will have every social beat at this event. The minute we arrest them, shit will hit the fan. Are you planning on giving any statements? Wouldn't it play in our favor to disclose why we are arresting them?" Damien asked.

Dillon took a step towards the group. "It would. The damage it could do to them politically would be worth it."

"I think we give a statement, DC and the FBI together at the podium the following morning. This way we have time to put our spin on it." AD Reynolds said.

"Our standard reply should be, 'a press conference will be following tomorrow morning at eight a.m. on the steps of DC. And with that, we perp walk them out the door," Chief Rosenthal said.

"Last thing, I would like to have more agents on hand for the arrest, just in case. I have no problem with you wanting to bring in some more from Division Central as well," AD Reynolds said.

Chief Rosenthal glanced at Captain Mackey. "We can round up some officers to help with the night of the gala."

AD Reynolds stood. "I think we have everything covered. Since we have the security company there helping us, we aren't going to need to barge in. This should put us in an excellent position of surprise."

"That is a good plan. Friday morning, we will have a conference," Captain Mackey turned towards his lieutenant.

Damien sat quietly in his thoughts. Oblivious to the question from the captain. He glanced up. "What? I'm sorry. What did you say?"

Captain Mackey's eyes narrowed. "I asked you if your interview with the Fatality Incident Manager went okay?"

"Yeah, it went fine. They have been told that the FBI is taking over the investigation because of Price's job and connection." Damien raised his eyebrows. "Good call by the way. It totally takes the suspicion off Joe and me and makes it look like you guys are assholes." He smiled at AD Reynolds.

AD Reynolds laughed. "Well, as much as I would like to take credit for that call, I can't. Director Sherman set that in motion. He figured with the way things were going, it was better to swoop in now and take over."

"It does work in our favor. Now Damien and Joe can defer all questions to the FBI or to the chief or me," Captain Mackey said.

Everyone in the room stood.

Damien stepped off to the side when the captain leaned towards him. "I need you to stay a few moments."

Damien acknowledged his captain's request. He winked at Dillon as she left the office. Turning his attention back to Captain Mackey he took the seat in front of his desk.

"Where did you go a few minutes ago? You seemed distracted."

"Oh, I was thinking about Joe. I know he is getting out," he glanced at his watch, "he's probably already out and home, sleeping. Milking this injury for all it's worth."

"Damien, I know you are guilt-laden about yesterday. But you can't hold on to that. It will eat you up from the inside out."

Damien winced.

"You can't let your head be somewhere else. I need you one hundred percent in this, or this arrest could be jeopardized."

Damien sighed. "Captain, I would never do anything to jeopardize this. Those fuckers, the Lockharts, killed a lot of people to push their own agendas forward. The last thing I want to see is anything mess that up. I do think we should make sure the news crews covering this event have the whole story."

The captain smiled. "And they will, Damien, in due time. But the information we release must be done so in a manner that will have the most impact on getting and keeping those fuckers behind bars. I am trusting you not to do something you or I will regret later. Go on. Get out of here."

Damien got to the door when Captain Mackey called to him.

"Damien, I hope that you have let the guilt of yesterday go. Joe is going to be okay, and no one blames you."

Damien lowered his head before speaking. "I have. I let it go. I promise."

"That's what I wanted to hear."

Damien started to leave and turned back to the captain. "What about the sketch and me withholding it?"

Captain Mackey shrugged. "I will make sure that the Chief is informed of things. Don't worry about that Damien." The captain waved him out.

# CHAPTER FIFTY-THREE

Thursday
Day of the gala


Damien pulled up out front of Joe's apartment. He had his hand on the horn when Joe bounded down the stairs.

Joe opened the door to the SUV with a big smile on his face. "Hey, what's up?" Joe leaned towards his partner and batted his eyes. "Did you miss me?"

Damien laughed and pulled away from the curb. "Are you kidding me? Not having to babysit your ass all day, I had no problem getting my work done. I didn't know how much you bug the hell out of me during any given day."

"Aww shucks, I knew you loved me." Joe put his fingers together and made a heart symbol. "I love you too."

"Oh fuck, are you high? Did you take your painkiller or something?"

"Nah. I'm a tuff boy. I don't need any painkillers. To tell the truth, it isn't that bad. I mean the wound is raw and sore. But Taylor replaced the bandage early this morning, and it isn't oozing too much. She made sure to wrap it securely, so it should stay clean and dry."

Joe looked out the window. "I know I have to pass a physical before I can be on actual duty, but I had no problem lifting, loading, or aiming my weapon. I'm not going to have a problem with getting back to work."

"I'm glad to hear that, my friend. The captain didn't hesitate to let you be part of these arrests. I would imagine on Friday you can do your testing or Monday even. That will give you the weekend to recuperate." Damien glanced over at him. "I'm glad you're okay. How about you don't get shot again?"

"How about we leave this fucking job? Because as long as we are in this profession, our asses are in the line of fire all the damn time."

"Okay, let me fill you in a bit." Damien explained to Joe the plan for the day. It included a lot of logistics centered around the gala, making sure everything was set up and ready to go without a hitch.

They pulled into Division Central and parked on the lower level of the garage. Navigating the halls of DC was never a dull moment. With Robbery, Vice, Narcotics, SWAT, and a large area for training and firearm maintenance training, there was always shit going on. Today, it looked as if Vice had a busy morning, or late evening, depending on how you looked at it.

"Hey, Lieutenant Diego, is that your new girlfriend?" Damien smirked at his counterpart as he and Joe walked by holding.

"Hey, you jealous of old Babs here?" Diego winked at the woman next to him.

Babs' flaming red, stringy hair hung matted off her shoulders. Her blue eyeshadow was a little heavy, and her black mascara was smudged under both eyes. "He can't get enough of me. That's why he is always arresting me." She leered at Joe and licked her lips. "Why can't you arrest me, big fellow? I bet I could make it worth your while."

Joe smiled at her. "Babs, I am not man enough to handle you. I would have to constantly think about something else so I wouldn't nut too soon."

She showed her rotted yellow teeth. "You got that right, handsome. But I'm always ready to teach you."

"I'll keep that in mind, Babs." Joe waved as they entered the elevator.

"I'm telling Taylor you have a new girlfriend."

Joe laughed. "Please don't. I want her to keep the illusion I can have any beautiful woman I want, not Babs."

When Joe and Damien entered the VCU, cheers erupted. The detectives had bought a bunch of balloons. Several said happy birthday or happy anniversary, they had strung streamers across Joe's desk.

Damien looked at the motley crew. "What the hell, birthday and anniversary balloons?"

Detective Hall beamed at them. "Hey, I wanted Joe to know how glad we are he is okay, but he isn't worth that much fucking money. Shit, these were on clearance."

Joe turned to Damien. "You didn't buy me balloons."

Damien headed into his office. "I buy you jelly beans," he shouted. Damien frowned at his desk. "I don't know where all this fucking mail comes from."

***

Damien heard a knock at his door as Dillon walked through.

"Hey, baby." She came around the desk, bending to give him a chaste kiss. "How was your day?"

Damien glanced at his watch. "Shit, it's five already? I spent the day catching up on paperwork. I think time stands still when you do that so that your ass stays planted at your desk. Your brain tells your body, *you have been here for thirty minutes, finish your work.*"

Dillon sat in the seat across from him and grabbed a handful of jelly beans. "I saw the balloons for Joe. The guys buy those for him?"

"Yeah, and they didn't want to spend a lot. Could you tell?"

Dillon laughed. "Happy birthday and anniversary balloons are always on clearance. But hey, it's the thought that counts. You about ready to head to the conference room? I saw a few of the agents have taken some seats in there."

Damien leaned back in his chair. "Oh yeah. I am so ready to arrest those assholes." Damien stood and grabbed his jacket. He came around the desk and pulled Dillon up towards him. He wrapped an arm around her waist. "Hmm, you smell fantastic." He inhaled her vanilla citrus scented hair. He nuzzled her neck and was about to kiss her passionately when Joe stuck his head in.

"Hey, you two lovebirds. No PDA in the workplace." Joe pushed them apart so he could get to the jelly beans.

"What the heck, man?" Damien stepped back so he wouldn't be knocked over. "What rule is that Mr. McFat Butt?"

"Ha, my rule. It makes the other guys and me jealous." He leaned into Damien, "You never kiss us like you do *her.*" Joe turned and squinted at Dillon.

She swatted his good arm and turned on her heels. "You're a dork, Joe."

They all headed towards the conference room which was fast filling up. As they stepped in, AD Reynolds and Captain Mackey waved them to the front.

"Okay, let's settle down. We have a lot to go over." Captain Mackey keyed up the overhead projector. "Here is the layout for the ballroom we will be entering. We will go through these doors." He pointed to a picture plastered on the wall indicating a set of doors at the far end of the room. "This team is Alpha. It consists of myself, AD Reynolds, Lieutenant Kaine, Detective Hagan, Agent McGrath, and SAC Marks."

AD Reynolds stepped up. "We will break off into two more groups. Team Bravo will follow us in through these doors. Once we go in, you see how the stage is configured," he pointed to the stairs on either side of the stage, "team Alpha will split and move up both sets of steps. Bravo team, I want you to move to stand in front of the stage. Making sure no one advances on us. I can't imagine these people will do anything, but you never know if someone wants to get involved, so be prepared."

Captain Mackey nodded. "There are going to be news crews there. Don't give any statements, but do not impede their progress of videotaping this event. Team Charlie, you will keep people from entering or leaving the event until we have the Lockharts in custody."

"Are there any questions? Anything need clarification?" AD Reynolds waited for a response. "Okay, Chief Rosenthal will be attending the gala. He's going to text the captain and let him know when the speeches are about to start. That's when we will enter the facility. I imagine that will be around seven forty-five, according to the update the security personnel gave us."

Captain Mackey shut off the projector. "We roll out in about fifteen to be in position. Grab some of the comms from here on the table. Team leaders use channel eight. Alpha team will give a countdown after we get the text from Chief Rosenthal. Coordinate amongst yourselves on transportation. If we need another vehicle, let us know."

"Captain, are you taking your vehicle?" Damien asked.

"Yes. AD Reynolds and I will lead in my vehicle. You can take the rest of the Alpha team."

Damien nodded. "You got it."

An electric static filled the air, ramping up the excitement of the operational personnel. When all the logistics of transportation had been figured out, the teams rolled out to their destination.

# CHAPTER FIFTY-FOUR

Gala

James Lockhart stood in his Dolce and Gabbana tux he had made for this occasion. He brushed a small piece of lint off his lapel, as a contributor droned on about computer software. "Excuse me, I need to speak to someone." He gave the overweight computer geek a belittling smile. "I'm so glad you came tonight. Please drink, eat, and enjoy yourself." James shook the man's hand. As he walked away, he wiped his palm on his pants.

He made his way to his wife, Amber. Who, even though she looked stunning in her long pink gown, was not the beautiful redhead he had sex with earlier in the afternoon. She stood next to his trusty assistant Tyler Bryce. James had recently found out about the affair the two were having, and although he should've been mad, he was grateful he didn't have to sleep with his wife.

The thousand-dollar a plate fundraiser was packed with A-listers and wannabes. James checked his watch. Seven forty-five. His lips puckered then flattened out. Glancing around the room he located each exit, and rechecked his watch. If he didn't have to give a damn speech, he didn't think anyone would even notice if he snuck out.

He eyeballed his father as he hob-knobbed with the elite of Chicago. James' mother mingled with everyone. A bitter smiled returned her gaze and wave. Why she put up with his father's girlfriends over the years, James didn't understand. He assumed it was the lifestyle she had grown accustomed to and had no desire to start from scratch. James couldn't blame her. He had the chance to leave this family and this life and chose the money and comfort over change.

Robert Lockhart made his way towards the podium. Stopping to shake someone's hand or pat them on the shoulder. James meandered, following his father's path through the swaths of people. Everyone either shook James' hand or patted him on the back as he passed by.

James noticed two news crews off to either side of the stage. Leave it to dear old Dad to get as much free press as possible. James was sure his dad told them they could eat and drink as long as they took photos and video. He was also certain his father had paid for those videos to make it to the top of the news hour. Politics was nothing more than money and power. Whoever had the most of both had the control.

Robert Lockhart stood at the podium. The clanking of forks against plates ceased as all eyes and ears turned towards the front of the ballroom. "First and foremost, I want to thank each of you who have come tonight in support of my son and his bid for Governor."

***

Chief Rosenthal sat at a table near the stage. He had two fully loaded plates in front of him and planned to enjoy every morsel. He pulled his phone from his jacket and sent a text. He replaced the phone and glanced at his watch. He figured he had about ten minutes before the fireworks began.

***

Captain Mackey's phone pinged. He glanced at the screen and nodded at AD Reynolds sitting next to him. They both pulled out walkietalkies and notified the other groups. Within minutes, several cars' doors opened and closed, filling the basement level garage parking area with echoes.

Captain Mackey lifted a hand to quiet the crowd of agents and officers gathered outside the entry into the hotel. They all wore vests with either FBI, VCU, or DC emblazoned on them. "Okay. You all know what to do. We want to get in and out as quickly as possible. Once we have the Lockharts in custody, there will be two patrol cars out front waiting for them. They will be placed into separate cars and brought back to DC holding."

AD Reynolds adjusted his vest as he spoke. "Do not speak to the press. We will hold a press conference in the morning, so if you are cornered by a news member, tell them that answers will be forthcoming soon. Got it?" AD Reynolds glanced around the group of law enforcement personnel. "Let's roll out."

# CHAPTER FIFTY-FIVE

"I am very pleased to stand here before you tonight. The support from the people of Illinois is a testament to the fantastic state I represent. I..." James trailed off as the doors to the ballroom opened up. Several men entered and made their way to the stage. James turned to look at his father. "Dad, what's going on?"

Damien, Joe, and Dillon followed behind AD Reynolds, Captain Mackey, and SAC Marks. Team Bravo brought up the rear. As they entered the ballroom, AD Reynolds and SAC Marks led the way to the left side of the stage with Dillon following behind them. Captain Mackey, Damien, and Joe moved up the small staircase on the right-hand side of the stage. Team Bravo took up positions in the front of the stage. Half facing the crowd and half facing the stage.

Robert Lockhart had been sitting next to his wife. He rose and walked towards the steps that AD Reynolds now advanced up. "What is going on here? How dare you interrupt this dinner." Robert took a small step towards his son when SAC Marks stepped up behind him.

The audience let out an audible gasp. The whispers of the patrons rose into loud murmurs. Dishes clanked as glassware fell from tables when several people stood quickly.

Captain Mackey reached the podium the same time as SAC Marks stood behind Robert Lockhart. Damien nodded to Joe. As Mackey stepped up behind James Lockhart, Damien and Joe flanked him on either side.

Both Mrs. Lockharts gasped.

"What is the meaning of this? Why are you doing this?" Francine Lockhart teared up.

Amber Lockhart reached out and took her mother-in-law's hand and pulled her out of the way towards the back of the stage. "Francine, we can call the lawyers. Don't get in their way."

Several male patrons tried to make their way to offer assistance, but were quickly stopped by team Bravo. Team Charlie had secured the other doorways, and people who wanted to leave the room were stopped and told to return to their seats.

Both news crews scrambled for the best angle. The camera operators zoomed in on Robert and James Lockhart. They had apparently gone live and the reporters assigned to cover the gala now scrambled to give updates to their respective stations.

The voices no longer whispered. The decibel level was increasing as the two Lockharts were surrounded by law enforcement.

SAC Marks reached for one of Robert Lockhart's hands bringing it behind his back.

"What are you doing?" Robert Lockhart tried to swing around and pull his arm out of the agent's grasp.

SAC Marks was too fast for him and secured his second wrist in the pair of cuffs.

James Lockhart stepped towards his father. "What the hell is the meaning of this? You have no right to arrest him." James Lockhart tried to push Joe out of the way but managed to throw himself off balance instead.

"Step back, Mr. Lockhart." Joe pushed his shoulder.

Captain Mackey positioned himself to the right of James. "Mr. Lockhart, you and your father are being arrested." Mackey motioned to Damien.

Damien stepped around and grabbed James' right wrist. Twisting a little harder than necessary, he secured the senator's arm behind his back. With speed and agility, Damien grabbed the left wrist and snapped the handcuffs on him. Damien nodded to Joe.

"James Lockhart. You are under arrest. You have the right to remain silent and refuse to answer questions. Anything you say may be used against you in a court of law. You have the right to counsel before speaking with the police. You may also have that counsel present during questioning. If you cannot afford an attorney one will be appointed for you. Do you understand these rights as I have stated them to you?"

"I understand the rights. You still have no basis to arrest my father or me." James Lockhart had a calm demeanor about him.

Dillon stepped toe to toe with Robert Lockhart and read him his rights. "Do you understand these rights, Mr. Lockhart?"

"Do you know who the hell you are messing with, little girl? I will have us out of custody within the hour." Robert Lockhart's nostrils flared.

Dillon stood her ground. "Good luck with that." She glanced at her watch. "Thursday evening, past eight thirty p.m. and charges that include murder for hire. I seriously doubt you are going to get out before the weekend."

Robert Lockhart now stood close to his son. "What murder charges? What the hell are you talking about?" He glanced at his son. "James, keep your mouth shut until the attorneys show up."

James Lockhart looked smugly at his father. "I'm not worried, Dad." He turned to look at Damien and Joe. "They don't have anything on me." A thin smile tugged at his lips.

One of the news cameramen stood directly in front of them, next to the stage. Damien lowered his voice, hoping the noisy crowd could drown out what he was saying. Damien leaned into the man. "I wouldn't be so sure of that, James. You see, we have the plane and vehicle you rented for the hitman you hired to kill Brock Avery."

James' face turned ashen and pallid. He straightened, angling himself away from Damien. He glanced over to see his father's incredulous stare.

Robert Lockhart confronted his son. "James, what are they talking about? What plane?" Robert's voice trailed off.

Damien glanced at the father and son. He spoke in a hushed tone. "It seems James here rented a plane using your Foundation to fly someone to Virginia the night before Brock Avery's house blew up."

Robert Lockhart's mouth fell open. "James, tell me that isn't true. Tell me you would never use the Foundation for that?"

Damien and Joe checked both of Lockhart's pants pockets.

Damien nodded towards Robert Lockhart. "Oh, he did more than that with the Foundation. It seems as though James here has been using your money for all kinds of interesting things."

Joe handed the wallet and keys from Robert Lockhart's pockets to one of the agents holding a small baggie. "Here's the kicker, Robert. He has worked extra hard at pinning everything on you," Joe said.

Robert's eyes zeroed in on his son. "Is that true, James? You would do something like that to me?"

James sneered at his father. "I refuse to answer any questions without the presence of my attorney."

"James, answer me." Robert Lockhart's face flushed. Spittle had formed at the corners of his mouth. "Answer me damn you."

SAC Marks led the senior Lockhart off the stage as he ranted at his son.

The news crew focused in on Robert Lockhart. The reporter shoved a microphone in his face. "Mr. Lockhart, can you tell me why the FBI have arrested you here tonight at your son's gala?"

SAC Marks nudged the reporter to the side.

The reporter stuck the microphone into SAC Marks' face. "Can you tell me, Agent, why you have arrested the Lockharts tonight?"

"Information will be forthcoming shortly. Excuse us, please." SAC Marks led the dejected man from the ballroom through a set of doors into the lobby.

Damien and Joe flanked the younger Lockhart and followed Captain Mackey off the stage and out the same set of double doors SAC Marks had gone through.

The lobby was filled with hotel guests and patrons from the dinner, the news crews catching every moment on their cameras.

They cornered AD Reynolds and Captain Mackey. AD Reynolds held up his hand. "There will be an eight a.m. news conference on the steps of DC. At which time, all questions regarding the arrests of Robert Lockhart and James Lockhart will be addressed. That is all for now."

# CHAPTER FIFTY-SIX

Friday Morning

At six thirty, news crews from around the state and national news had lined the street. They clamored to claim their spots on the steps of Division Central. Microphone stands, cameramen, and reporters packed themselves in like sardines on the steps and sidewalk, all vying for the best spot. News vans lined the street. Making it necessary for DC to assign traffic cops to keep the flow of vehicles moving.

Damien and Joe sat in Damien's office eating the breakfast they had picked up on the way to the VCU. Damien wiped the corners of his mouth. "Why the hell do we have to be at the press conference? We aren't going to speak. You know that, right?"

"Especially at the butt crack of dawn." Joe swallowed his bite of breakfast sandwich. "Solidarity, bro. They want the FBI and DC to show a united front." Joe stuffed half of a hash brown into his mouth.

Damien lifted a single brow at Joe. "Seriously, dude, you're going to choke one day. Man, take smaller bites."

Joe frowned at him. "My esophagus is a perfectly working muscle. I never have any trouble swallowing."

Damien turned away and burst out laughing. "Is that what your boyfriend says?"

It dawned on Joe what he said and he snorted. "Fuck you." He took another bite of his sandwich. "Where's Dillon?"

Damien was still chuckling at his own joke. "She had to go into the FBI office. They wanted her there by six thirty to go over everything that would be covered in the press conference."

"Is she speaking?"

"No. I don't think so anyway. Like us, she will be there to look pretty." Damien winked. His desk phone rang. "Kaine." He nodded. "Yes, Sir. We will meet you at the doors." He threw his trash into the bin and stood. Stretching, he grabbed his jacket.

"Is it showtime already?" Joe stuffed the last of his breakfast into his mouth.

"Yup. You ready?"

"Fuck no."

"Me neither." Damien led the way to the front steps.

***

Everyone from DC and the FBI had gathered at the top of the steps. The podium had been placed in the center allowing for the mass of media to swarm around them, almost encircling them.

First, AD Reynolds stepped to the podium and adjusted the microphone. The press corps continued to fling questions at them. He remained quiet until they stopped the chatter. "Thank you for coming out so early this morning. As you are aware, Robert and James Lockhart have been arrested.

"They are both charged with Federal and State charges connected to their actions five years ago and to more recent events, that will be disclosed at a later date. Evidence has been uncovered that shows they used their power and money, and colluded with others, to help James Lockhart get elected to Brock Avery's Senate seat."

Questions flew in rapid succession to one another. The news reporters yelled out, all clamoring for answers. AD Reynolds held up his hand. The crowd buzzed. "We cannot give many details at this time as it is a State and Federal matter. However, the charges against the two men have not come lightly. We are aware of their status in the community and recognize that some may find it hard to believe they could be involved in these crimes."

"Can you tell us if the murder of Glenn Rossdale is related to the charges against Robert and James Lockhart?" A reporter yelled out.

The crowd quieted, waiting for the response.

AD Reynolds nodded to Captain Mackey and stepped aside so he could take over the podium.

Captain Mackey adjusted the microphone so he didn't have to bend over. "Lieutenant Kaine and Detective Hagan have been working tirelessly on the Rossdale case. I can't discuss an ongoing murder investigation, but there are some parallel patterns that we continue to investigate."

Captain Mackey was about to speak when a reporter asked a question.

"I have recently come across some information, Captain. Can you tell me if it is true that James Lockhart hired someone to kill Brock Avery's bodyguard five years ago, subsequently leading to Avery relinquishing his position in the Senate and paving the way for James Lockhart to win it? And can you also tell me if Robert Lockhart set Avery up in his business in Virginia to keep his silence?"

Captain Mackey's eyes hardened as they narrowed on the reporter. "I'm not sure where you have received your information from, perhaps you would like to share that?"

The reporter stepped forward. "No, Captain. I don't plan on sharing my source. But I would still like an answer to the question. Is it true?"

Captain Mackey leaned into the microphone. "There will be more information to come as the FBI and Division Central uncover more facts. Thank you for your time."

The captain turned and motioned to Damien and Joe to follow him. Close on their heels AD Reynolds and Dillon followed suit.

Once inside the confines of Division Central and away from the prying microphones of the press, Captain Mackey turned to his lieutenant. "Where the fuck did they get the information, Damien?"

Damien stepped back. His eyes darted between everyone and back to Captain Mackey. "Why the hell are you asking me?"

"Who else gave him the fucking information? You and Joe figured that shit out after speaking with Gage Price. Who else if not you?"

Damien's jaw stiffened. "Are you fucking kidding me? Why the hell would I release that kind of information to the press? That could mess up our whole case. Now those fucking Lockharts have some idea where this investigation is going. I can't fucking believe you would think I would do that."

Dillon and AD Reynolds stood by. Dillon was about to speak when AD Reynolds gently tugged at her shirt.

Damien looked directly at the captain. "Well, there is one person who knows everything."

The captain crossed his arms. "Who?"

"The fucking killer, that's who. Who the fuck else knows details like that? Details we just gathered after talking to Gage Price?"

The captain's mouth turned down as his hands fell to his side. "Fuck. Damien. I'm sorry. I was way out of line." Captain Mackey scrubbed a hand over his face. "Fuck, Fuck, Fuck. I heard that question from the reporter and immediately thought you guys did it to bring extra heat on the Lockharts. I'm sorry." Captain Mackey turned and paced the area.

Dillon stepped near Damien but didn't touch him. "He's right, you know. This killer has been two steps ahead of us throughout this entire investigation. It doesn't seem far-fetched that he called in the tip to the news."

Captain Mackey's shoulder's sagged. "I am truly sorry that I blamed you, Damien. I was wrong. If it was the killer that means he is watching this investigation. And more than likely continuing to watch you two."

AD Reynolds pinched the bridge of his nose. "If that is the case, that means you two still have a target on your backs and will continue to do so until you find out who he is and stop him."

Everyone absorbed the moment. Captain Mackey and AD Reynolds headed off to their offices, leaving Dillon, Damien, and Joe behind.

Dillon turned towards Damien and reached out stroking his arm. "Don't take what the Captain said personally. The minute he realized there was a chance it could be the killer himself, he regretted his comments."

Damien nodded. The bitter taste still lingered in his mouth. It may be a while before that taste left. "Yeah. Sure." He looked at Joe. "What do you have to do today? Technically you aren't cleared for work."

"I'm going to head over to the personnel office to find out what I need to do to get cleared. If I need a ride home, I will tag you and let you know." Joe lightly kissed Dillon on the cheek as he headed along the hallway. "Check you guys later."

Damien turned and faced Dillon. The highlights in her hair sparkled under the bright overhead bulbs. "I imagine that question by the reporter is going to cause a lot of commotion over at your office."

"Oh, hell yeah. I imagine SAC Marks is on his way now to the station to see if they can get any information as to how the tip came in or where it came from. If it came via the computer, and this guy used a VPN, we may never know the area it came from." Dillon grabbed his hand and walked with him to the elevator. "I need to head back to the office, and I may not be home at a reasonable time. I'll let you know later."

Generally, she didn't kiss him in public, but the blue in his eyes beckoned her. She rose on her tippy toes and kissed him. More passionately than she should have. "I love you. I will call you later."

"Bye, babe." Damien entered the elevator wishing he had a shot of whiskey to wash the nasty taste of betrayal and distrust from his mouth.

# CHAPTER FIFTY-SEVEN

Friday Evening

The day had been long and full of fires. The press conference the day before had created a shit storm, and all day Damien chased down as many leads as he could. Joe hadn't been cleared and was instructed on Thursday to go home until Monday. *Lucky fucker,* Damien thought as he drove home. "I wish I had an extended weekend."

He pulled into his garage. A text from Dillon pinged as he shut off the engine.

*I wish I could be there to have dinner with you. I love you.*

He responded and tucked his phone away. Entering the house, Coach sat at the ready. Scowl and all.

"Hey, Fatty. How's it going?" Coach weaved in and out of his legs, then darted past him to the kitchen. "Okay. Man. Give me a second. I will feed you." Damien grabbed a can of wet, stinky, fishy food and filled his beloved pet's bowl. "Damn, that shit smells. How do you stand it?"

Coach growled as he ate, scarfing every morsel.

Damien went into the office and poured a double shot of whiskey. He sat at his desk and looked for the journal from Rossdale. "Fuck. Where the hell is that?" After a few more minutes of shuffling things on his desk around, he remembered it was in the safe. Opening the safe he immediately saw the container of rice. "Shit."

He reached in and took out the container holding the secret jump drive Price had given him. Damien opened it and shook off the rice. He wiped it off and inspected it. He couldn't see any moisture, so hopefully, no damage was done. He turned on his laptop. As he waited for it to boot up, he stared at the drive in his fingertips. His stomach rolled as stomach acid bubbled up his throat.

His computer lit up. He logged in and held his breath. Damien plugged in the jump drive and stared. His lungs burned as he thought back to what Gage Price had said. Rossdale came across this name during his research when trying to identify the man who killed Zach Franklin. He released the breath he had been holding and clicked on the file.

The filed opened and Damien read the note attached. His heart stopped. Beads of sweat formed on his lip and forehead. The coil in his stomach ignited and burned. His eyes widened as he stared at the one name on the screen.

DILLON MCGRATH

Damien remembered the warning:
Trust no one with this information.


THE END
**Other books by Victoria M. Patton**
**Damien Kaine Series**
Innocence Taken
Confession of Sin
Fatal Dominion
Web of Malice
Blind Vengeance
Series bundle books 1-3

**Derek Reed Thrillers**
The Box

**Short Stories**
Deadfall

If you enjoyed this book, you would be doing me a great favor by posting a review wherever you purchased the book.

## ABOUT THE AUTHOR

I spent eight years (four Active/four Reserve) in the Coast Guard and later received my BS of Forensics in Chemistry. For the past thirteen years, I've been a stay at home mother. I live with my wonderful husband, my twelve-year-old son and my thirteen-year-old daughter. I also share my home with three dogs, Georgie, Gracie, and Bella, and Squeakers the cat. Check out my websites below and the other books I have out.

www.whiskeyandwriting.com
www.victoriampatton.com

Made in the USA
Middletown, DE
15 September 2021